FALLING TO EARTH

Kate Southwood

FALLING TO EARTH

Europa
editions

Europa Editions
214 West 29th Street
New York, N.Y. 10001
www.europaeditions.com
info@europaeditions.com

Copyright © 2013 by Kate Southwood
First Publication 2013 by Europa Editions
Second printing, 2013

Library of Congress Cataloging in Publication Data is available
ISBN 978-1-60945-091-5

Southwood, Kate
Falling to Earth

Book design by Emanuele Ragnisco
www.mekkanografici.com

Cover photo © Elzbieta Sekowska/iStock

Prepress by Grafica Punto Print – Rome

Printed in the USA

For Aksel, Maren, and Inger

FALLING TO EARTH

MARCH 18, 1925

The cloud is black, shot through with red and orange and purple, a vein of gold at its crest. A mile wide end to end, it rolls like a barrel, feeding on rivers and farmland. Tethered and stabled animals smell it coming and lurch against their restraints. Swollen with river mud, it moves with a howl over the land, taking with it a cow, a cookstove, a linen tablecloth embroidered with baskets of flowers. A section of fencing, a clothes hanger, a coffee can. A house lifted up and dashed to earth. The side of a barn.

The people in the town scatter; some find shelter. The men and women running through the streets are mothers and fathers, desperate to reach their children at the schools. There is no time; the cloud is rolling over them. The men and women screw their eyes shut tight and some scream, but the wind screams louder and flings metal and wood and window glass though the streets. A Model T and its driver are hurled through the window of the hardware store. Telegraph poles snap and sail like javelins into houses. An old oak rips in two like paper torn in strips. Grass is torn from the ground.

The school, the town hall, the shops at the rail yard fold in on themselves and the people inside. And as the cloud passes, the fires begin, lapping at the broken town.

BOOK ONE

1

Mae pulls the lace curtain aside to look out the window and up at the sky. "It's awful dark out there," she says.

"Come away from that window," Mae's mother-in-law, Lavinia, says. "I'm not afraid of any rainstorm. If we were back out on the farm, I might be persuaded, but this is different. A town is different than wide open spaces."

"A funnel's a funnel. It doesn't know the difference between the country and a town," Mae says.

"Yes, but you don't hear town folk talking about funnels, now do you? It's the people out on farms who see them."

Lavinia pulls her glasses down on her nose and tilts her head back to look at her work. "Hand me another dark blue," she says to her granddaughter Ruby and points to the basket of wool scraps on the floor beside her chair. Ruby spins around on her knees and takes a long scrap off the top. "Like this?"

"Thank you, snookie. I bet you're not sorry to be missing school." Lavinia smiles at Ruby over her glasses and waits for Ruby to smile back at her. "I know I'd hate to have to walk home in this weather. Do you want to try braiding with me?"

Ruby looks at the basket and the braided wool snaking from Lavinia's lap onto the floor. She wrinkles her nose in answer. "I'm bored. Why couldn't I just go back to school today?"

"Land sakes, child! You'd rather be out in this weather than home with us?" Lavinia is laughing, inwardly gratified that Ruby would rather be at school.

"You know you can't go back until your scabs are falling off," Mae says. "Chicken pox is catching."

"But I feel fine!"

"You don't look fine. Go look in the mirror. They'd send you home right away if you tried."

"Why'd Ellis have to go and get dumb chicken pox anyway?"

"It wasn't my fault!" Ruby's brother Ellis says, "Whole bunch of kids got 'em."

"Well, now you'll be done with it, all three of you," Lavinia says. "All done with the polka dots. Why, I should be calling you Dot now, shouldn't I? And Ellis, you could be Spot."

Lavinia sees that Ruby is annoyed by the joke, but five-year-old Little Homer is smiling, waiting for her to name him.

"Ruby, don't look at your Gran like that," Mae says.

"Oh now, I didn't mean to hurt your feelings, snookie. You just go on with your marbles." She turns to Little Homer and says, "What do you want to be? There's not much left after Dot and Spot."

"Poke."

"Dot, Spot, and Poke?"

Little Homer nods, smiling at her and waiting for her to get the joke, then laughs with her when Lavinia slaps her knee and yells, "Poke-a-dot!"

"I don't want to be Spot," Ellis says, "Sounds like a dog."

"Well, fine, you and Ruby can just be Ellis and Ruby. Right, Poke?" She winks at Little Homer, who nods again, pleased that he's the only one playing the game.

Lavinia laughs at Ellis, stretched out flat on his belly, half under the davenport. "Lose one?"

"Got it." Ellis sets the marble with the others he has clustered outside the ring of twine and picks up his shooter. "How many twisters have you seen, Grandma?"

"Me? Oh, I thought I saw one once. Far off in the distance,

though, so I couldn't be sure. Grandpa Homer teased me and said I just wanted to see a real one so badly, I imagined it. I've been in plenty of storms, though, down cellar, waiting them out with a lantern. That's no fun, wondering what you'll find when you come out again." Lavinia stops braiding and sits looking at the opposite wall with her hands in her lap.

"They used to tell you to close all the windows in the house if a cyclone was coming, but then someone figured even if the funnel didn't skirt your place, the winds would blow the glass out, so they started telling us to open all the windows." She laughs and slaps her knee. "All that got us was a dirty house, I'll tell you. Why, we no more had all that black grit cleaned off of every surface before the next storm came up and we were flinging open the windows and running for the cellar again."

"You ever seen a twister, Mama?" Ellis asks.

Mae shakes her head. She has not once looked away from the window. She's exasperated by Lavinia's cheerfulness, by her refusal to do a thing as simple as look out the window.

Little Homer goes to stand with Mae and asks, "What are you looking for, Mama? What's one look like?"

"I've never seen anything but pictures, but they look like long, twisty cones, sort of bendy and fuzzy gray. They're wide at the top and skinny at the bottom where they touch the ground and stir things up." Mae draws a quick circle on the top of Little Homer's head and remembers to smile at the boy with her eyes.

"Daddy says if you want to know when there's a storm coming, you can listen for the birds and watch what they're doing," Mae continues. "If they're all twittering and fussing and the leaves on the trees start to spin so you can see their undersides, then you know a storm is coming. But if the light outside turns green and things seem kind of eerie, that's when you know you've got cyclone weather."

Mae turns back to the window, shakes her head and glowers

out. If only her husband Paul were here to talk sense to Lavinia—not that he outranks his mother the matriarch, but at least then there would be two of them she'd have to listen to. "You should really have a look, Mother. I don't like this," she says.

"I can see from here, and what I see doesn't look like cyclone weather. I think we're in for a walloping thunderstorm, but we don't have to be chased down a hole like scared rabbits."

"Maybe it wouldn't hurt to go down for a little while," Ellis says. "Just a little while." He's sitting up on his knees, and he's already dropped his marbles back into their fabric bag.

"Mae, come away from that window right now. You've got Ellis spooked. It's not even the right season for it. The newspaper didn't say anything but that we'd get a good soaking today."

Mae exhales, drops the curtain and goes to sit on the davenport. It's only a little after two o'clock, and they've got every lamp in the front room on. She shakes her head again, thinking of Paul and wondering what the others will be able to see on her face. Lavinia continues her rag braiding, tying on new scraps as she reaches the ends of old ones. The room is quiet; not even the children are making any noise. Lord, if Ruby and Ellis were in school, Mae thinks. That many more to worry about.

They've never yet taken shelter down in the cellar, but this is why Paul built it, she thinks. He'd had to take a little ribbing for it down at the lumberyard when he was building the house. Overkill, they'd chuckled at him, enjoying themselves. He'd just laughed along with them and kept smiling when he explained that if he had the ground, a shovel, and the lumber to make the cellar doors, why, he figured he could spare a day's labor. The children have only ever looked into it now and then when Mae has gone down to sweep it out and check for damp. They've never ventured down; they know its purpose and somehow that's made even the boys always shudder at the dirt

floor, littered as it always is with pill bugs, and at the spider-
webs stretched everywhere like sails.

The lamplight seems brighter as the sky darkens. Little
Homer is the first to go to the davenport and sits right up
against his mother. When Mae takes Little Homer on her lap,
Ruby and Ellis go to sit on either side of her. Lavinia stops her
work and they all look around the room, at the clock and the
windows, without looking into each other's faces. The rain,
which has been falling steadily all day, washes over the windows in sheets. The sky is black. There is a terrific crash of
thunder, and they begin to hear sounds they have never heard
before, and Mae says loudly, "Mother!"

When Lavinia stands, they all bolt. Mae shoves the candlesticks from the dining table into Ellis's hands and snatches the
box of matches from the sideboard.

"Go, go!" she shouts at the children who run for the kitchen.

"I need an umbrella!" Ruby says. Mae pushes her toward
the door, "You can have a towel later," she shouts at her,
"Go!"

They run huddled in a knot around to the side of the house,
shielding their eyes from the rain, soaked when they reach the
storm cellar. Mae yanks at the cellar doors, holding one open
and Lavinia holding the other. The children go down first, then
Lavinia, then Mae, who pushes back against the wind on the
doors until she is all the way down and the doors slam shut
behind her, and she drops the crossbar into place. Mae strikes
a match and pinches hold of it tight to stop her trembling.
"Let's see how wet those candles got," she says.

"I held the wicks inside my hand, Mama," Ellis says. He
holds out both candles to her. "I guess I dropped the candlesticks."

"Better the candlesticks than the candles. Good boy." Mae
takes one lit candle and lets Ellis keep the other. "Let's all sit
down. Are there enough crates?"

Lavinia looks up at Mae from her seat on a crate, then down again. "I'm sorry, Mae. I'm sorry," she says, shaking her head. "Lord, what if they hadn't been home sick?"

"We're all here now," Mae exhales and tries to smile. She sits down and holds Lavinia's hand in her lap.

"Not Daddy," says Ruby. "What about Daddy?"

Mae looks directly at Ruby. "You know that Daddy is downtown at the lumberyard."

"We didn't open the windows," Little Homer says.

"No," Lavinia shakes her head.

The children are frozen, too frightened to move closer to one of the women. The sound they heard while still in the house has advanced, roaring its way above them. There is a crash against the storm door, and they all scream, ducking with their arms held over their heads. Ellis drops his candle, and in the weak light left from the candle Mae is still holding, she sees his terrified face. Ruby is crying. Lavinia has Little Homer's face pressed into the front of her dress as if she can shield him by blocking his sight. Mae reaches out her arms, and Ruby and Ellis come to her immediately. She blows out her candle and drops it so that she can hold both children tight against her. In the darkness, Lavinia cries, "Dear Lord! Oh, dear Lord!" Then the roaring moves on, like a train careering over their heads. The sound recedes, and eventually even the wind seems to subside. When there is no longer any sound except rain on the cellar doors, the children hold utterly still, waiting to see what will come next.

"I don't think we can go out yet," Mae says. "We could still be in the eye of it."

"What if Daddy came home? He can't get down here with that bar over the door!"

"Ruby, hush. He wouldn't have tried to come home in this. He'd have known he couldn't make it in time."

"He could come home quick in the truck, couldn't he?"

"No," Mae says quietly, as much to warn Ruby against further questions as to answer her. "It's not safe to drive in storms like this, he knows that. He'll have found shelter at the yard."

Mae can feel the fear in the children's wire-hard bodies. I'd like to know where he was meant to find shelter, myself, Mae thinks. Not in the store, with those windows along the front; nor yet in the yard, among the stacks and rows of lumber.

"You all remember how strong and smart your daddy is," Lavinia says. "He can out-think a storm, easy. And imagine how glad he is right now that we had this cellar to go to." Her voice is decisive, but she can't entirely mask the quake she means to conceal.

When the rain finally stops coming in between the cellar doors, Mae rises and touches each of the children. Her eyes close, and she breathes in and out rhythmically, preparing herself. She lifts the crossbar and pushes against the doors, but cannot budge them. She pushes again, braced with one foot on the lowest step, and still they will not open.

"Something's fallen across the doors. Probably that crash we heard." Mae labors against the doors, shoving with her arms locked straight above her head. A gap opens between them as she pushes up, and they can see a tree trunk lying across them. Lavinia pulls the children back as far as she can. Debris rains in on Mae's head, and she thrusts against the doors but can't dislodge the tree trunk. Finally, Ellis pushes with his mother; they bounce against the doors with their shoulders and backs until they hear a scraping sound on the opposite side. "It's starting to give," Mae pants, turning to thrust at the doors again with her hands, bit by bit, rolling the tree trunk off the sloping doors and onto the ground. Mae leans against the doors, gulping air, and pushes one side up and open so that the children can run up out of the cellar. She reaches a hand down again for Lavinia, to help her out and over the fallen tree.

"Where in the world . . . " Lavinia says, looking around. All of their trees are still standing, festooned now with debris and broken branches.

"It's not ours," Mae says.

Debris and dirt are still swirling in the air around them. They shield their eyes, looking around, too shocked by what they see to move.

"Oh, Lord, Oh, Lord, Paul! Where are you?" Mae moans, clutching her mouth with one hand, her stomach with the other.

Ruby runs back with a metal object in her hand. She holds it up, a long black thread trailing from it. "What is it, Mama?" she asks.

"It's the shuttle from a sewing machine . . . " Mae says in a murmur. She takes the shuttle, turning it over and over in her hand, as if by touching it, it will tell her something more. She feels dread rising from her gut and registering in her face. She hands the shuttle to Lavinia. "The thread's still in it."

The children pick their way around the side yard, looking for wind-borne treasures under the branches lying everywhere. Lavinia is shaking, mumbling, "I never . . . I never . . . " She turns to look at the house, knowing, feeling at first glance that it is whole. The roof is littered with branches and twigs, the clapboards and windows are smeared with mud, but the house is whole.

"Saints be praised, Mae! Look at the house!"

"Shhh, Mother," Mae says, holding out a hand. "What's that sound?"

A woman is moaning across the street somewhere behind them, and as Mae and Lavinia turn to look, the moaning turns to screaming. Their neighbor Alice Duttweiler is there, staggering toward her house, which has gone all wrong. Turned facing another direction, one whole side missing, like a doll's house, to show what's inside. Alice sinks to her knees in front of the house and then rises to run back to the other side of the yard, her arms held out in front of her like she's trying to catch something. Alice's cries land in Mae's gut like fists. She feels Lavinia take hold of her arm. "Oh, sweet Jesus," she says with her hand over her mouth, "The baby."

Downtown, the cloud has passed, but the air is still choked with dirt. Paul pulls himself up slowly from the ground, still gripping the pole he'd taken hold of when the cloud was almost on top of him. His arms and hands ache from gripping the pole so tightly for so long. He's looked out the lumberyard windows at that very telegraph pole day in and day out for years, and now both he and the pole are still standing, the imprint of the pole on the side of his face. He looks at his hands, held out in front of him. He sees them but can't feel them, skin and shirtsleeves mud-black, his arms shaking. He touches his head, his neck, and holds out his hands again to see if there's blood. Retching on the air he's breathing, he begins to look around.

Everything is happening slowly, so slowly. Live wires dangle from utility poles, twitching in the wind. Buildings that stood solid only minutes before are now so much rubble and kindling. The trees left standing are choked with garments, newspaper, even the limbs of other trees that the black branches have snatched out of the wind. The sounds of wailing begin to reach him. Voices screaming, calling out names or crying for help. A blackened figure staggers in the middle of the street, a woman with her long hair clumped at the back of her head, the remnants of her clothes trailing.

Paul blinks as if he is waking. He'd gone outside before the cloud hit, heard it coming, seen it boiling along the ground. He'd been frozen where he stood, knowing the cloud would be on him, around him, before he could get back inside the store.

He'd taken hold of the telegraph pole next to him then, and let himself fall prone to its base while he'd turned his face into his arm and hugged the wooden pole.

He'd been facing into the cloud and he'd known that that posture might save him. The wind had raised him off the sidewalk and snapped him hard like a flag, but he'd held tight, waiting for it to set him down. Now he turns, expecting to see the lumberyard in ruins behind him, but it's whole. The storefront, at least, of Graves Lumber is whole, and so is the Liberty Theater beside it, though their fronts are smothered in mud.

Paul hears a man shout, "Watch the hot line!" and turns in the direction of the voice. A downed power line trails near a cluster of figures struggling around an overturned automobile; shouting, pulling, they are trying to free someone trapped inside. Paul looks past the figures in the direction of the school and takes off at a run down the middle of the street. He passes a man lying on his side, wide eyes in a blackened face, staring blankly past a metal rod driven through his chest. Paul doesn't stop; if the man is not yet dead, he will be soon. Bodies lie all around; Paul leaps the sickening hurdles. Among the dazed people are men and women who, like Paul, are rousing and running for the school. They shout their children's names as they near the collapsed building and the bodies sprawled there on the ground. They run among the stunned survivors, looking for their own. A woman is frozen, screaming under a tree at a child's body caught high in its branches.

"They're not here," Paul murmurs. He's remembering at last that his children were kept home today with chicken pox. "They're not here!" he shouts. His voice is suspended somewhere between shock and jubilation and makes a man standing nearby take notice. The man is calm, holding a small girl in his arms. "They're pulling more kids out of the building over there!" he yells, climbing over the debris toward Paul.

"They were home today!" Paul yells back. This man has

found his own child in the wreckage, and his child is alive. The cellar, Paul thinks. Please God, the cellar. The man stares at Paul and then suddenly shouts, "Go home! Go home! Go!"

Running the length of his own mutilated street, Paul tries to look straight ahead at what he's running toward. He can't make any sense of the nightmare vision, but neither can he look away. The cloud has been capricious: the houses on one side of the street have been knocked into piles of sticks, the bricks blown out of the sidewalks and trees snatched out of the ground like hanks of hair. On the other side, the houses are still standing, some shoved over sideways or twisted. Their roofs are mostly gone, and the first fires have been touched off by the snapped electrical lines and cookstoves lying in the wreckage. A few of the people he passes walk naked, crazed, calling out names. An arm rests in the crotch of a tree. Paul tries again to shut out the grotesques, running toward home, running through the searing in his lungs, desperately afraid of arriving.

Nearing the corner, he sees someone behind the house, a child standing there, and then another. He's crying, running toward those small heads. Once he's between the house and the garage he sees them all, all five of them, standing in different places in the yard. His mother looks at him, but Mae is the first to recognize him and she cries out. He's laughing now and they're all shouting. He holds each head, kissing them in turn, laughing, then suddenly he stops and a terrible look darkens his face.

"I have to go back," he says to Mae, and he's running again, running back toward the school.

2

Principal Claude Frayley stands grief-stricken outside his school, his trouser legs snapping against his shins, staring at the remains of the building. The air has finally begun to clear, the wind having carried away most of the filth and debris and deposited it in the nearby fields. How can it look this way, he wonders. How can the sides have simply folded in on the middle like that? The section of wall still standing with its window glass intact baffles him. He feels betrayed; he's looking at the school as if it can answer him, as if it is mocking him. It seems to him that, as an institution of learning, his school, a fine old school, should somehow have had more structural stability than that. Now it seems it was only an edifice after all, as frangible as a child's sand castle before an advancing wave.

He is aware in a vacant sense that there is activity around him, that there are voices intruding, annoying him. He is struck from the side by another person stumbling into him, and turning to issue a reprimand, he sees it is a woman who has struck him. Or perhaps it was only the legs of the dead child she holds in her arms.

"Help them!" she screams savagely at him. "What are you standing there for? Help them!"

Frayley is still desperately hoping that someone will come to lead him away, to tell him that it's all a horrible mistake and that he can go home to rest. He could just walk home as he does every day, to the white clapboard house on his oak-lined street. He could go right up the stairs to his bedroom, turn the cool porcelain knob on the door and just go in. He could hang his suit jacket on the beechnut chair by the window, take off his shoes, and lie down on top of the bedspread, just lie still with his hands folded on his chest and his feet crossed at the ankle. He could close his eyes without worrying about sleeping and listen to his mother at her work in the different rooms of the house.

He looks all around himself but sees nothing here that he can do. What can a man like him possibly do to help people who are screaming and children who are dead? A man nearby, seeing Frayley's paralysis, walks over to him and hands him a child. "Take him," he shouts, already walking away. "He says he's got an older brother here somewhere. Their parents might be here looking for them."

A live child, then, a boy. The first thing in his mind is the scrubbing the child will require; the mud around his eyes is like a minstrel's blackface. Rather than allow the next thought to blossom in his consciousness, rather than wonder who is still alive to assume responsibility for this child, he thinks logically and retreats into his official position.

"Whose classroom are you in?" Frayley asks, but the boy says nothing. He sets the boy down. "Did you hear me? I asked whose class you're in."

"Miss Geiler's. I'm Charlie Needham, sir. Don't you know me?"

He sits down on his heels to look closely at the boy. "Yes, I know you," he says. He takes hold of him and swings him up again, aware now of what he can do for him.

"Your brother's name is Joe, isn't it? Joe Needham!" he shouts, then shouts it again above the din of the other voices. He sets out to walk the periphery of the school property with the boy in his arms. He stumbles a little at first; his legs won't obey him properly. What he will do if he manages to make a circuit without a response, he does not know. He's begun to shake but has remembered that he should conceal this from the boy. "Joe Needham!" he cries, knowing that the boy in his arms is quiet because he hasn't yet realized what the adults knew immediately; that the question of who has died is not nearly as important in this moment as who has survived.

"Needham?" a man yells, running toward him. "Over here!" He takes the boy and runs a hand over his head. "Oh, thank God, thank God," he says. "You come with me, Charlie. I found your dad."

Frayley looks up and sees to his horror that he is standing near the school, much closer than he had intended to come. Another man is walking toward him, another bloodied man holding another child. It's not properly a child, though it's a child's body. He feels his arms reaching to accept the child and then realizes that the man is leaving.

"Wait! What do I do?" he pleads.

"Find someplace to set her down," the man says. His voice is thick, anguished. He's shaking his head. "There are more coming."

Now Frayley understands what he can do for these children, the last thing he can do for them. He kicks debris away to clear a space in the grass well away from the school and lays out the girl's body. He straightens her dress over her legs and takes off his suit coat to lay over her, but it doesn't cover the length of her body. Her legs stick out at the bottom. He pulls the jacket lower, to cover her legs and feet and to allow her face to be seen so that she can be identified. He then disturbs his coat one last time, to remove a notepad and pencil from the inside pocket.

He pushes her hair back away from her face, wipes his palms off on his trousers, and smoothes her face again. Mattie, he thinks. Mattie . . . "Second grade," he says aloud. "Dawkins." He writes out her name and tucks the sheet of notepaper inside the neck of her dress. Satisfied that the white paper is visible there, he rises, ready to receive the next body. He clears space each time, kicking at things with his feet, laying the children's bodies out properly, side by side with their legs and arms straight. He realizes the row will be all the more horrifying if it gets too long and decides it might lessen the impact to begin another row below the first. He clears the space alone with his hands, tossing debris and bricks well away from him. He kneels down to look at each one of the children's faces, to wipe them free of blood and dirt if he can, so that he can write another name on his pad and tuck the paper into their clothing.

There is a girl with a smashed-in head he cannot hope to identify. He covers the pulpy remnant of her face with his handkerchief and forces himself to examine the pattern of her dress, the buttons on her sweater, hoping they'll provoke a memory from when the children arrived at school that morning. He's kneeling, holding her hand when he sees the ring. He writes just that, "ring," on his pad, hoping that someone will look and be able to say which girl wore a ring like that, so that she can be buried with her name.

He watches the fathers and mothers tearing at the collapsed building with their bare hands. When he is handed a living, injured child, he gives it away to someone else standing there to take wherever it is they're taking the living. Two men carry a badly injured teacher out on a door. Her eyes are closed, not because she has lost consciousness, but because she has squeezed them shut to keep herself from moaning. The digging begins to slow. There are no tools, no shovels, and both men and women are beginning to stop, sitting anywhere, exhausted, allowing their bloodied hands to be wrapped.

Frayley climbs over the wall then, into the ruined building for the first time. He tries to lift a fallen beam. Grunting and shaking, he heaves at it until it finally budges. Amazed that he was able to lift it, he looks behind him and sees another man, holding up the other end. The man nods to him to start carrying it out and they climb, in turn, over the caved-in wall to set the beam out somewhere on the grass. They work together without talking, the man helping him, doing most of the work in fact, but never refusing his weaker partner. When they find a crushed boy under the next fallen beam, the man cries out. They pull the boy's body out together. He's one of the bigger boys and heavy to carry. After they've laid him out with the other children, the man stays where he is, kneeling by the boy's side. Frayley thinks he sees a flicker of relief in the sorrow on his face.

"Do you know who he was?"

"No," the man says, sitting up on his heels and wiping his brow with his forearm. "He's not mine, if that's what you mean. None of mine were here. They've all three got chicken pox."

Frayley looks at the man, bewildered, waiting to understand.

"Paul Graves, Mr. Frayley. I'm Paul Graves." Paul claps him on the shoulder.

"Your family . . . "

"Alive, they're all alive. That's why I'm here. As soon as I saw they were okay, I came running right back. I feel a fool now for having left in the first place. They didn't need me; I could have been here."

"But the chicken pox . . . There were more families down with it, several of them." Frayley grasps Paul's arm. "That means there were others who weren't here today!" His eyes are wide with relief; he doesn't understand why Paul is looking at him that way and shaking his head.

"Mine were down cellar," he says.

"I don't understand."

Paul speaks the next difficult words carefully. "There's not many as has cellars in Marah. There wasn't much time, either."

This brings Frayley, finally, back to his own house and what he will likely find, or not find there, when he returns. Having seen the ratio of living to dead here at the school, he feels certain now in which column his mother's name will be recorded. The arbitrariness of his mother's probable fate, alone when the storm hit in the old frame house in which he was born, the utter blamelessness of it sickens him, pointing, as it does, to his own culpability. His stomach heaves and he cups a hand over his mouth, managing to turn quickly enough that he retches in the grass below the line of bodies. When he's wiped his mouth on his sleeve, he looks up to see the people behind him, fathers and mothers standing below him on the slope, looking silently at the rows of children he has laid out.

"I was sending them home early," he bursts out. "It had gotten so threatening, and I was thinking of the farm children going home in the open bus, and I dismissed the school early. It was only ten minutes before the bell. I thought they were probably all just looking out of the windows anyway, waiting to go, so I had the bell rung early." He is holding his hands out, palms up, beseeching.

"Then how come more of them weren't outside?" one of the fathers asks.

"I told them they could come back in. It was raining so hard and it looked . . . I told them they could come back in and wait it out. But then the walls began to quake so . . . " He sees the children running back inside the school, running past him, squealing and laughing at having gotten soaked through in just those few seconds outside. Then their faces when the storm came howling. He had looked along the corridor at the children lining the staircase, and then it all went dark. He remembers the screaming and the first sounds of breaking glass. Then the deep rumbling, the shuddering walls, and his own voice screaming for them to get outside again. The staircase plunging, the walls sheeting down, and him caught, quite by happenstance, in the only safe place, under the framework of the main doors.

It's so hard, he thinks, to know which thing was the most wrong. But then he sees it in their faces and feels it in his hands that laid the children out. He feels someone take hold of his arm and looks to see Paul Graves, the only man present who can offer him absolution, there beside him. Paul is looking, too, at the parents standing there, he's looking back at them and frowning. Frayley feels a tug on his arm and allows Paul to lead him away.

C hill floorboards under bare feet. Bathroom taps screech. Boiled coffee, a triangle of toast. *Eat your egg, eat up.* Wet comb through the hair. *Take your umbrella, good-bye, good-bye.* Now only a handful of hours later in the same day people are doing things they would not have dreamed themselves capable of when they sat down that morning to their breakfast. They do what they must; the uninjured and the walking wounded organize themselves. There is no time to talk over what needs to be done or to decide democratically who will do what. People are where they are and their surroundings decide for them. If an injured person needs to be moved to a place of safety but there is no way of moving him, a man standing there will look around, see a door lying nearby, and shout to another man to help carry.

A woman will find herself pressed into service by a doctor, running in the street from one injured person to the next. She will be astonished at the things she can bear to look at, surprised at how she can maintain an impassive expression while she's tearing away their clothing to reveal the horrifying wounds.

The injured themselves will find that they can lie silent and wait for help, because what little morphine there is is running out and there is nothing to be gained by wailing. Owners of automobiles and delivery trucks will volunteer their vehicles as ambulances; those whose homes are still standing will offer them up as provisional morgues and as shelter for the living. A man still too young to have been tested by life will find that the disaster has left him clearheaded, that he can see the things happening around him as if he is standing above them, and that people listen to him when he tells them what they should do.

They will keep on into the night, without pausing for food or rest, but the injured will nonetheless continue to die of their wounds. The streets will be largely impassable and the ambulances will not get through. Neither will the men who come in with wagons to carry away the injured because their horses will scream and rear, even if their heads are blanketed, even if they are led by hand, at the smell of so many dead.

That the black cook at the Blue Front Hotel is a powerful man, that he struggles tirelessly—though injured himself—to save the guests trapped inside will not prevent the kitchen floor from giving way and sending the great iron cookstove into the basement, burning alive the people who had fled there from the storm.

That the fire brigade will use dynamite to choke the biggest fires downtown will not stop the fires that are spreading among the houses. People completely stripped of their clothing will wander the streets wrapped in blankets and rugs, and dazed children found miles away will be unable to say if the storm blew them there or if they walked.

People will know that many other towns to the east and west will have lain in the path of that cloud and that help will be slow in coming. And when the evening train arrives from the north, its cow catcher thrusting debris ahead of it along the tracks, the dumbfounded engineer will take the first of the injured on board and reverse the train all the way back to the nearest town, promising to come back.

It will occur to some that life, ordinary life, is going on for people other places; that the news has not yet been printed in the papers or broadcast on the radio, and that breakfast was a lifetime ago.

Mae fills her largest pots with water and sets them on the stove. She shovels more coal into the firebox and then sits at the kitchen table to rip a top sheet into rags. She bites the sheet's edge each time before she tears, rather than nicking it with scissors. The fabric is dry on her lips; it smells like the linen closet and a good day's work. It's like preparing for a birth, she thinks, listening for the boil to start. When she's reduced the sheet to a pile of cotton squares the size of washcloths, she looks in the icebox. The chops she'd bought that morning on their plate, a half a pound or so of butter, two bottles of milk, one half empty, bacon, a bowl with six eggs. In the pantry there are opened bags of potatoes and flour, sugar, coffee, tea, and cornmeal. Soup, vegetables, and salmon in cans. Boxes of cornflakes, tapioca, Cream of Wheat. Cookies, three loaves of bread. None of it will last long.

Mae thinks that perhaps she should be behaving differently—not calmly, in any case. She supposes she's stunned, really, and that Lavinia is stunned, too. But it's Lavinia's calm she's mirroring, although there's a sadness, too, in Lavinia's face she can't figure yet, something that didn't vanish entirely even when she'd seen Paul. Once they'd gone back inside the house, it might have been possible to pretend it was just another day. Nothing was changed inside, after all. The world outside the house had gone all wrong, but inside everything was the same. No, not everything, Mae thinks. They were not the same. They had stopped being themselves once they'd fought their way out of the cellar; opening those doors again had been the last thing they'd do as just themselves for a good long while. Standing there in the yard, they'd been like figures glued inside a snow globe with the remains of their neighbors' shredded possessions drifting down around them. Now they're safe inside but avoiding the windows and their view of the exploded streets around them. It's strange to feel fear, she thinks, now that the storm has done its work and passed, now that they've seen that both Paul and the house are whole. What exactly it is she's fearful of is difficult to say. It's not the lack of electricity or food, it's nothing inside the house. It's not even awareness of what they in particular have been spared, but it feels like fear all the same.

Mae had been all of seven when she'd first seen a person dead. She'd woken to sounds that had nothing to do with a normal day and found her mother in the dining room, covering the wide oak table with a clean sheet so that they could lay her grandmother out on top of it in her nightgown, her hair still woven into her thin silver-gray sleeping braid, her ashy feet splayed out where they rested on the heels. When the undertaker had arrived and gone in with his black case and clanking bottles, they'd pulled shut the pocket doors behind him and left Mae to wonder silently how her grandmother would look when he was done with her. They had kept Mae busy with them all that morning, her mother and her aunt, cleaning the house and especially her grandmother's bedroom, which would be used for the viewing. *He's giving us time*, her mother had said of the undertaker, but time for what? Dead was dead as far as Mae could tell. She couldn't fathom the rush to push strange liquids into her grandmother's veins and build a box for her to lie in while relatives hurried into town on trains, as if her grandmother would somehow become more dead, or perhaps even less so, if everyone took their time.

Mae closes her eyes and lays her hands on the pantry countertop. She skates her hands out over the surface. The wood is cool, worn smooth with work and washing. When she opens her eyes again, the light falling in from the pantry window seems to her to be the same light she's seen on the counter and shelves for years. The gray half-light of an overcast day that would be too dim for work except for the familiarity of the shelves and their contents. She stands here in the pantry most afternoons, leaning with her head and shoulder against the window frame, to all appearances avoiding her work but really letting the view of the houses and the cobbled street decide what she will bake that day. She's never had more than a valance on the window before, but now she knows she'll need a simple calico curtain to block the window, even though that will also block the light.

She can hear Lavinia with the children upstairs opening dresser drawers and closets, pulling out linens, towels, and clothing to donate. Mae takes a stack of folded paper bags from the pantry upstairs, and they put the things they've piled on Lavinia's bed into them. There isn't as much as she would have thought, not as much as she had hoped. Of course, they should pile absolutely everything into those bags, everything but the clothes on their backs. It's hard to know where the line between thinking of their basic needs and stinginess lies.

"What else should we do?" Mae says. They are proceeding on instinct, preparing for a clothing drive before they've been told there is one. They've seen the smashed houses all along White and Elm, looked from the corner up and down both streets and not needed to walk any further, not needed to wait for someone to come to them and tell them what to do. When Paul had turned to run back toward downtown yelling, "Stay put!" when they were still giddy and wild with laughter at seeing him whole, Mae had stood watching him recede and then, when he was gone from view, looked at the way the storm had reshaped the landscape, as if it hadn't just smashed the houses, but had somehow blown things further apart. The spaces in front of her, cleared in their brutal way, were more open, and as Paul had receded, the town had seemed to recede with him.

Now she's standing, looking at the paper bags full of things that, up until this moment, they had bought or made and laundered and used themselves. She's aware of her breathing, of her uninterrupted breathing, and the feeling she still has in her legs of wanting to run. She had wanted to run with Paul, to run without stopping, to feel her legs reaching and hear her shoes striking the pavement, to simply run as she had run as a child, with abandon and no thought of destination. The children are all either sitting or leaning on the bed, each of them touching one of the bags in some way, poking the point of the bottom corner or running a finger along the crisp, cut line at the top. They're looking at the bags, wondering what other possessions they'll be asked to put in them and give away.

"I don't know what more to do," Lavinia says. "Surely Paul will come home soon with news from town?"

Mae laughs and says, "Paul won't come home until someone forces him to, you know that."

The children are worried, that much is clear. They've seen everything Lavinia and Mae have seen, looking up and down the ruined streets. But whatever the children saw was diminished the moment they looked back at their own house again, when they looked up at Mae or Lavinia, or even when they heard their father's voice coming from the mud-covered man who ran shouting into their yard. They will never think, never say, Mama, what will we do? They can't guess at anything larger than what they see, can't reason that hardship can and will follow for them, too. Like Mae, they heard the screaming from across the street, they saw Alice Duttweiler running up and down her own front yard, shrieking that her baby was gone. Mae can't tell them yet that the baby is surely dead, carried off God knows where by the cloud. She can't ever tell them that what looked to them like her holding Alice and comforting her, was actually her fighting to restrain Alice, preventing her from running back into her kitchen for a knife, telling her Nash will come, I know Nash will come. And when Nash Duttweiler did come running, just as Paul would do, and Mae had crossed the street back to her own yard, the children had petted her hands to comfort her without any understanding of all the reasons she was crying.

Mae jumps. Someone is pounding on the front door. She runs down the stairs and slows when she sees the outline of a large policeman standing on the porch through the sheer curtain over the front door's glass. Lavinia and the children are behind her by the time she opens the door.

"Ma'am," The man nods. "Any dead or injured here?"

"No, we're all fine," Mae says, her heart pounding. The day's first official business.

"Is your husband at home?"

"No. He was . . . He went back downtown to help somewhere. I have no idea where he is."

"We need your porch, ma'am." He looks behind Mae at the children, and when he looks at her again, he's hesitating.

Lavinia says quickly, "Come with me, you three. Let's see if that water's boiling."

The policeman lowers his voice and Mae steps out closer to him.

"We're asking anyone who didn't get knocked flat for space for the bodies. There's nowhere else to put them, and frankly, it's cold enough that they'll do better outside."

Lavinia had said as much, that they'd be laying out bodies on the porch before the day was out. Mae feels herself nodding and hears Lavinia clattering pot lids in the kitchen. She hears herself saying, "Yes, it's a good-sized porch," and stares out over the policeman's shoulder, but there's no one else coming up the sidewalk. Now the cloud has finally reached them. Having passed them by before, it's reaching back now to deposit its dead at her door. She hears the policeman saying, "Wait for the undertakers. You'll be on a list," and thinks that she and Paul would have been hanging up the porch swing again in a month or so, and wonders how they'll ever stand it now. The policeman going back down the steps brings her back to herself. She goes into the kitchen and finds that Lavinia has set the children to peeling potatoes.

"I'll try to manage alone as long as I can," she says, taking the old metal washtub from the pantry. She and Lavinia carry the steaming pots of water out to the porch between them and tip them into the washtub. They've made the last trip when the next knock on the door comes. "Stay here and do what your Gran says," Mae tells the children, taking her stack of rags from the table. She hasn't told them what the policeman wanted and is hoping Lavinia will do it for her somehow. The curtains are drawn in the front room on all the windows that overlook the wraparound porch to prevent the children looking out. There's nothing but the sheer lace curtain over the glass in the front door, but there's nothing to be done about that. Mae sees another man through it, waiting for someone to answer the door. He's standing there alone, just as the policeman was, and when she opens the door, he greets her with another "ma'am." He's already laid the body of a woman to the side and is saying, "There's some coming without their clothes," and she answers, "We've got clothes," thinking of the paper bags and of her grandmother on the dining room table. Across the street, there are people crawling over the wreckage of their house, making piles of what belongings they can salvage on the grass. Next door, the Eberhardt's porch is being put to the same use as hers. Mae looks away; she doesn't need to see what they're doing over there, she'll be doing it herself in a moment.

"Straighten them out if you can," the man is saying, going back down the walk. "Some of them are already going stiff."

She's crying again and her blood is thundering in her ears. Her face is convulsed and there's no way to stop it, so she lifts her apron to her face and waits. It occurs to her that she has not yet had word about her friend Bess and she is ashamed not to have thought of Bess before this. She glances at the woman the policeman laid out long enough to be sure she doesn't recognize her and looks away again quickly. A list of painful truths races through Mae's head, among them the fact that Bess and her husband Stuart never dug a storm cellar for their house. Whether Stuart was inside or out when the storm hit is impossible to say, the only certain thing is that he was at work at the rail yards and not at home with Bess. Mae can picture the McCorkle house in every detail, she can picture Bess in it, and now she's working hard to stop the image of that house in ruins from entering her mind. Bess and Stuart's house is not so far away, only a couple of blocks north of downtown. She's praying, but it's all wrong. She should be pleading, bargaining with God, for Bess's safety, but instead she's praying that Bess's body doesn't end up on her porch. Thank God, she thinks, that they hadn't any children.

The boards Paul painted gray are there beneath her feet and there's a creaking sound coming from somewhere that sounds like the porch swing, and in her head she sees Paul, leaning back with her on their swing, rocking them slowly with just the heel of his work boot saying, *We got the best corner lot in town, we've sure got a view.* But the woman is waiting and there are more coming, so she dips hot water out of the washtub with a pail and kneels by the woman's side to begin to wash her. Someone's child, someone's sister, she thinks, wiping the woman's muddy palm with her rag and then someone's wife when she comes to the other hand and its ring. She washes the woman's face and neck, and when she hears the front door open, she looks up and Lavinia is standing there with her hand over her mouth. Mae asks her for a bedsheet and when Lavinia brings it to her she asks for the paper sacks they packed earlier, all of them. She straightens the woman's legs and folds her arms over her stomach with the wedding ring showing, then stretches the sheet out over her and puts a chunk of brick and a snapped piece of two-by-four she has found in the yard on one side to keep it from lifting in a breeze. It's a double sheet, one of hers and Paul's. How many times has she folded it before, with Lavinia on the other side of it, or alone. How many times has she smoothed it, fresh from the linen closet over their bed.

Virginia Eberhardt is looking toward downtown from her own porch, hands on her hips, a print scarf tied over her hair. Mae goes inside quickly before Virginia sees her looking, before she has to hear that Virgina is still waiting for news of her husband and their son. Leaning against the inside of the closed door, Mae is holding her hands in her apron, hands that she held in the tub of hot water and rubbed hard with a clean rag before she rose from her knees to come inside. The others are still in the kitchen. It'll be getting dark in another hour or so. Mae wonders how she'll be able to carry on outside in the dark, how long she'll have to carry on, and whether she'll be bent over a body when Paul finally comes up the walk for the night. She can hear Lavinia talking quietly to the children, talking somehow about ordinary things so that she can keep them away from Mae. She goes back out when she hears men coming again up the front walk, tells them to lay the next body alongside the first, and when one of the same men comes again a little while later and stops to look at her after he's laid out the next body, she sees that he's sizing her up, deciding how much she can take. She lets him have a good look at her, and when he's seen that she's tired and frightened but not broken, she says, "It's all right," and he nods and goes back down the walk. She knows they'll bring her the worst ones after that, and they do, bodies they've already covered before they come up the walk, some smashed, some without their limbs and some, like they'd said, without their clothes. She washes them all as best she can, puts clothes on those that need them and covers them with sheets. There's a child, a girl, she has to wash and then cover with a dress that she'd made herself and that Ruby has outgrown. They worried about sending me a man with no arms, she thinks, but this is the one she's crying over, the muddied skin and broken legs, the tiny, slack mouth. When the porch is full, the men stop coming. She never counted the bodies and won't lift the sheets to do it now. There are fifteen or so; it doesn't matter.

Mae had never eaten the sandwich Lavinia brought out to her, couldn't bear to pick it up with her hands, although she could have held it wrapped it in the napkin laying under the plate. She's light-headed now, wondering what time it is. She's worked through till dark, and now the moon is rising, bright and hard as a button above the broken houses. She's hardly had to speak to the children, who watched her carry out more pots of hot water from where they sat at the kitchen table, all of them clearly, and for the first time in their lives, doing exactly what they had been told. Now she's shaking, her knees are bleeding, and her apron and dress are filthy and wet to the hem. When she goes in, Lavinia is there, talking to her in a soothing voice as if Mae is an exhausted child who needs to be coaxed into bed, telling her that the children are eating their supper and then walking ahead of her up the stairs with a lit candle. There are several inches of hot water in the tub, fresh clothes folded on the lid of the toilet and a cup of coffee and another sandwich on a plate sitting on the children's stool. Lavinia pulls Mae's sweater off for her, puts the candle on the windowsill and raises a hand to Mae when they hear a knock on the door downstairs. "I'll go," she says, "You take your time."

Mae feels as if she could sleep right here in the water, even if it went cold, just sleep and wait for Paul to come lift her out and carry her to bed. She knows, though, that there will be more for her to do, despite what Lavinia said, and she's agitated by the voices coming now from downstairs and the next knock on the door. She hopes they're coming already to start taking the bodies away, but knows as soon as she thinks it that they're not. Neither was the candle Lavinia put in the window downstairs meant for Paul. She closes her eyes and sees her mother's face, hears her saying, *He's giving us time*, saying it in the way an adult says a difficult thing to a child when the child needs to understand that she is not to ask any more questions. Mae knows now that there is such a thing as more dead, and that once you've laid the body out and washed it, you need to rush to build the box and dig the hole and pray that the trains are running on time.

5

Night falls. The sky above the town is clear, left scoured by the cloud, and as the light fails, it begins to color again, a delicate blue that deepens quickly, tumbling through navy into black. The scavenging continues through moonrise, but then tapers off despite the brilliant light falling on the town. Men and women take what possessions they can carry, gather what members of their family remain, and set out into the streets in search of shelter. Each person carries something. An older child will carry a sack of food, a man will strap rolled blankets and rugs together to carry on his back, a woman will hug a bundle of clothes to her belly as she goes, and even the smallest child will be given something to carry; the family's Brownie camera if it can be found, or a cooking pot.

In the night they falter, fearful of the next step, mistaking fear for uncertainty. They have always done for themselves and find that they must now contract a debt. They haven't yet understood that the very people who are waiting to help them are anxious themselves, worried that the help they offer will be thought too mean. A man making his painstaking way through the streets weighs what will injure him least: asking a man he has known for years for space on the floor and a supper scratched for his children, or being greeted by strangers with government uniforms and government cots who have arrived on trains for the sole purpose of giving aid. Any meeting will be precarious. The men begin to realize that what is truly unbearable is what they risk seeing in each other's eyes. A man who must beg shelter for his family draws himself up tall in front of another man's door, summoning his dignity before he knocks, knowing full well that his eyes will still betray him. The man who opens the door, if he now possesses only that door and walls and a roof, finds that his eyes fall hungrily on the other man's children and that he is the poorer of the two. And the sympathy of a stranger, however earnest, becomes intolerable if the stranger is careless in veiling his relief that he will leave soon on another train.

The women watch as they walk, making note of every possibility, ready if the men should waver to say carefully, *I thought I saw a candle back a block or so.* They watch and they worry lest the children tire and begin to fret about their bellies, or ask *Where are we going to go?* not yet realizing that the children won't complain because more frightening to them than hunger or even the storm is the possibility that their mothers and fathers will allow themselves to be defeated by it. The children see the fear the adults are too weary to conceal. They see without understanding that their fathers and mothers are working out if they can trust their beating hearts, figuring just how much of the self is lost when a house is smashed or a child is snatched up into the air.

The children do not doubt the evidence of their own bodies. They see what the adults cannot: that one is responsible to a beating heart, that the simple act of walking means moving forward in more than just the literal sense, and that even the act of reaching into the wreckage of a house to save a book or a tea kettle is a kind of beginning.

The sight of a lantern outside the one church that was spared will stop a damaged man cold, knowing as he does that it means he is welcome to spread out his bedroll inside on a pew. He will stand a moment in the street with his remaining family, watching the flickering light outside the doors, feeling hardness overtaking his face and anger balling up in his gut.

Hell no, not in there, he'll say, frightened suddenly of where he is laying blame. A woman damaged in the same way will turn inward and simply take the first shelter she finds, keeping a stupefied silence throughout the night, fearful of uttering any sound lest she become deranged.

Not everyone remains in the town. Proud men who find themselves alone will go out into the fields where fires built by other men like themselves signal a space cleared for sleeping. There they'll wrap themselves in the blankets and rugs they've scavenged and share what food they've managed to find. It will occur to some of them that this was the boyhood idyll: to sleep in the open air with one's fellows, to have no clothes other than those you wore on your back, no responsibility to anyone but yourself or to anything but the fire. They will spend the night repeating the horrors of the day, unable to sleep because of the coldness of the ground and because of the terrible beauty of the night sky above them. Still others will leave Marah entirely, fleeing on foot along the train tracks or driving out in automobiles or wagons they've managed to wrest from the wreckage, putting a long and permanent distance between themselves and the town.

None of them can know yet that aid will come from every possible source and that even poor people far away will hear about the storm and find they have something to spare. Without discussion or formal assent, the people of the town act on a simple, instinctual code: that a door knocked upon is a door opened, that food is not to be hoarded, and that succor can be found wherever a bonfire or a candle are lit. The living fan out across the town and come to rest. The end of the first day.

6

Death had come by stealth when Paul's father, Homer, had been found out in the field, taken by a stroke. There had been no long illness to give warning, no opportunity for leave-taking, but his death nonetheless had a quality of inevitability about it and had been the kind of shock you could expect to recover from reasonably quickly in every-day ways. Now, because death had come in a ravenous cloud, Paul, Mae, Lavinia, and the children are sitting in candlelight, with the curtains drawn and the bedroom door shut, trying to give some privacy to the other families who have taken shelter in the house. Mae, sitting up with a pillow between her back and the headboard, has an arm around Ellis on the one side and Ruby and Little Homer on the other. Little Homer lies closest to her, half on her, his head on her belly and a leg and an arm draped across her lap. For once, they're all lying still, not vying for the place closest to their mother. They are so still you might believe that they had fallen asleep there, that some-one would lay a finger over their lips and shush you if you entered the room too quickly, but their eyes are open, every one of them. They're staring, seeming not even to blink. Something about their eyes suggests that they might spring up at any moment, despite the heaviness with which they lie against Mae. Ellis seems to be looking at the closed door. Ruby is watching Lavinia, who sits in the corner in an armchair brought up from the living room, worrying an earlobe with a trembling hand. Little Homer, like Mae, is looking directly and alertly at Paul. He realizes that none of the children has spoken since he came home.

Paul looks at Ruby and Ellis and remembers the careful, pleased way his father had held them both as blanket-swaddled babies. And after both their births, when there had been three generations of them sitting there together, he had looked at Lavinia who was smiling at them all and realized she was savoring it, too, gratified at their increasing. That Mae had been pregnant with Little Homer when his father had died was a comfort in its way. He'd known, at least, that the last one was coming.

It had been Mae who'd named the baby, though he supposed most people thought it had been him. She'd taken his hand at the funeral supper in the church basement and pressed it against her belly for him to feel the baby's heel pressing hard from its side. "Doesn't that hurt?" he'd asked, and she'd smiled and shaken her head no, but pressed back anyway with her fingertips to tell the baby it was time to stop. "It's a boy," she'd said and smiled at him in a way that told him she was right. "We're going to call him Homer."

Life goes on, Paul had thought at the time. So many things at once. His father, dead, abruptly. The farm, his mother's to decide about now. A boy, another son, and his name. It was all right, though, not being in control of everything. He could settle again into his own life now and do the things he needed to do to keep moving forward. That his and his brother John's debt from starting up the lumberyard was repaid was a comfort, too. They had gotten to see their father's damp, proud eyes when they'd handed him the last envelope of bills, their loan paid in full and ahead of schedule. "Well, I'll be," he'd said and shaken both their hands.

Paul wonders how much of the day the children can have comprehended. What began as a miracle for him has more likely seemed like magic to them; the destroying wind brought only rain and strange airborne treasures into their yard. They can have seen the other houses around theirs, they can be told that well over half the houses in town have been smashed, that an as-yet-unknown number of their schoolmates are dead, without their being able to attach any particular meaning to any of it. What was horrifyingly concrete for him would remain hazy and indistinct for them for a time, and perhaps should remain so for as long as possible. He knows that meaning and consequence will continue to filter into his own consciousness as well, that it might take the rest of his life to make sense of this.

Soon enough he'd be the one to tell his children which of their friends were lost. Knowing that had made him avoid looking too closely at the children laid out at the school. Certain knowledge now, right now, was still too much. Holding the crushed body of a boy of twelve or thirteen had been too much. And in the end it wasn't really grief for the boy that had overtaken him but a sad kind of joy at knowing that he'd still hear Little Homer and Ellis's voices break one day; that he would see his sons grow taller and faster than he himself had ever been.

Now his children are lying, all three of them, heavy and warm, against their mother. It's a temptation to look at them all and try to erase them, one after the other, from the scene, to imagine other ways the day might have ended. But the occasional sounds coming from the rest of the house, the sounds of grieving that draw a moan out of Lavinia each time they hear them, tell him quickly, shamefully, that that is folly. It's late, getting on toward midnight finally, not twelve hours yet since the storm, but it's time for sleep.

The weight of the coming day should make it impossible for him to sleep, but it won't. He could sleep right here in this chair all night, probably without moving even once. He thinks of John and his wife, Dora, again as he has off and on throughout the day, and again, without any whiff of the old rancor. He thinks that their moving to California was providential. He hasn't seen it for himself but has heard from others that the houses on their old street were hit hard, that there's nothing left except the odd black tree trunk sticking out of the ruins. He hasn't yet told any of this to his mother, although he knows it's possible she's already guessed.

What can have been in those children's minds in the last seconds before the school collapsed, he wonders. Had any of them, any one of them, understood what was about to happen? There hadn't been any such moment for Paul. He'd known somehow as he sank to the sidewalk with his arms around the telegraph pole and laid there on his belly to wait out the tearing wind that he'd done the right thing. And knowing now that he hadn't just been lucky, that if he'd stayed inside the store he would have been safe there too was terrible to bear. He was fine. He would have been fine no matter what.

The night had turned heartbreakingly clear, and when there was nothing more he could do at the school, he'd walked home in the moonlight. The first relief trains had pulled in by then, as close as they could come to the shattered depot. Doctors and nurses had come in on those trains, and the worst of the injured had gone out on them when they'd pulled out again. Medical supplies were beginning to flow into town, and he'd heard reports that surgeries were in full swing in the undamaged parts of the hospital and the high school. He'd been offered a blanket, which he'd declined, and hot coffee and a doughnut, which he'd accepted. His hands had been bandaged, and while he'd sat there on the ground, he'd slowly taken in the blood-red crosses on the nurses' still-spotless white uniforms, and had found himself close to weeping at the wave of relief, the miraculous relief that had come when he'd surrendered to their care.

As he had walked home, he'd laughed a little at the moon's

consideration, illuminating the ruins around him as it had, making the giant splinters shine where they lay so that he could safely pick his way home without streetlight. He'd felt nothing in the air. If he closed his eyes to the wrecked houses around him, he'd wondered, would he feel a weight in the air, a heaviness or any whisper at all of what had happened that day? He had looked up instead, past the few bare trees at the blue-black sky and the moon, but there had been nothing, only the lingering smell of burning, and looking far up above himself, he could let that remind him of other pleasanter things.

His street had been strange and still; he'd met no one at all while walking its length. It might have seemed that everyone but him had been blown right out of Marah except for the small flicker of candlelight in the windows of intact houses. There would be candles lit at home, too, he'd thought, and when he realized that he was almost there, he'd slowed. It had surprised him how quick his walk had been, but then his landmarks were mostly gone, and it had been like walking the street for the first time. He'd stopped half a block from home to look from a distance at the Duttweiler house on the far corner. He had seen it earlier in the daylight, but he'd been preoccupied then and hadn't given any real thought to it in comparison with his own house. It had, after all, been only one of a long string of bizarre, sad things he'd seen in the first hours after the storm. Standing there in the moonlight it had seemed terrifying and comic in equal measure; a freak of a giant's dollhouse. On the corner opposite his own house, the storm had slung the Duttweiler house around as if it weren't even fixed to its underpinnings and ripped off one side entirely, only to cross the street and do nothing more than dirty his house and the next few after his.

He'd finally seen his own car pointing the wrong way in the driveway then. It had surely been like that when he'd run home the first time, but desperate as he was to see his family safe, he hadn't seen it. Spun around, just spun around in the same place he had left it parked there on the driveway between the sidewalk and the garage. It had stopped him cold when he'd finally seen it, the one funny thing he'd seen all day, and he'd felt the ache it left in the bottom of his stomach and stared a while before he went up the walk to the house, where he stopped again when he saw the sheeted bodies laid out along the front porch. Not yet, not yet. He'd thought he was prepared for that; he'd known they would be there as they were on the other porches he'd passed on his way home, lined up tight, like matchsticks. Paul had closed his eyes then in resignation, knowing as he suddenly did how Mae and Lavinia had been occupied since he'd kissed them in the yard.

By the time he'd walked into the house, he'd had the last of the day's bad surprises and was able to look at the group of people gathered in his living room as if he'd been expecting them, because he had been. He had been certain Mae and Lavinia would offer up every extra bed, every chair, every inch of floor for people to sleep on in his absence. Now they were there with their bundles stacked in neat piles in the corners of the room, waiting, polite as invited guests, for him to come home before they spread out all over the floor for the night. The problem of it, Paul had thought, closing the front door slowly behind him, lay in how to greet them. How does a man greet people he's known all his life when they're standing in his house because they've lost something, lost everything perhaps, and he has not. How do you stop the black joke entering your head, *Welcome folks, sorry about the electricity and the stiffs*, and get past them all without their feeling they have to thank you, because all you want to do now is to get behind a closed door with your own family. How do you look at neighbors and former schoolmates when you know that, tomorrow morning, they'll be buying wood from you for coffins.

There had been no way of knowing what he was looking at

when he'd finally turned and met their eyes; a child without a brother, a man without his wife, a woman without her child? What could he say to them, now that happy commonplaces were impossible, now that *That boy of yours has sure shot up* had become *Where is your son?* In the end, it had been a statement and not a greeting that was spoken first, and he'd realized to his shame that what was unpleasant for him was impossible for them. It was Vida Long who'd spoken first, who'd come toward him to take his bandaged hands in hers and had simply said, "You were at the school." He'd looked at her eyes, swollen, red, long past crying now and seen that she'd found a way to thank him without saying the words, and that what she was thanking him for was not the roof over their heads. She was a tiny woman, a few years younger than Mae, and knowing then where her children were, he'd thought, *Now she'll always look older.* But standing there with her tender hands holding his, wearing the same navy-print work dress she'd had on when the storm hit, she had seemed to tower over him somehow, humbling and magnificent, holding in all there was now to hold inside her.

It's past midnight now. Outside, it's still. Maybe no more so than any other chill night in early spring before the windows can be left cracked open and the sounds of insects and birds can come into the house, but it feels unnaturally quiet, as if the storm's roaring voice has frightened everything into silence. Inside it's hushed. The occasional sounds that reach them from the rest of the house are the sounds of stifled grieving, and are hard to bear. The children's eyes have finally closed. Time to peel them off Mae, put Ellis and Little Homer to bed on the floor, and Ruby in with Lavinia in the next room. Suddenly, Paul wants to wake them instead, to shake each of them so that he can see their eyes again, and take hold of them so hard he risks crushing them. He's never felt any particular way toward the Almighty, but he's shaking now with gratitude and Mae is crying and he hears himself saying thank you and thank you and thank you.

7

Three and a half hours. Three states. Two hundred and nineteen miles. Well over two hundred dead in Marah alone, and counting. *Started over in the Ozarks, they're saying, jumped the Mississippi into Illinois, hit the Big Muddy and Little Egypt, petered out somewhere across the border in Indiana.* News circulates, and the good fortune of the living is thrown into bare relief. *They found out who that little girl was out in Harrington's field. The one who wouldn't talk. Someone finally recognized her, and they sent her out on the train to her grandparents in De Soto. Can you imagine?* People stand in lines at the grain elevator downtown, waiting for the Red Cross blankets and donated clothing to be had there. Each arrives with facts and particulars to trade, hoping to talk more about others than about themselves. There is solace in greeting friends and occasionally even relief to be had in the absurd. *I heard Opal Tolliver still won't come out of her bedroom closet. Her son's tried telling her its foolish, her squatting in a closet when the rest of house is lying flat around it like playing cards, but she won't listen. Figures it saved her life, and there he is, stuck bringing food to the closet every day.*

Newspapers from surrounding cities make their way in on the trains and the people read, amazed and gratified, the many accounts of the storm and the messages of sympathy and condolence that President Coolidge has accepted on their behalf. *Will you look at that. They heard about us all the way in Italy and Japan.* The wondrous news multiplies with reports of aid streaming in from the state, from neighboring states and towns, the nation. Drives for donations in aid of the survivors of March 18th spring up from St. Louis to Chicago with churches, schools, even newspapers organizing seemingly overnight. *Folks aren't careful, they'll be needing aid from us pretty soon.*

The men and women visit cautiously with each other while they wait in the lines, surprised by life's pulling them forward and wary of moving too quickly, like a widow flirting over her husband's grave. They feel the ruined town spreading out behind them and beyond it the endless ruined farms and the dead livestock still lying in the fields. Each fears the day and the night that will follow; the snow or rain that will fall, the cold, the uncertain food. The newspapers have told that the National Guard is mobilizing. They are coming, they are coming with tents and food, and although each person can imagine sleeping in a tent, each wonders how long they are meant to live in them and how exactly a hunk of canvas and a handful of poles can form a bridge back to employment and a solid roof.

The aid workers, doctors, and nurses streaming into town, housed and fed in sleepers and dining cars sent in by the railroad. The grim lists—dead, injured, missing, found—revised and stuck again to the doors of the library. The men and women huddled in front of the doors, jostling for the place in front, impatient fingers trailing down the lists, and the wretched faces of those pushing their way back out of the crowd.

8

A scraping sound wakes Paul, scraping and wood being thrown on top of wood. Like something at the lumber-yard, the clatter of plank against plank. Little Homer has climbed into bed with them again, although Paul can't remember when. He's coming slowly out of his dream, a dream he's glad to be leaving. He can hear Little Homer's breathing, a dry open-mouthed rattle just this side of snoring. Mae is lying as she always does, on her side facing out toward the wall, and Little Homer is snug up against her back with his hand on her shoulder. It's still dark in the room. It's past six-thirty, but the alarm never went off and the curtains weren't left open as they usually are to let the morning light start to wake him even before the jangle of the alarm. Paul remembers then; he feels his body remembering the storm even before he can finish the thought in his head. His dry mouth and throat, his bruised arms, his injured hands. He breathes in deeply and exhales, feeling his heart beat faster with dread of the coming day. There is a ribbon of daylight all around the curtains. The air in the room is blue. Paul has never thought of the air as having a color before. He's assigned colors to the sky or to clouds before, but never the air itself, having only thought of air in terms of light before, whether it is bright or dark and how it changes with the movement of the sun. But the air around him now is blue, a deep, palpable blue that looks as if it would smudge if the daylight weren't already hurrying it away.

Paul wonders if he isn't the only one awake in the house. It's been a handful of hours since everyone went to sleep, and although there are the occasional sounds from people outside already beginning to pick through the rubble, it's quiet inside the house. He won't move yet, he thinks. He won't even stretch. Let them get all the sleep they can. There were enough disruptions after midnight, people crying out in their sleep at intervals throughout the house, the few children mumbling loudly through nightmares, never waking entirely, just fighting in confusion until a hand on their chest and a low voice in their ear settled them again. *Try to sleep*, he'd said to Homer and Ellis, touching their faces. His boys had lain there, eyes wide and listening, and Paul was sure Lavinia and Ruby had also lain awake. Paul exhales again. He's not sure what there is for people to get up for, what jobs there are left to go to, and Lord knows when there will be a school again. People will try to salvage what they can from their houses, he supposes, without having any place to put things. Each day's efforts will surely seem pointless, like being told to move a heap of boulders from here to there only to learn that the next day's labor is to move them back again.

Paul's stomach is tight. He will have to get up, and soon. Getting out of the house again may even be worse than coming home was last night. He can wash and dress quickly as usual, he can even leave through the kitchen door, but he will not be able to avoid seeing in all those eyes the knowledge that, unlike him, they have no place to go to. He realizes he's still thinking about the lumberyard as it was yesterday, as it was before the storm. Yesterday morning had been Wednesday. Just Wednesday, pleasant and indistinguishable from any other working day. He'd been up early and out the door with the smells of coffee and eggs and bacon still in his nose, the children sleepy at the table, Mae and his mother already distracted by the coming day's work. The customers coming and going under the bell on the door, the sounds of the saws, his routine with all the weight of the familiar. Greetings and small talk, the occasional car passing outside the windows. Only the talk about the weather was bitter now, the jokes they'd made about forgotten umbrellas, and, *Hurry, get where you're going before it starts to rain.*

But he'd left the lumberyard without locking up yesterday, without doing anything more than looking back, astonished, at the front of the building before he took off running for the school. He hadn't given it another thought the rest of the day, not even when he'd taken his keys and coins out of his pocket and laid them in the dish on the dresser. Up till this moment, he hasn't given a thought to the people who work for him, to which of them was inside when the storm hit and who was still out back in the yard among the stacks of cut lumber. He hadn't seen them again, not even later that day, downtown or at the school.

He'd neither seen nor thought of Irene after he'd left her inside the store, sitting behind the counter at the adding machine. He'd only gone outside to stand on the sidewalk to see why the sky had gone so dark, why the wind had picked up and there were so many dead leaves flying by the windows suddenly. He'd intended to have a look and then go right back in, to laugh and tell Irene they were in for a good soaking, and then to call the other men inside the store.

He'd meant to go back in but he'd been frozen there, looking down Union Street in the direction of home when he'd seen the cloud. He could see nothing else, no sky at its edges, no space below or above it, just the seething black cloud rolling towards him, swallowing the street. The screams behind him had brought him back to himself, and it was then he'd thought to grab the telegraph pole because he was two steps closer to it than he was to the store, and he'd fallen with his arms around it the way he used to fall on the football in high school.

Now he's lying on his back with his arm across his face, gasping like he's been running.

"Paul," Mae is saying, "Paul!" She's up on her elbow, pulling his arm away from his face. "What is it?"

Homer hasn't woken, he's lying there rolled over on his back now, still sleeping with his mouth slightly open. He'll wake and remember the storm soon, too.

Mae is cupping his cheek with her warm hand, kissing his temple.

"I never went back," he says. He's sobbing now and trying to stop, but he's making more noise having to breathe through his clamped teeth. Mae moves her hand to his shoulder. He knows she's watching him, waiting. If she gives him time, he'll be able to explain, he'll be able to tell her that he's not talking about the school. He knows he's confused her, and if she asks again he won't be able to control himself at all. But she isn't asking, she's waiting. He's finally able to take his hands away from his mouth, but he can't look at her yet, he can only look up at the ceiling. The air has lost its color. It's just a dull half light now, waiting for someone to push the curtains back.

"The lumberyard," he says in a whisper, as if he's only trying not to wake the boys. "I never went back to the lumberyard yesterday."

Mae is still silent. He's sure she knows that he's talking about the people he left there and not the place, and that she won't try to reassure him that if the one escaped unharmed the others would have as well. Mae has never asked him to justify any feelings of responsibility before, and she won't make him defend remorse and shame now. Just as she let go of him when he set off running back to the school the day before, she'll send him off again this morning without complaint to do whatever it is he has to do, and she and Lavinia will run things at home. Funny that the day can, in this one respect, be so much like any other.

"I have to go." He looks at her finally, but now she's not look-ing at him. She's breathing slowly and looking down at Homer, mostly to look at something other than Paul. She hasn't taken her hand from his shoulder, but he can see she's unhappy, that she's trying hard to keep anything she's thinking from showing on her face. Her eyes flicker up briefly and then down again and she nods. Paul sits up and pulls Mae up to him and holds her with Homer lying between them.

"I'll get up with you," she says.

"No, don't. You can wait a little."

"Wait for what? They'll hear you downstairs, and I'll have to get up anyway."

"I'll be quiet."

Mae shakes her head and gives him a rueful smile with her eyes. "No, you won't," she says.

They're there when he opens the door. Lon, Clarence, Irene. Only Dennis is missing and in the shouts that follow Paul's crossing the threshold, someone manages to say that he went out on a train to Carbondale with his injured wife. Paul can do nothing but stand there while they clap him on the shoulder and beam at him, feeling relief run through him slowly, moving out from his core like warmth on a winter day when he's come back inside to a fire in the fireplace and knows he'll get warm and stay warm for the rest of the night. Paul sees the other people in the back of the room, smiling shyly at him.

"We slept here," Clarence is saying. "Our places are all flat-ter than flat, so we all just came back here. There was the heater and plenty of floor space and the sink in back."

Clarence's voice recedes as if he's walked into another room. Paul hasn't seen these people for a good while, and has rarely seen them here at the yard, but he's looking now from face to face and back again: Lon's wife, Clarence's wife and teenaged son, even Irene's mother. Clarence is still talking.

He's normally taciturn, the one they rib because of his one-word replies. Now he's rattling on apologetically about something, twisting a piece of cloth in his hands.

Paul smiles at him, and everyone laughs when he says, "Took a cyclone to loosen your tongue."

"We'll pay you back for the coal, or you can take it out of our pay—"

"I'll do no such thing." Paul's eyes are stinging again, he hopes he can keep the shake out of his voice. "I wish there was room for you all at my place, but we're full up. This sure as hell isn't much, but I suppose four walls and a roof is better than flat. You did right, coming back."

It's almost like seeing family after a long period apart. Paul can't imagine he'd have felt any differently if he'd come through the door to find his brother John waiting for him there with his wife, Dora, and their two boys. Maybe he didn't come back after the storm, he can't ever change that, but he can't see that they blame him for it, and the lumberyard he and John built was there for them to come back to. What would John say if he walked in here right now and saw the men they hired together still here. Irene, too, still at the first job she'd had coming out of secretarial school in Carbondale.

"I was just headed out, hoping to get some word about you," Clarence says. "We didn't know what to think. Or more like we knew what we thought, and we were trying not to think it."

Serious again, Paul is jolted back to the storm. Irene is looking at him like he's performed a miracle right out of the Bible.

"You were right outside," she says, pointing toward the door. "I saw you there on the sidewalk, right outside and then you disappeared. "

What must you all have seen since then, Paul thinks. He'd walked the long way down White Street all the way to Union to get to the lumberyard, right down the middle of the street, or the closest he could come consistently to the middle, having had to walk around and climb over debris the entire way. He had not been alone out in the streets this morning as he had been late last night, when there had only been the wreckage and the moonlight and a burnt smell hanging in the air for company. There were people out all along the streets, walking gingerly on the wreckage, searching in the daylight now for whatever they could save. Ragged things fluttered from the trees wherever there were still trees. There were the same kinds of clattering sounds that had woken Paul earlier, coming intermittently when someone threw aside a piece of wood. Paul even saw a woman sitting on a piano stool on top of a flattened house. He had imagined if he'd walked up and asked the woman, she would have told him, *Yes, the storm set this stool right here on top of my house. So I'm sitting on it.* The daylight had been unforgiving. There was no longer even the sense that it had all just happened; it seemed as though it had been this way for the longest time and that everything would stay this way for years.

Paul says, "I can hardly believe it myself, but that's what happened. I just took hold of that pole and somehow or other I managed to hang on and here I am," wondering how many times he'll be telling this story again in the coming days, how many more incredulous faces he'll have to meet and convince. He sees the faces before him, rapt, while they try to picture him out there, belly to the sidewalk, riding out the cloud by just wrapping his arms around a pole, amazed that he'd been out there the whole time just feet away when they'd taken it as read that he'd been carried off in that first moment. He's beginning to see himself that it is all astounding, not just the telegraph pole and the lumberyard. They're still fixed on the image of him hanging onto the pole and haven't remembered he must also still have a house if he's said it's already full of people. How strange, Paul thinks, he's the only one of them standing here who hasn't lost a single thing.

Someone has contrived to make coffee on the heater and

odd bits of food are shared around while they finish the job of clearing the floor of bedding. When Irene's mother, Mrs. Dower, finds the broom, Paul knows better than to stop her giving the floor a going-over. They all seem perfectly normal to him, aside from the timidity they're still trying to banish because he came in and found them standing among their bedrolls. Their homes are gone, and yet they seem pleased to be here and pleased to see Paul. Not one of them looks as tired as Paul feels, although they must certainly have spent yesterday in much the same manner he did. Paul finds that he feels timid himself, having interrupted their rough housekeeping when he walked through the door and turned it all back into a place of business. He finds he hasn't the words to ask what they did in the first moments after the storm or in the long hours that followed, because asking will take them back to those very moments when they didn't know, when they couldn't know yet who had survived. *Flatter than flat*, Clarence had said. You can't ask a man for details when those details will leave him standing in front of his ruined house again in his own mind, when he'll be forced, then, to say something about it and you will be forced to reply.

He wonders how long they can continue with this kind of chatter. How long they can smile at the fact that they're all still there, that there's hot coffee and that Irene's mother pulls a quick broom. None of them will be the one to break this mood, Paul is certain. The bell on the door will be the thing to do it, because when it rings, when the next person opens the door and comes in wanting something, that something will be wood for a coffin. Paul needs to ask Lon and Clarence both what they think, how they should go about it, but he can't force himself to ask them into the backroom with him to do it. They've sold lumber intended for coffins before, though never so many as they will need now, and never so many for children. But what he can't do for himself, Lon and Clarence are doing for him. He sees first Lon, then Clarence moving toward the backroom, slowly, with their hands in their pockets and their mouths gone into thin hard lines, because the reason for it is unpleasant. Clarence looks up at him before he goes through the doorway, waits for Paul to show that he will follow before he goes through himself. And even then, knowing that they are waiting for him, Paul enters the room not knowing how to begin to talk about the lumber they will need to measure and cut, over and over again, to sell for coffins, and the coffins that they will likely have to build themselves, to sell ready-made to undertakers and to new widows, and everything sold on credit because the banks were hit and no one can get at their money.

The little room is still dark; hardly any light can get through the muddied windows. It puts Paul in mind of waking in the blue air with Little Homer breathing deeply beside him in the bed.

"I dreamt that every last thing was gone," he is mumbling nervously to Lon and Clarence. "My house was ruined and my family was gone."

There had been varnished woodwork everywhere and the kind of carving he'd always wished he'd learned to do, carpets everywhere riding on long, gleaming floorboards, velvet curtains on tall windows. He'd heard his name then, someone calling his name from outside, and when he'd gone outside the house, the city he lived in was gone. The other houses around his were entirely gone. There was no sign that they had ever been there, nor were there people anywhere. Just pale, flat earth as far as he could see, parched and cracked by a hard wind. He'd turned then to escape it, to run back into his house and lock its door against the wasteland, but when he turned, the door was hanging crooked on its hinges, and the paint on the clapboards was faded and flaking. The curtains were torn and flapping out of jagged window glass. He'd known then that Mae and the children were no longer inside the house, that they had disappeared just as the people in the town had disappeared to a place he would never find. The sound of a shutter banging on the house had been the last thing he heard before he woke.

He sees them standing there and sees a new expression overtaking their faces as they look at him. He hears his own voice, and although he has already begun to regret it, he continues. "I had nothing." He knows he should have found a way for them to speak first and tell him what they saw, and though he knows it clearly, as clearly as he still sees himself standing in the wasteland in his dream, as if he is the only one among them who could have dreamt it, he says again, "I had nothing."

9

Each night after the storm, the men come out to wander the streets, surveying the damage as if the ruined houses will tell them something new. They set out determined, intending to take in what they will see as nothing more than an implausible exhibition dreamed up for a World's Fair. They vow to go further afield this time, to gain a broader view of the devastation in order to place their own losses in better perspective. Each man hopes the present quietness will allow him to view his neighbor's tragedy as if he is a tourist, but the horror embedded in each inconceivable sight shrinks them into shuffling old men.

Those men among them who are deputized bear arms: rifles and pistols removed from their own wrecked homes before looters could find them. Even without the firearms, the deputies would be recognizable by their gait, the particular stride conferred by their jurisdiction. Unlike the other men, they are imperturbable, having been given a purpose, and they have the luxury of empathy, their dignity restored by their office.

The deputies learn to read the faces of the men they meet and tailor their questions according to what they see there. If a man has an angry look, they'll ask, *You had trouble with looters?* because anger is a concrete thing and means the man has not stopped fighting. If a man has a bewildered look, they are mindful of his dignity and of what he has likely lost. They'll venture to touch a man like this, to lay a hand on his shoulder and say, *We'll dig out, you know.* And if a man's face is still convulsed with grief, they are as tender with him as if he were a child. *You know they're giving out tents downtown, don't you? And camp beds and cookstoves, milk and bread?* If the man nods, they'll ask, *How many beds you need?* as a way of inquiring how many of his family were taken by the storm.

Until the looting started, no one thought of needing deputies. The first cases defied belief in most of the people who heard of them, and in their disbelief they repeated the stories until they began to take the shape of storm lore.

Taking the rings off corpses, I heard. Going along from porch to porch where the bodies were laid out and yanking the rings right off their fingers.

I heard there was a stranger coming through and cutting off fingers to get the rings. Heard he got himself shot.

The men wander the streets each night, their own at first and then the surrounding blocks. They marvel at the houses pushed over sideways, the houses without roofs, the holes in the ground that are just the wound of a basement, ripped open and full of junk. Here, concrete steps and a metal railing leading nowhere; there, someone's yard with the grass entirely gone and an old tree torn clean in two. Sometimes they see folks with cameras, taking pictures of kids in front of ruined houses.

Just stand there a minute. No, you can't go climbing up, it's just a pile of sticks, it's not safe.

At first it's just town folks, taking pictures of their own places to send to relatives. The men understand that this is born of the need to witness and record the devastation. Pictures like these will be sent in letters to relatives in other states; they will be put into albums to show to grandchildren in years to come. But now it's folks from out of town coming in their clean clothes and their polished cars, gawking and taking snapshots of their children like they're standing at the rim of the Grand Canyon. The men walk past, shaking their heads, and some of them mutter their dissent loud enough to be heard. *We ain't a sideshow, you know.*

A man who has been in a stupor since the storm will see a family of tourists perched on a ruin, children posing for their father's camera, and his breathing will fall into shallow stabs, and his hands will shape themselves into loose fists as he glowers his defiance at the father. He will mutter something and clench his jaw, and then mutter it louder until he is shouting *You got no right!* and other men passing will take his arms and pull him away with them, speaking to him in the low, confidential tones of a parent calming an angry child.

When it falls dark each night, the men gather around fires they light in the middle of the streets from the downed branches and debris all around them. News can be had here, stories exchanged, and a man can warm himself while talking to his neighbors. A man deep in mourning is welcome the same as a man who is only angry. Here the grieving man is not expected to meet his neighbors' eyes. He can bring his face out of the shadows into the orange-yellow light knowing that he'll be allowed to stare into the fire alongside the others and unburden himself of his sorrow or not, as he chooses. It may be that some of the other men were there when the grieving man failed to find his children alive. It may be that the other men's hands are also torn from ripping at the beams and crumbled bricks of the school, and dragging out the bodies of the children.

These other men will understand when the grieving man says, *I keep seeing them, whole, when I sleep.* And when he says, *I see them, smiling, walking to me out of a ruin,* they will nod their heads deeply, having seen it, too.

Mostly the men around these fires want to detach themselves from their losses by talking about those worse off than themselves. Standing in the glare of the fire, they don't see the wreckage illuminated behind them. *I heard as folks' clothes was ripped right off their backs. Walkin' naked as God made 'em, right down the middle of Main Street,* one man says. *I heard that, too,* the man opposite him replies. *Course most everybody was covered up good with mud and dirt, wherever their clothes had got to.* They shake their heads at the stubbornness of those too prideful to accept a tent and cookstove from the National Guard. *Any roof, even a canvas roof, is better than sleeping rolled up in a rug next to a bonfire in a field,* a man says. *Well, they don't want charity, they say,* is the answer. *They'll come around soon enough, we keep having these flurries at night.*

The men end by talking about the things they cannot believe. *They're saying it was worse than a battlefield,* one man ventures, hoping for confirmation, although he is ashamed that he has spoken so baldly. *Well, I was over in France,* another man quietly answers, pausing. *I never saw anything over there to match it.* The men are aghast, but grateful for the veteran's authority in resolving the question. If they'd had exemptions in the war, well, that was all right. They can say now they've seen worse and survived.

The men are emboldened; some of them look at each other now and not into the fire, embarking on the one topic too incendiary to be decent.

Is it true what they're saying about Paul Graves?

All true.

What's that?

Didn't get hit.

You mean his place? His house didn't get hit?

That's right.

Not just his place. The lumberyard, too. Neither one got touched.

I heard his Ford got hit.

Moved. It got itself moved, not hit.

His kids weren't even in school that day. Home sick, all of 'em, and down cellar.

One man whistles in spiteful amazement. *That's luck for you.*

Another man looks from face to face and says, *Well, that can't be. There can't be just one.* The others look back knowingly, in gentle derision of his disbelief.

That's what everyone's saying. What Graves says himself.

The unbelieving man frowns into the fire, shaking his head slowly, laboriously. To accept this news as true is to magnify his own anguish, to bitterly underscore the randomness of the storm. The other men in the circle know this already, and they watch as understanding settles on the last man among them to hear the news.

That just can't be, he says. *He can't be the only one.*

10

Three-footers and six-footers, that's all he's got measurements for, all he's ever made. Paul is leaning on the counter, papers spread out between his hands. Lon is looking on next to him, worrying the eraser on a short pencil with his thumbnail.

"Seems like we need a couple more sizes," he says. He glances up at Paul who nods but keeps frowning. "Three foot's too big for a baby and too small for a ten-year-old."

"Go ahead," Paul says, "Figure out two more and we'll get cutting. But make them simple. We don't have time for toe-pinchers."

Lon pauses. As soon as he steps away, work will begin in earnest. This is what they will be doing, all they will be doing, and the Lord only knows how long they will be doing it. Paul looks at him and asks, "Anything else?"

"Are we building them or just cutting the lumber?"

"Both," Paul says. "I figure we'll do both until someone tells us different."

They look at the door and the windows on either side of it. They can hear occasional foot traffic outside, but it's impossible to see any people who might be passing, the windows are so muddied. It has always been Paul's habit to look up each time the light in the windows changed, to see who was passing on the sidewalk, who might already be turning to open the door. Paul has always looked up quickly, so quickly that he's known who was coming in before the bell has even had a chance to ring. He knows the look of most everyone in town, no matter if they're wearing a straw hat or a muffler, and he can name folks a block away just by their gait or the way they stand. He'd learned it watching his father, who always seemed to know exactly who was coming up the long dirt road to the house when everyone else was still squinting, only certain of it being a man or a woman. Once Paul had moved to town, it became a regular feature of his days at the lumberyard, making Johnny and everyone who worked for them shake their heads and smile as he called out greetings to people before they'd gotten a foot over the threshold.

Now Paul is of more than half a mind to silence the bell over the door, to stuff newspaper in its cheerful throat. Always before he's greeted people as if he's been expecting them, but now he'll have to meet their gaze knowing already what it is they've come for. He decides instead to prop the door open to prevent the bell from ringing, and to let in some extra light, if nothing else. Pulling the door open, he's startled by someone pushing on it from the other side. A man in uniform comes in, a National Guardsman, smart and clean, wishing him a good morning, saying his name is Captain Kemmel and asking who the owner is.

"I am," Paul says, taking him in. "Name's Graves." The Captain takes hold of Paul's hand and grips it a touch more firmly than he needs to, a touch longer. He looks hard at Paul, and Paul knows he's being measured. He thinks he sees regret in Kemmel's eyes, an apology of sorts for having had to begin with an assessment. They're of a similar age, both wear a wedding band. Paul recognizes something of himself in Kemmel's face; this man also has children, of that he's certain. They're of a kind, Paul thinks. He sees the beginnings of a smile around Kemmel's eyes, that he's also recognized himself in Paul.

"I suppose you've been expecting me," Kemmel says.

"After a fashion." Paul had thought he'd understood that

absolutely everything had changed, but he still hasn't. He realizes now how foolish, how hopeful he had been, thinking it would be his regular customers and friends coming through the door. How many of them must be dead, he wonders, if the government has sent this man to order their coffins.

"How many men do you still have?" Kemmel asks.

"Two, besides myself," Paul says. He remembers Clarence's son, Sam, then and adds, "One of them has a boy here, sixteen years old. He can help."

Paul is reasonably certain he's answering Kemmel's questions because he's being asked them only once. Still, the Captain's voice is coming to him distantly, as if they're separated somehow and not walking side by side through the office out to the yard. Two hundred coffins, Kemmel is saying. More than two hundred.

They're looking over the stock in the yard. They've been clearing debris from the yard all morning and Clarence is still at it now, making room for the pallets on which they will stack the cut lumber for coffins. Kemmel is asking how much of the stock was ruined in the storm, and before Paul can say that they haven't gotten that far, he has to stop Irene going by with a bucket in each hand.

"Not yet," he says, holding up a hand.

"But the windows!" Irene protests.

Paul exhales hard to keep himself from frowning. "Just one, then. And just enough to let in some light."

Paul hears the bell ring as Irene goes out the door to the sidewalk. He's wondering how much longer he's going to be answering questions, how soon he can get out there to stop her from doing too good a job on that window. Yes, he keeps answering. Yes, they've got enough handsaws to work with while the electricity is out. He and his men are uninjured. They'll finish moving the spoiled stock and start cutting when they uncover lumber they can use. They're walking back into the office now and the Captain is talking to Lon about coffin sizes. Irene keeps coming through with her buckets and splashing water onto the window outside with a cup to soften up the mud. She's scraping the mud off now, dragging it along the glass with the edge of a scrap of wood.

Captain Kemmel is congratulating them on their good fortune and shaking hands again.

"It's lucky for us all that you weren't hit," he's saying. "There will be Guardsmen detailed here to cut lumber, then they'll start building the coffins once you've got enough cut to get them started."

Paul knows there'll be some who will want to build coffins for their own dead, as he and John had for their father. Then, of course, there had been time to do the thing properly. Now people will be forced to knock out what amounts to crates, rough ones at that.

"There's one coffin already built," Kemmel is saying. Paul and Lon look at him and even Irene pauses on her way back out with her buckets full of water.

"You didn't hear? There was a funeral going on in the First Baptist Church when the storm hit. The coffin's still inside the wreckage." They all stare at him. It might be funny later, each of them knows, many years on, when the idea of a coffin inside a collapsed church won't leave them wondering who it was who was lucky enough to get himself boxed up the very morning of the storm.

Captain Kemmel is moving toward the door, nodding at Irene's buckets and saying, "Wash all you want with that water, miss, but don't drink it. It's contaminated."

Now there's the water to worry about, too, Paul thinks. And the coffee they've already been drinking this morning. "I have to warn Mae," he says aloud, wondering just what it is they're meant to drink if it's not the town water. But there's the yard to clear and the lumber stock to sort and boards to cut and

bang into boxes so all the corpses around town can start to disappear off people's porches. Kemmel motions Paul outside
with him and then says in a low voice, "I'll send a man out to
your place with water." Kemmel holds up a hand when Paul
begins to protest at the preferential treatment and says, "You're
needed here. We'll be discreet about it."

Paul goes back inside, looking at his hands and starting to
unwrap the bandages so that he can get his work gloves on. He
can see Irene plainly through the big front window now. She's
gotten rid of the worst of the mud and is moving the rest of it
around on the glass with a rag.

"Knock on that window, will you?" Paul says to Lon and
heads toward the back. "Ask her to start getting together some
rope."

They decide on a rotation—one man measuring, two sawing, one stacking—to avoid fatigue. Paul sees the others hesitate, not knowing what task Sam should be put to.

"You can pull a straight saw, can't you, Sam?" he asks,
holding out a handsaw to the boy.

"Yes, sir," Sam says, taking the saw with a glance at his father.

"Thought as much. All right if I pay you a wage today?"

It's hard not to wink when Sam thanks him, but Paul manages to nod at the boy instead and give him a smile with his
eyes. They settle in to work, and when a group of Captain
Kemmel's men arrive, they see Paul's rotation in operation and
immediately set to work in two more groups of four alongside
Paul and his men.

Irene comes through at intervals and forces them to rest
and drink some of the water the Guardsmen have brought
with them to the lumberyard before they relinquish one task in
the rotation and begin another. Paul is streaming with sweat.
They all are. He can't think when he's ever cut this much wood
with just a hand saw. He looks at each board passing through

his hands knowing that although he's built coffins before or sold people the wood for them, he's never cut a board before and known, even as he cut it, that it was going straight into the ground to rot.

He and John had built the lumberyard knowing that the lumberyard would build Marah. They had both taken pleasure in seeing frames going up on lots here and there in town, knowing that they had cut the gleaming boards. Surely John, like Paul, had taken his family on evening drives, pointing out the houses that had been framed with wood from their lumberyard, laughing when the children begged him to show them another and another. Marah was built and Marah must be rebuilt. But for now there is only digging, the furious digging in the cemeteries.

Irene's voice beside him startles Paul. "Your wife is here, Mr. Graves," she says.

"Mae? Here?"

"She's outside, out front."

"Why doesn't she just come in?"

Irene starts back into the office, calling over her shoulder, "She says she's not staying."

Mae is there, in the street, holding the handle of Homer's wagon.

"I didn't think I'd see you at all today unless I stopped by now," she says. "I have to return some water that was delivered to us by mistake."

No, Paul thinks, not much discreet about a National Guardsman coming to the house with a large container of water. He sees that Mae has empty stock pots stacked in the wagon as well, to take drinking water home in again. He grins at her, grateful and proud.

"Can you manage all right?"

"I walked right down the middle of the street all the way here." Mae says, and nods at the Liberty Theater next door, where a couple of men are at work cleaning the sign. "They're making progress here, too, I see. You could probably let Irene have another go at the windows this afternoon."

Paul watches her until she turns the corner onto Walnut Street and disappears from view. He exhales heavily and when he passes Irene on his way back out to the yard he says, "My wife tells me they're cleaning next door."

"Are they?"

"You know they are. And next time, tell me yourself. You don't have to wait for Mae to come by."

Paul keeps his mind on his family through the afternoon to distract himself. He can only guess when he'll be able to go home again, what on earth they'll be doing all day while he's gone. Mae and his mother can hardly want to keep the children inside, but neither can they send them outside with the stench that's building all around and the porch to keep them away from. He swings his hammer harder every time he thinks about the porch. The coffins are being taken away almost as fast as they can build them. Just as well; he wouldn't want to turn around and see a stack of them there.

He wonders how far the news has gotten, how much of the country has heard it now. John and Dora must surely be frantic out there in California. With everything down, there's nothing to do but hope they can get a letter out to them, and he imagines Mae and his mother have already thought of that. Send a letter to John and Dora out on a train to the next town that has a post office still standing and then wait. The reply's not the important thing, of course, just the words going out: *Family fine, house and lumberyard also fine.* We've been knocked back a few centuries, but we're all still standing here and breathing.

They've got me building coffins, Johnny, Paul thinks. We're hard at it with the cheapest pine and handsaws. You were right to leave, your old house is gone. Imagine that—I'm finally glad you left.

Paul knows now that the way his mother has been shaking since the storm has as much to do with John as any of the rest of them. She'd been against John's moving out to California, just as Paul had been, but held her tongue and let Paul be the one to try to talk him out of it. John had argued that Paul was only worried about the lumberyard, but it was up and running and everyone knew that either Paul or John could have continued without the other. It was their family Lavinia had been thinking about. Even though Homer, Paul's father, had died, they were increasing: John with his two children, and Paul now with his three, and neither Paul nor his mother could stand the thought of their diminishing again. He and John had argued bitterly, and it was only when Lavinia had happened to come by the lumberyard and walked in on them fighting that they had stopped. Neither of them could be sure whether it was what she had heard or the mere fact of their arguing that had made her face look like that, but they had stopped then and there. The last words spoken on the subject that day, before Paul finally agreed to buy out John's share of the lumberyard were John shouting at Paul, "I didn't make you stay on the farm. Don't you make me stay here in Marah!" If Lavinia can't stop her shaking now, it's because she's grateful, finally grateful after all these years for John's stubbornness, for his forcing himself to turn a deaf ear to Paul and moving anyway.

Paul is blinking hard so he can see, stopping his hammering to wipe his nose on his shirt sleeve. The sounds of others hammering and sawing continue around him. He looks at the length of the boards in front of him and sees that he's building a coffin for a child. It comes as a surprise to Paul that this could be worse, more painful somehow than it had been to carry a dead child out of the ruins of the school. He realizes now that he had deceived himself then, persuading himself as he carried out the children that death weighed no heavier on each one of them than sleep did on his own children when he carried them to bed. Now there's nothing to do but continue, finish the thing and let them take it away.

"Mr. Graves." Irene is there again, but this time her face is serious. "You're needed out front."

"Who is it?" Paul asks her.

"It's Russell Meeker. He's here about a coffin."

Irene seems to be stunned by having to deliver the message. "It's all right," Paul says and lays his hand on her shoulder. If she's distressed by the very thing they were all braced for, it's only because of her youth and because she allowed herself to believe that Captain Kemmel had put in the total order himself. He walks out of the light of the yard back into the dark office and through to the store. He sees Meeker at the counter, recognizes his outline in the light coming in from the window behind him. Paul walks around the counter slowly, giving himself a moment to take in the changes; the sunken line of Meeker's shoulders, the effort with which he holds up his head.

"Hello, Russ," he says, and offers his hand. Meeker takes it and looks at him, beginning to shake his head as if he is saying No. His head keeps shaking, back and forth, as if it's only a tremor, but his eyes are still telling Paul no.

"Is it for Gertie?" Paul asks gently, and Meeker begins to nod instead.

"I can't stand to build it myself," he says, his voice quiet.

"You don't have to," Paul says. "I'm building it now."

11

A gray cat flicks its tail in the dust. An old man sitting nearby on a salvaged straight-backed chair sees the cat and recognizes his own lassitude in the cat's half-closed eyes. Nowhere to go, nothing to do, he's been rendered little more than a child by the industry of the relief workers around him, left to fill his days with watching. He flicks a pebble at the cat who springs up and bounds away, settling in an identical pose further down the street, out of range.

The men and women in the town are watchful, wary of the western sky. Fearful now of every cloud, they look up at intervals, scanning the horizon. People sifting through the wreckage and those setting out to fetch water or food mark the changes in the sky throughout the day. Children forget to look for animal shapes in the cottony masses at rest in a pale blue sky, finding no pleasure in following even the whitest clouds. At day's end, people gather in the streets, equally fearful of a dark sky and unwilling to take shelter for the night.

Dark clouds draw a crowd. *Time was I'd have just gone inside if I saw a cloud like that.* They stand there, half transfixed, half skittery, their breath going shallow until it begins to rain and they can shake off their fear with a shiver and laugh at their foolishness before they disperse. *Half a minute there, I was ready to run.*

They are wary, too, of being out in the town, of being abroad during the day when strangers come touring in their automobiles. The Guardsmen are there to send them away, but they continue to arrive daily by the carload. Those who cannot account for missing loved ones fear the wreckage. *They can hope all they want she was blown away. Won't know for sure till they haul off that house.*

Fathers and mothers who are told they should send their children out on trains to get them back to school hesitate. When they're told that they must, that other people in other towns have already done so, they resist. The children hear the talk and stay close. They feel their fathers and mothers gripping their shoulders as they weigh the thing, trying to imagine watching their children pull out of town on a train. When someone argues, *There's folks willing to take them in for a while, under proper roofs. Think how much school they're missing! How much more they'll miss before the school can be rebuilt here*, one of the fathers will finally say, *Nothing saying we can't teach them right here.* The children's fear eases then, when they are all certain that their fathers and mothers will refuse. *They can set up one of those big tents for a school. Give us all something to do till we can rebuild.*

Those in the town who have camped before for pleasure recognize the enforced dullness of each day, but also that the boredom and privation are expanding now without their consent. The chill evenings, when it is still too early for people to return to the houses they are sheltering in or to the government tents they have pitched in the fields, are the longest part of the day. The dreariness everywhere heightens the people's restlessness, and restlessness gives way to unease.

The Liberty's showing a Buster Keaton tonight.

Got no money.

Don't need money, they're showing it for free.

That so. Which one?

Sherlock Jr.

Seen it last year.

Well, hell, so'd I. I'm only going to get where it's warm for a while.

The Liberty Theater is full to capacity every night, often with the same people, though the movie showing doesn't change. They sit with their coats on and their hats in their laps. With the electricity restored, the theater is intact, exactly as it was before the storm, and leaves people feeling that they have entered a time machine of sorts. Once the lights are dimmed, it is possible to sit in the dark and imagine that the town also lies just as it was, intact beyond the theater's closed doors. Some of the people forget themselves and laugh at the movie, lulled by the dark and the familiarity of the theater.

A woman flings open the theater doors one evening, halfway through the movie, and runs in screaming, *Tornado!* The men and women rise without looking at each other and rush out of the theater into the street to look at the masses of dark clouds crouching above the town. While they are looking up, judging whether to run or stay, the clouds burst open. There is no glee among the people because of the rain, no relief that the clouds' only intention is to soak them, only despondency that they are no longer rational, no better than cattle in their panicked response. Too wet now to return to the theater's upholstered seats, the words *guess I'll just go home* begin to form on each tongue. There are a few rueful snorts among the men, because home now means a tent in a rainstorm, before they all turn to scurry away along the dark, wet streets.

12

They're leaving," Paul says, closing the bedroom door behind him. "The McKinneys say they're leaving after breakfast."

Mae is making their bed, tucking the bedspread under the pillows more painstakingly than she needs to, weighing her words.

"I know," she says in an even voice.

"You know? How do you know?"

"They told me last night before I came up to bed."

"Why didn't you tell me? I could have talked to them before they'd made up their minds!"

"I didn't tell you because I wanted you to be able to sleep. And their minds were already made up before they told me."

She stands straight and looks at Paul with an expression he has seen before that is both gentle and troubled. She's warning him, he knows, not to try to coerce the last of the people sheltering with them to stay longer. He knows he'll likely meet the same resistance in his mother, whether or not she and Mae have had a chance to talk together this morning.

"Ed and Grace aren't children," Mae says. "We can hardly force them to stay if they want to go."

"But go where? There's nothing for them to go to."

"A tent and cots aren't nothing."

"I thought we'd made them all welcome."

"We did."

Paul sits on the edge of the bed and pulls Mae down to sit

beside him. She exhales and looks at her hands lying clasped on her knees. She'd formed her habit of sighing and exhaling during her pregnancies. She'd said each time he'd pointed it out, "Was I sighing? I suppose I was only trying to draw a proper breath." But she'd never lost the habit, and in the years that had followed it had come to signal her turning inward. Whenever he asked her now whether something was wrong, why she was sighing, she only answered in a distracted voice, "Was I?"

Stay here, Mae, stay here, Paul thinks. He pulls her closer and presses his forehead to her temple, looking down so he won't have to see if she becomes annoyed. "Where did my girl go?" he murmurs.

"It's wearing on everybody, having to be considerate all the time," Mae says. "If it were me, I'd be lining up for a tent, too. Think what you'd be asking of them if you talked them into staying. Roll your blankets in the corner folks, and don't come back till supper."

"We never even hinted at such a thing!"

"Of course not. But those are the rules they all followed. I didn't like it either, watching them leave after breakfast, wondering what in creation they could find to do between then and supper time. We tried, your mother and I both tried to convince them it wasn't necessary, that they were welcome to spend their days here with us, but in the end we weren't their family and they weren't really guests."

Paul takes Mae's hand lightly in his and she exhales again.

"I understand they have their pride," Paul says, "But it's cold out there."

"They'll have a wood-burning stove in their tent. Lord knows there's enough stuff lying around to burn."

"Yes, and if they stayed they could have electric lights and a bathroom."

"Oh, for pity's sake, Paul!" Mae shakes her hand away from

Paul's, gets up off the bed, and finally looks at him. "They can no more stay here than we can get in line and ask for a tent! Ed and Grace McKinney don't need saving. They're not even all that bad off, compared to some. They lost their house, not a child, and they can rebuild."

Mae looks at Paul sitting there, looking down at his hands. She feels remorse for wanting to leave without setting things right, but decides she's leaving anyway.

"I have to get breakfast," she says.

Paul returns to the kitchen table to sit with his cold coffee. Breakfasts since the storm have become hurried affairs, no matter how they try to make a normal meal out of their random fare, and now Paul is the only one in the kitchen. Milk and bread from the National Guard today, plus their own potatoes, fried, and his mother's strawberry jam spooned sparingly on the bread. He can't figure yet what it is that's got him so upset, whether it's folks no longer accepting his help or simple guilt. Even if it were both and he could say in exactly what proportion each thing weighed on him, it wouldn't matter. Living in this house, untouched as it is, was easier to bear when there were people sheltering there with them. He could at least point to a reason his and a few other houses on their block had been spared and say to the people sleeping on his floors, "I'm so glad we had a place for you to come to." He's no longer the man with everything to share, he's just the man with everything.

The McKinney's had left with smiles and handshakes, calling their good-byes as he and Mae had stood on the steps and watched them go up the middle of the street toward town, their bedrolls tied and carried under their arms. The house had seemed cavernous to him when he'd turned to go inside, and judging from the way Mae had stopped to look around the living room, rubbing her palms on her apron as if to dry them, she had felt it, too. Strange to think that a house with three adults and three children still in it could seem this empty. Of course it wasn't just that the bedrolls had been removed one by one as people left to take up residence in one of the tent cities springing up on the edges of town; the porch, relieved now of its corpses, was empty, too.

Paul gets up from the kitchen table and goes into the broom closet, looking for a scrub brush and a pail.

"I'm going to scrub the porch is all," he says to Mae who hears him rummaging and comes in. "Nothing else yet. I think we should still wait a while longer to finish clearing the yard."

Mae nods, silent, with her hands in her apron pockets.

"About the yard," he says. "I don't think you should plan on planting much this summer. Not flowers, anyway. Just tomatoes and such in the vegetable patch."

He's been fearful of saying this, knowing how it will sadden her. When he thinks of summer, he thinks first of Mae and her hands full of flowers. He'd been sincerely puzzled when Ruby had been born and Mae hadn't wanted to name her something like Rose or Violet. He'd even teased her a little about it. Then there are the floral fabrics she favors for her dresses and aprons. Even her hair, bobbed and wavy, reminds him of flowering vines and the tendrils on young growing things. It will cost her something, he realizes, to spend a summer without her flowers.

"There are flowers starting to come up now, all around the house. Do you want me to pull the bulbs?"

Paul shakes his head. "Maybe you can just cut them to have in vases inside once they're up."

Paul reasons that he and Mae are thinking alike, that it will be heaven knows how long before either of them can look at the porch without remembering the row of bodies, draped in white bedsheets. She'd been the first to say that the porch swing shouldn't go up this year, and that she didn't know when she'd be able to enjoy being out on the porch again. For Paul's part, he couldn't imagine being seen publicly to be enjoying life too soon, not tending ornamental flowers and certainly not sitting in a porch swing for every passerby to see. Same with the house and the yard, at that rate. If he'd swept the porch hard with the old broom from the garage and if he was scrubbing every inch of it now, it was only so he could stand to walk on it again, not because it was time to set things to rights.

The neighborhood is quiet, not peaceful like it's always been, but empty. No children's voices to be heard, no cars rolling over the cobbles in the streets. If there is a din to be heard, it's in the tent cities now, he supposes, although things might be somber there, too, what with waiting for the burials to begin. He'd like to go out there and have a look around one of the tent cities and see how folks are fixed. Lon and Clarence are living in those tents with their families, and Irene and her mother. Russ Meeker, too. He could probably walk over there with them after work one day soon and have a look without being too conspicuous. Just see them home, have a laugh at their all being down-the-row neighbors now, and leave. Then again, maybe not. There'd be others there he'd know, folks he'd have to greet and explain himself to and convince some-how that he wasn't there touring like the gawkers.

Paul wonders what Mae ever did with the bedsheets she used to cover the bodies out here on the porch those first few nights before the Guardsmen took them away. He doesn't sup-pose they'll find their way back onto any of the beds. Not any time soon. Would boiling be enough to satisfy her, he won-ders? There'd be no way of knowing until you were standing there with the sheet in your hand, dry, ironed, and folded, about to snap it out over a mattress. It might be an idea to con-fuse things, to wash those sheets again with others from the linen closet so you couldn't know for sure which was which. It might also be an idea just to burn them. Paul drops his brush in the pail and gets up to look over the porch rail at the debris alongside the house.

He has less and less excuse now for putting off clearing the yard. Once the electricity was on again at the lumberyard, finishing the cutting of lumber for all the coffins had been quick work. They were cutting government lumber by then, sent in in boxcars, and the National Guard had simply requisitioned the use of the lumberyard as a place to build the coffins and sent Paul and his men home. With nothing to do now until those boxes are in the ground, with having to wait for shipments of lumber to replenish his own stock, and with there being no takers for the help he has to offer, he doesn't know how he can wait any longer to begin work at home, cleaning up the place.

This is the moment he has been dreading, the moment he's been delaying, hoping others on his street would spare him by beginning first. It had worked out all right at the lumberyard where he'd made Irene and the others wait until there was cleaning underway next door at the Liberty before they got started. Even then, he'd prevented them from doing too good a job. Paul saw how they were itching to clean the place; having lost everything of their own, they were that much keener to see the lumberyard restored to its old self. He'd had to say it out loud finally and explain to them all that the storm had left him walking a high wire of sorts, and that for the time being, and no matter what they were doing next door at the Liberty, his having an overly clean storefront amounted to preening. And now, because he is not needed at the lumberyard, and because everyone knows he has nothing else to occupy him at home but the yard, he will be seen as calculating if he waits. Paul empties his pail, throwing the last of his wash water out over the brown grass in the yard in a thin gray curl and says, "Damned if I do, damned if I don't."

Mae is helping the children put on their coats in the kitchen when he goes in to get a stack of old newspapers and the matches.

"Your mother needs a rest," Mae says. "I thought I'd take the children with me down to the relief tent today."

"Why don't you leave Ellis with me. He can help me burn some of the junk in the yard."

Ruby and Homer protest immediately at the unfairness of being singled out for the dull walk to town, and Mae shushes them just as quickly.

"You two can ride in the wagon all the way downtown," she says.

"We don't both fit!" cries Ruby.

"You will if you sit sideways," Mae says. "Now quit your complaining, or you can both walk there and back."

Paul follows them out the back door to the garage. There is debris all around the house. He and Ellis would only make visible progress if they worked into the night, but he supposes they have no choice but to make a start. Mae sits Ruby and Homer in the wagon facing opposite directions with their legs dangling over the side and pulls them down the driveway after her and into the street.

Paul waves them off. "Help your mama get the food," he calls. "Then you can help me outside when you get home."

He stands there with Ellis watching them go and knows that Ellis is waiting for him to say what they need to do to start the fire. Paul tells himself that the way the yard wants clearing is not unlike the way the porch had wanted scrubbing, and that maybe all that will happen as a result is that others will start on their own property once they've seen a fire in his driveway. Then his eyes close and he hears himself exhale just like Mae and he hears a voice saying, *Nothing to rebuild, so he prettied up his yard.*

They start with the downed branches and twigs lying everywhere and Ellis seems already to know how to stack the pieces, and in which order. "That's right, that's right," says Paul, watching the boy. Once they've got the fire going in the same spot where Paul burns fallen leaves every autumn, each of them takes a bushel basket to gather more debris from the yard.

"Dump it over to the side there when your basket is full," Paul says, pointing away from the fire toward the top of the driveway. "We'll let the fire burn down a while before we throw anything else big on." When there's enough debris gathered to keep the fire going a good long while, they stand together and watch the fire, Ellis holding a garden rake and Paul, a shovel. "Anything rolls out of the fire, you just push it back with the rake, okay?" Ellis nods. "Anything big rolls out, we'll scoop it up like we're holding giant spoons and dump it right back on."

"What'll we do with the stuff that won't burn, Daddy?" Ellis asks. Paul looks at the boy and sees that he's trying to keep an impassive expression on his face, pretending that neither the question nor its answer are of any particular importance when he clearly started thinking about it long before he'd asked.

"Metal and stuff like that?" Paul asks.

"Yeah. Metal and stuff."

Paul looks away from Ellis and back at the fire to keep himself from grinning. The boy is so serious, so grave with his hands on the shaft of the rake like he's holding a ceremonial object.

"Well, now . . . " Paul says, furrowing his brow to let Ellis know he is thinking. "What do you figure we oughta do with it?" he asks.

"We could make a pile of it. Keep it separate."

Paul nods. "That way we could drive it all out to the dump, later."

"Yes, Daddy," Ellis says.

"Then that's just what we'll do."

"Could I throw one metal thing on the fire, Daddy? Just to see what would happen?"

Paul allows himself a smile. Ellis hasn't entirely lost his serious expression, but he is beginning to look more like a seven-year-old again. "Go get yourself a good one," he says.

"Started clearing things up, have you?" a woman's voice calls once Ellis has run off. Paul looks up to see Virginia Eberhardt looking at him from her porch next door.

"Thought we might as well get started," Paul says, walking away from the fire to the hedge that divides the Eberhardt's yard from theirs. Virginia is still in her bathrobe. Paul looks toward the fire; Ellis is back, crouching there and peering in at whatever object he has found to throw in it. Virginia has exactly the same cleaning job ahead of her, washing mud off her house and clearing her yard of debris, but newly widowed and childless as she is, Paul has no idea who can help her. He realizes his error then and feels his stomach drop. If he had been killed downtown in the storm instead of Henry Eberhardt, Henry would have been cleaning up in Mae's yard before he touched his own. It's too late now, the first fire was lit in his own driveway, not Virginia's. If he makes her the offer, it will be an afterthought, born out of guilt and not selfless duty to his neighbor.

"Might as well," Virginia says. "It's quite a job, and I don't suppose you have much else to do."

"Ellis wanted to, you see," Paul hears himself saying. "He built the fire almost by himself." Paul's eyes dart over to Ellis and then back to Virginia.

"Did he, now? Well, I'll be."

It's over almost as soon as it's started, ending with Virginia drifting back inside her house. Paul stands there by the hedge, unnerved by his error and by the fact that the very comment he'd feared had come, and come immediately. There is a small, cold feeling growing in his gut that feels like fear. He knows the feeling; he felt it once before, the time he'd wandered away from the farm as a child. He had been about five, the same age Little Homer is now. All he'd meant to do was walk for a while on the county road, then turn and come back again, just long enough to see if it felt different to do it alone than it had the times he had done it with Johnny. He'd walked a long ways and, when he'd turned and could no longer see the farm buildings but only the towering corn on either side of the road, he had believed himself to be lost. He'd stood there not knowing what to do, not thinking clearly enough to realize that he'd never even turned off the county road, feeling that new feeling in his belly when he'd heard his name called and seen his mother hurrying along the road toward him. He'd remembered that moment since, and the way that cold feeling began to dissolve the moment he'd seen her.

They'd gone out searching for him when they'd realized he was gone, his father and mother setting out in opposite directions, praying that he had stayed on the road and not strayed into the corn. Once they were all home again, his parents were serious but hardly scolded him at all, which had the inadvertent effect of frightening him more than if they'd simply punished him. They had agreed not to let on what a scare he'd given them and had also understood that they couldn't simply forbid a curious boy to go off wandering alone again. They'd told him instead to stop more often when he was alone, to look up and make certain he knew where he was before he went any further. Paul had taken them literally out of remorse as a child and had thereafter kept faithful track of his whereabouts, and by the time he'd reached adulthood, the incident had turned to metaphor; an illustration that he could overcome indecision or uncertainty by turning, figuratively now, to see where he stood in relation to where he had been.

Now it seems that his parent's advice belonged only to the

time before the storm, before the roads around him were scoured off the map. If he feels uncertain now, it's because he is lost, as lost as any other person in town, and no simple act of turning around, literal or figurative, will right him. He sees it every day, in every face he meets. Virginia, widowed now and dressing in her bathrobe. His own mother who needs to rest mid-morning on a weekday. Mae going silent and exhaling all the time. Russ Meeker, standing in front of Paul at the lumberyard and shaking so because of Gertie's coffin.

When Paul had told Russ he was already working on Gertie's coffin, Russ had looked at him, astonished. Paul had startled himself, saying those words. He had felt a fierceness rush through him as he said them, suddenly determined that he should know which child would be buried in that one small coffin.

"Come out back with me," Paul had said, knowing that if the others in the yard, and the Guardsmen in particular, saw Russ looking at the coffin, he could be certain it would be used for Gertie Meeker.

Russ had frowned for a moment, looking at the back of the store where Paul was gesturing before he agreed. All work had stopped when Paul led Russ out into the yard. The men stood there with their tools at their sides, watching the man in the dark overcoat walk between them and stop where Paul had been working.

"Just tell me where you want it sent," Paul had said, knowing he would take it along himself, that he'd carry it alone on his shoulder through the streets if he had to.

"They've got her over at the high school. I suppose you should send it there." Russ had stood staring at the partially built box, holding his hat in front of him with both hands. "I can't pay you for it yet," he'd said.

"No one can pay for anything yet," Paul had said, shaking his head. "We'll worry about that later."

Russ had looked around himself then, scanning the yard as if he'd misplaced something. Paul had thought at first that Russ was so distraught he couldn't see the way out, but then he saw the simpler truth; that Russ was truly lost, having to force himself to believe the fact of his daughter's death. When Russ had turned to leave the yard, Paul had bent down swiftly to pick something up from the ground and followed him out. When they shook hands on the sidewalk in front of the store, Paul pressed a scrap of wood no longer than his thumb into Russ's hand before he turned to go back inside. Just a small piece of pine from a board he'd been cutting that the saw's teeth had snagged on earlier and that Paul had broken off and thrown on the ground.

"Daddy, why did you tell Mrs. Eberhardt it was my idea to burn this stuff?" Ellis asks, still crouching by the fire, and Paul answers him, feeling again like that boy on the county road who has just looked up but doesn't know yet that his mother is coming.

"I don't know, son. I just don't know."

13

The women wait silent in their lines, holding their children by the hand. Women with babies ride them on their hips and bounce and sway when the babies begin to fret. The women shift their weight from one leg to the other and shuffle forward in child-sized steps when another box has been handed out and the woman holding it, *Excuse me, Pardon me*, is making her way out of the tent. The women cast sidelong glances at the box as it passes, trying to catch a glimpse of the foodstuffs it contains today. A cabbage, some cans. The woman passes too quickly for them to see more than that.

Mae stands Ruby and Homer on either side of her so that they can't fuss at each other. Homer pulls on her hand as he bends to look at something on the ground, and Mae pulls him up without a word. Their line moves forward, inside the big tent now. Mae smiles at each of the children once they're in the shade of the tent as if to say *Almost there*. She hears mumbling from the line next to theirs and a voice spits, "What on earth does *she* need food handouts for?" Mae turns, wide-eyed, knowing instantly that they will all be looking at her, and they are. Hard, righteous faces in a row hoping to shame her.

"Same as anybody here," Mae says in a loud, steady voice. "The stores all got flattened."

She squeezes Ruby's and Homer's hands hard; she feels them looking up at her for an explanation, but she lifts her chin and stares straight ahead at the Guardsmen packing boxes. She'd like to snatch Homer up in her arms and pull Ruby right back out of the tent, march them home and away from this spectacle. Her teeth clench, and Ruby whines, "Mama . . ." pulling at Mae's fingers clenching on her hand. Mae lets go a bit, and the line moves forward again.

She can see them filling the rows of boxes from the crates full of foodstuffs. Bread, potatoes, milk, carrots, and cabbages. She hears the Guardsmens' voices, *There you go, ma'am. You ladies can bring these boxes back next time.* Her heart is knocking hard by the time it's her turn to receive a box. "Thank you," she says to the Guardsman who gives her a kind smile, mistaking the look on her face for shame at accepting charity. Mae feels all the eyes on her as she pushes her way out of the crowd, pulling Homer and Ruby in a train behind her.

The box is heavy, but Mae keeps hold of it and says, "Get in," to the children who stand staring at Homer's wagon. She walks briskly across the grass, yanking the wagon clear of the curb when she reaches the street.

She has as much right as anyone to be taking his box home, of that Mae is certain. Milk for the children and fresh bread are not things a body squirrels away in a pantry or cellar for later. She's certain of this and also that she's afraid of what she'd see if she once looked back at that tent. Mae walks with the heavy box the whole way home, carrying it first under one arm and then the other, holding her head high but nonetheless unable to stop the tears running into the neck of her dress.

Paul is jabbing the burn pile with a rake when she comes up the driveway. He follows her in after hearing her slam the kitchen door and stands there, silent and patient, while she takes cans out of the box and slams them down onto the kitchen table. His face, when she looks up, wears an inexplicable expression: part pity, part need, as if he had seen the whole thing and didn't need telling.

14

A young minister sits among his elders. Baptist, Methodist, Lutheran, Presbyterian. Sitting on straight-backed chairs, they hold the lists of the dead. The young minister, Josiah Ollery, is no longer listening to the discussion of times and days and where exactly to bury the people who belonged to no particular church. He's looking around at the other men's faces. They're not untouched, themselves. One man here will bury his wife, another, his son. Everyone of them but Ollery must rebuild his church.

The minister to Ollery's left, Pastor Harland, touches his arm gently, and then withdraws his hand.

"You think we're wrong, spending so long on the details," he says.

Ollery shakes his head.

"Perhaps we are," Harland says.

"Of course we have to bury the dead," Ollery says. "I just can't work out what to say to the living."

"What have the living said to you?"

Ollery looks back at the older man. He's not so distraught that he can't see Harland's face clearly and each astonishing thing that lies in his expression. Harland sits with his hands clasped and his knees crossed. He is not the least bit agitated or anxious, like the rest of them. Ollery sees Harland's habitual kindness and atten-tiveness in his eyes, but there are new things there as well: a calm acknowledgment of the storm and an acceptance of the things he has seen since that day. In the time Ollery has known him, Harland's tranquility and faith have struck him with a force like physical vigor. Harland's frailties—that he walks with a cane, that he stands so thin inside his suits they seem to belong to another man—have always surprised Ollery.

"It's not what anyone has said so much as what I'm waiting to hear," Ollery says. "What I'm afraid they'll say."

Now that they are all silent, waiting for him to speak, he realizes that there is truly only one thing, one question, that scares him. But what scares him most, whether it is the question itself, the endless futility of answering it, or the very real likelihood that it will never be spoken aloud and only screamed inside people's heads, he doesn't know.

When he says it finally, "Why?" he's thinking of the people who scowl at his church as they pass it. The blazing, angry faces of those who pass and the stunned, blank faces of those who do come in. Either could demand an answer of him, either could stand in the doorway of his church and shout, *Why?* It could come from anyone at any time.

"If someone asks you why, you can answer him honestly and simply by saying that it was God's will," says Pastor Coffman opposite him.

Ollery feels himself beginning to wince and closes his eyes hard. He had hoped he wouldn't have to be the one to do this. He hadn't wanted to be the one to force the discussion. He looks up again at Coffman and lets some of that same blazing anger come into his eyes before he says again in a level voice, "Why?" No one can mistake his meaning this time. He, the youngest among them, means to challenge them.

They are all looking at him now, but he fixes his eyes on Coffman, waiting for an answer. Coffman, like Harland, is over sixty. His wife died in the storm, horribly, they say. Ollery, whose young wife is injured, but alive, knows it is likely cruel of him to force this question on a man who would clearly rather not think about it at all.

"Please understand," Ollery says to him, "I don't want to cause you any more pain. But we have to guide all those people out there through pain like yours. We have to be able to answer them."

Coffman sputters, his voice rising. "But answer what? Why did it happen? Why did God allow it? Why did this person die and not the other? I don't dare say: we can't understand God, we can't know the mind of God!"

Ollery lowers his eyes briefly. Pastor Aufrecht, seated next to Coffman, looks around, flustered, from face to face. "At least the days of people saying it was a judgment are past," he says.

"Are they?" says Pastor Stephens. "I'm not so sure."

Stephens is the only one among them who will bury his child. His teenaged son, they say, survived the storm but died when part of the high school collapsed on him as he was working to free another boy from the wreckage.

"Ollery's right," Stephens says. "But we don't need to just be prepared for 'Why?' we need to be prepared for absolutely anything. People will come out of this thinking and saying strange things, irrational things, even that this was somehow a judgment. People who were perfectly reasonable a week ago will be changed. A thing like this changes people."

"They're already changed," Ollery says. "They're angry, some of them. Don't forget, I see this in a different way than the rest of you because my church is still standing. I thought people would flock here to take shelter at night and pray during the day, but they haven't. Not nearly as many as I'd thought."

"All right, then," says Coffman. "If someone asks you why, what will you say?"

"I haven't the faintest idea. How can I convince people that God has not abandoned them when it seems that he has?"

"Don't forget that God is still present in all of us," says Harland. "He is present in every one of us who has done something to help a neighbor since the storm."

"Perhaps it's the suddenness of it," says Stephens. "Suddenly, on a day like any other, life as you knew it is gone and your loved ones are gone and there was no time to say good-bye."

"Yes, but people die suddenly every day," Ollery says. "A man crossing a street can be struck and killed by a car. It's the scale of things here that makes this different. The insurance companies will be calling this an act of God, and that's what it appears to be, an act of God."

"It was an act of nature," Aufrecht says, frowning.

"In a world made by God," Ollery says.

"I truly take comfort in knowing that my wife is with God now and out of her pain," says Coffman. "They're all with God now. Can't we try to comfort the living with that?"

"Some of them, yes," says Ollery. "But as you said, we can't understand God, so how can we understand his taking these people away from their families?"

"They were his to take," says Harland.

"How do I explain that to a child? That what God wants is more important?" says Ollery.

"You might as well ask why God allows sickness as why he allowed the storm," Coffman shouts. "God never meant this world to be our final home. This world is not our final home!"

Ollery shouts back, "Yes, and if there were no bad in the world we would never experience the good as good!" He exhales and lowers his voice. "They've heard all those things many times before. I mean something else, something that they haven't already heard or thought of themselves."

Aufrecht clears his throat before he speaks. "If you don't think faith is enough, then perhaps you should try reasoning. God once created a perfect world in the Garden of Eden. We're outside the Garden now. There's an angel with a fiery sword to keep us on this side, and this is the side where bad things happen. Earth is not Heaven. There are no tornados in Heaven."

"I thought you said we were past thinking this was a judgment!"

"It's a paradox," Stephens says. "God gave us the gift of water. People drink it, but sometimes people drown in it. God gave us the gift of fire, but the same fire that warms us and cooks our food can burn our house to the ground."

"That just turns a problem into a puzzle." Ollery says.

"Josiah–" Harland says, softly.

"I can hardly say that to a widow with no home!"

"Josiah," Harland says again. "You know that if you answer from the very deepest part of your heart, you will never answer badly."

Ollery looks back at Harland, at that lined, gentle face and everything it contains. He feels chastened, although no one has chastised him.

"You must first be honest with yourself," Harland says in the same kind voice. "They're not the ones you're truly worried about. None of them can scare you by asking why. But you can scare yourself."

15

I
t is a fine day. The minister has said as much, although he probably shouldn't have. *The changeability of all things*, he said, and Mae wondered what prevented the fathers standing there from taking his neck into their hands. So far he hasn't reminded them that the Lord giveth and taketh away, and she prays that he won't.

"We are met in this solemn moment to commend these departed souls into the hands of Almighty God, our heavenly Father. In the presence of death, Christians have sure ground for hope and confidence and even for joy, because the Lord Jesus Christ, who shared our human life and death, was raised again triumphant and lives for evermore."

Mae has heard these words before; when she buried her mother, and then her father. That they were some comfort then and no comfort now is no mystery. She cannot look away from her children. Ellis's almost-new trousers already looking too short. Ruby's hair so fair and sleek with combing. Little Homer, the very image of Ellis at that age. She is persuaded, although they are sober, that they all look as normal as can be. What can they possibly be thinking, anyway, she wonders. Do they even understand that the front porch is clear now because men came and took away the bodies that were laid out there and boxed them up? Mae's expression is fearful; her stomach is clenched, her breathing shallow. If she looks up, she'll see the coffins again, all the coffins in their rows.

Paul stands looking down at the ground. Mae sees the sleeves of his suit coat moving slightly as his clasped hands squeeze each other, gripping in time like a pulse. His hair is sleeked down, too, as much as it will allow. How she had scrubbed the children's necks and combed and combed their hair that morning, dipping the comb into water, parting and re-parting and combing again. But none of them had complained and none had ducked out from under her hand when they'd had enough and run away to play. They had all stood still and careful in their good clothes and watched her and Paul with their small mouths tight until it was time to walk to the cemetery.

Lavinia had come down the stairs with extra hankies that she pressed into Mae's hand and Paul's, looking quickly up at Paul with her hand on his lapel, then looking down again.

"You're sure you want to walk, Mother?" Paul had asked, and Lavinia had answered, "Yes, and anyway, the roads still aren't all passable. We don't know what we'll find."

Mae can't figure Lavinia's expression. The trembling that overtook her in the first days after the storm has stopped and her face is finally calm, as if she understands something about this day that no one else does. She buried her husband at our last funeral, Mae thinks, I suppose she'd thought till now that hers would be the next. Little Homer, Mae's Homer, is standing by Paul, staring at the faces around him. Mae can't reach him to tap his shoulder and shake her head at him to make him stop. She knows what he's looking at: the faces of their neighbors, the parents of his friends, who stand there silent with wet faces. *But men don't cry, Mama,* she can hear him saying. *My daddy isn't crying.*

Mae holds Ruby's shoulders tighter. She looks down at Ruby's head. She won't look up, she can't look up. If she does, then someone, someone's mother, will be looking back at her and at her three, whole children who are standing here with her. At her husband who can still put food in their mouths in the house he built that's still standing.

"And we give thanks for the miracle of the Graves family, dear Lord, who alone among us suffered no loss of any kind," the minister is saying. Mae's breath catches at the mention of her name. The Lord giveth.

The very air, the fine spring air has become oppressive to Mae. She feels herself pressed in against from all sides, sure that everyone is watching her to see—to see what—if she comprehends? Her narrow escape, or was it wide? The duty now incumbent on her family, her great good fortune and the shame she should feel because of it. Mae feels a tightness in her chest that only grows and grows the more deeply she breathes to make it stop. She realizes that the tightness she feels is in her heart, that she can feel her own heart; not beating, but hurting.

Mae looks away from Ruby's head at the coffins now. She blinks fast and hard to keep from crying. She looks at the coffins and feels dread. All the new boards that Paul had cut after the town had laid out their dead. The pale boards that the Guardsmen had hammered urgently into coffins. The number of the dead so great that this is only the first of many burials to be held.

The cemetery has become a peculiar sort of wasteland. Nearly all of the trees are gone, the ground has been mostly cleared of downed branches, and only splintered tree stumps remain. The largest headstones, the ones belonging to the oldest graves, lie toppled, waiting to be reaffixed to their bases. And then there is the earth, all the mounds of earth gouged out of the ground and lying humped along the trenches. Mae's own people are buried here, on the other side of the cemetery. Homer, too, in Paul's family's plot. But today is not the day to visit the family plots. They'll come back another day to check on things, although Mae knows as well as the others that everything will likely be fine. The crocuses she planted there will have started to come up, green spears surging up from the bulbs, even as the new ground had had its maw forced open to receive the dead. *Thank God it's spring,* Mae has heard people saying, *Thank God the ground wasn't frozen.*

There are National Guardsmen standing behind everyone else, near the road. They are likely the same ones who dug with the steam shovel the army sent in. The steam shovel is gone, at work now in the other cemetery across town, and the Guardsmen are standing in a solemn row, no less ominous because, for the moment, they have laid their shovels aside. They come forward when the time for the committal comes, and Paul, the other men, and the larger boys lift the coffins, one by one, and whenever possible, carry their own dead to the grave. Seeing Paul carrying a coffin brings Mae back out of herself, and she begins to hear the sounds of mourning building from the women around her.

"Thus says the Lord God to these bones," the minister calls out. "Behold, I will put my breath into you, and you shall live. And I will lay sinews upon you, and cause flesh to come upon you, and cover you with skin, and put breath in you, and you shall live, and you shall know that I am the Lord."

A smallish woman runs toward the nearest row of coffins, and lays across the smallest one, kneeling on the ground, seeming to embrace it. Mae doesn't realize that it's Alice at first, until Nash Duttweiler comes running to her, trying to pull her away. Mae realizes she hasn't seen either of them since the day of the storm. She'd been so grateful when Nash came, so relieved that he was alive to take Alice from her so that she could concentrate on willing Paul to emerge, whole, from the ruins. And then when Paul came running home, just as Nash had, and she'd realized that all of them, all six of them were alive, she'd stopped thinking about the Duttweilers. She hadn't given them another thought, not the rest of that evening as the bodies were laid out on their porch, not in the following days when she'd had a house full of people. Nash and Alice should have been the first of the neighbors to come to them for shelter, and Mae wonders now how she could have forgotten them so entirely.

"No!" Alice is shouting, throwing Nash's arms away. She staggers to her feet, holding the tiny coffin and screaming, "Where is my coffin! Where is my baby! I have no one to bury. I want to bury my baby!"

Mae moans and holds a hand over her mouth. It was hard to know which image from the storm horrified her most: the men and women killed because they had gone running to the school to retrieve their children, or the people found, some alive, lying in the streets with objects driven through their skulls, or Alice, right across the street, thrown across her own backyard by the cloud, rising, unharmed, to discover that the cloud had carried her baby away. Mae and Paul had heard the stories told and retold around the town, as if people had to hear themselves telling what had happened to them before they themselves could believe it.

When Alice finally releases the coffin, Nash passes it slowly, reverentially to a waiting man, as if he's handing him a sleeping child. He turns back to Alice and lays his hands on her shoulders. He lifts his face as if to look upward, but his eyes are closed.

"Heaven help them," Lavinia says at Mae's side.

"Heaven help us," Mae whispers.

Someone says Mae's name again, and she jumps. She turns and Sally Prosser is standing there. Her face is menacing; Mae sees both mirth and outrage there.

"Graves," Sally says again. "I hadn't thought of it before now. Your name is Graves."

Lavinia puts her arm around Mae's waist and says quietly, but fiercely, "A person can't help their own name."

"You've no one to bury," Sally says. "We've all seen you now. You needn't come again."

16

There is the fizz of sparks that goes up each time a man
flings new junk into the flames, a crack that precedes
the soft thud of charred wood collapsing at the fire's
base, then the scratch of a voice; a rawboned older man stops
to speak with his arms braced straight on bent knees.
"Someone should walk around town with a box of matches,"
he says. "Just set light to whatever isn't whole, and spare us the
trouble of hauling it off." A younger man claps him on the
shoulder rather than reply, and they turn again to throw debris
onto the fire.

The men working the burn are weary. Sweat lines run gray
through the grime on their faces and necks. They don't speak
much because of the bandanas tied over their noses and mouths
and because of the pointlessness of conversation. These are the
uninjured men, men of every age who set to hauling with
trucks, wagons, or wheelbarrows, loading up the crates and
bushel baskets the children filled with whatever they could lift
and driving it all out to the burn.

The men know that if they keep their minds on the job at
hand, on feeding the fire with the junk dumped onto the dirt
out of wheelbarrows and truck beds, on breaking up the largest
pieces by stomping on them or splintering them painfully
across their bent knees, they will think less about what the junk
is. If they stand so close to the fire that they squint from the heat
and the smoke, they're less likely to see clearly the faces of the
women and children standing in a ring around them. This wad

of scorched paper was never a book; throw it on the fire. That bit of white-painted wood was never a window frame; throw it on, too. That smashed ladder, that bit of crate. Break the feet off that table pedestal, leave the knob on that cabinet door and let the fire have them.

The women are heedful, watching for anything that could be spared. Was that bit of fabric a tablecloth? What was that flash of color at its end, embroidery? No, it's gone now, just look away. That broken rocker, whose place did that come from? Scrutinizing turns their faces sour; resentful eyes follow the arc of every scrap into the fire. They have all picked, bitter or bewildered, through the wreckage, their houses now nothing more than giant splinters. They have learned to walk on the ruins the way you walk on new, deep snow that can't support you. And slowly, slowly, they are becoming as hard as the men who can look at a ruined thing and say it is ruined without stopping first to say, *We had that thirty years.*

The women force the men to rest occasionally, carrying water buckets among them and waiting insistently until each man has tipped his head back with the metal dipper to his mouth. The men stand with their hands on their hips, breathing in and blowing out hard, and wipe their faces on shirt-sleeves or with bandanas kept clean for as long as possible in hip pockets. It's almost bearable, throwing all your neighbors' wreckage on the pyre rather than burning just your own. Makes it just a job that needs doing and not such a mournful thing.

With no provisional school to attend, the children are kept all day at the burn by parents still too stunned to let them out of their sight. The women hold the children back, upwind from the fire, but still the big boys, enthralled and skittish, dart away from their mothers to throw things at the flames. They know no precedent for this type of conflagration. Not the leaf burns that smolder each fall in their fathers' driveways, nor any bonfire they've ever seen before, not even the fires the storm birthed. They watch the adults to work out what to think, but are too young to make out anything from the stony faces around them. The children tug at the unfamiliar, ill-fitting clothes their mothers pulled hastily out of the piles at the relief center. They wriggle where they stand to test the women's hold on them, ready to dart out if they see anything small they can throw at the fire.

After a while, the children begin to see the truth of the men's movements, begin to see the hatred in their stooping, turning, and throwing. They decide that what the men hate is the fire and that hatred, not determination, is fueling their movements. When they understand this much, they also understand that it is hatred that makes the women grip their shoulders so and stare ahead, silent. This pacifies the children, because they think that this is all there is to hate, and that they can do as much and hate the fire, too. They cannot fathom that the men and women hate not the fire but the storm that necessitated it; the women, because the storm has taken their past from them and the men, because it has obliged them to begin again with nothing.

What the children cannot fathom, they don't contemplate for long. Like things that should have made people glad but didn't; when folks from towns and farms as much as fifty miles away drove into Marah in the first days after the storm, laps piled up high with clothing and blankets and baskets of food to leave behind, and grown men and women had to stop and wipe their eyes.

When the women sense the hatred in the children's wiry bodies, they loosen their hold a little and then a little more until the children pull away, drawn inexorably toward the fire. They pick up sticks and rocks to hurl at it and the big boys cautiously approach the men, wary at first of being warned off, but then daring to pick up pieces of junk to fling. One of the big boys yells, "Hah!" when the scrap of wood he tosses sends up sparks and then the other boys start yelling, too, throwing whatever they can lift, mocking the fire as much as feeding it. The girls dare not venture away from the women, but they smile furtively with their eyes, gratified and admiring, at the boys' daring. The boys dance and stomp and whoop and yell, their voices joining and rising with the sparks and smoke until one man finally bellows, "That's enough!" and chops the air with an angry hand.

They all stand then in a silent ring under the darkening sky, to watch the heedless fire.

17

Lavinia waits for Paul to finish and come in. She daren't go near the door, or she'll be beckoned out, too, and made to comment again on everything Paul has surely just said. He can't ever just come home anymore. Delayed each and every day by stunned well-wishers and gawkers, both of them nuisances in their own way, he delivers the same painful litany from the front porch: Yes, just a miracle. It is true, we are all fine. The house, too, and the lumber-yard.

When she hears him begin on the "thank you, I will. I surely appreciate that. We're all praying for you," she watches for the front door to swing open. Paul takes a backward step into the house, still calling out, still waving. He's framed by the glass insets in the heavy oak door. "So long, now," he calls, but he won't close the door until the people he's been talking to have moved along the sidewalk and looked away. He won't close the door in anyone's face, he says.

"We could start selling tickets," she says when he turns and sees her there. "Give the money to the relief effort." There is a smile for Paul, playing at the edges of her eyes, but her mouth is pursed in wry defeat. He'd never take advantage of another living soul, but neither would he ever admit being taken advantage of. Generous to the end, like his father.

"They just can't believe it, Mother. That's why they keep coming; to see for themselves. They'll keep coming, too, for a good long while. Why, it hasn't even been two weeks yet. Folks are still just crawling out from under." Paul holds his cap lightly in one hand, then the other.

"What is it? Has something happened?" Lavinia says.

"Nothing, Mother, nothing's happened. It's just that so many people have said it. We're the only ones who made it through. You don't even have to look at the rest of the town to see it; you just look right here at our street. Pretty much everything around us got flattened. Our neighbors' homes just turned into so many sticks. The Duttweilers' might as well have been leveled; they can't live in that house, spun around like that. And then there's our place. Dirty is all. Just needs a wash to get the mud off.

"Then there's folks that lost more than everything, you might even say, because of what they found when they went home. It's one thing to have come home and found your house tossed into a neighboring field. Even with the windows blown out and the stuff inside all broken up, a body can salvage what's left and shelter there for a while. But what about folks like those miners over in Atkinson? Didn't even know anything was wrong topside until their power went out. So they climb out of the mines and find that a twister's been, and their homes and women and children are gone.

"And what about the Welches? What happens after you've come home and found Grandma sitting right where you left her in her rocker, except both the house and Grandma's head are ripped off and blown to kingdom come?"

"Paul, don't!" Lavinia pleads, warning him more than she is scolding. "We all saw horrible, horrible things. I saw things I could never have invented. No, now you wait. I know it's not the same. None of the injured or dead were our people, but they were our friends. We've got to live alongside the ones who lived. We'll carry this to our graves, every one of us."

Paul looks down at his cap while he speaks, taking it more firmly in both hands.

"At first, I couldn't stop thinking about the car. How on earth that storm twisted the house across the street and spun our car around, right where it stood in the driveway, but didn't touch our house, I'll never understand. I stopped thinking about it when I realized it was funny, the part about the car. It was harmless, after all, just a remarkable, funny thing that happened. No one else seems to have a funny story, though, only us. And it's not just that we didn't have to bury anyone, or that the house and the lumberyard are still standing. We're whole! We've all got our legs and arms and our prospects intact. And, yes, we saw the same things as everyone else, but we saw them, Mother, we watched them. They didn't truly happen to us, not in the same way. I'm just starting to wonder why."

"Why? What ever do you mean, why?" Lavinia doesn't hold much with introspection, especially in times like these when folks should take things for what they are, be grateful or be sad, and move forward. "And, yes, it most certainly did happen to us. We may not have lost anyone in the family, but we all lost friends." Paul finally looks up at Lavinia's wary frown.

"You've got a guilty look on your face, Paul," she says. "I sincerely hope you're not trying to find blame or fault here. No, don't just shake your head. You listen to me. There's no why about it. Our good luck was chance, that's all. We had the same chance, good or bad, of coming through as anyone. We had a cellar and we got to it in time, but we might just as easily not have." Lavinia sees more people outside, slowing as they approach the house. "Come away from that door," she says to Paul and pulls him to the side and out of sight. "They'll be ringing the doorbell next, asking to be shown around the place."

"But that's just it, Mother, even if you hadn't gotten to the cellar in time, you'd all still be fine! You could just have sat there in the living room like you were, never budged, and that storm would have hopped over you just the same."

"Paul, don't be simple! What if that tree had been dropped

on the cellar door before we got outside? We'd have been out there for who knows how long, not knowing what to do, not able to hear ourselves think for that wind. We could easily, any of us, have been hurt or even killed by something flying through the air."

"I know it," Paul says, looking his hands, wringing his cap.

"I'm not sure you do. I hope you won't go trying to find meaning in any of this. It was random, that's all it was. Randomness and luck saved us, and you and everyone else will profit by remembering that."

Paul looks up at Lavinia, cautious and wary. There's that look again, Lavinia thinks, the second time this week.

"If you're going to chide me, get it over with," she says.

"What do you mean?"

"That's the same look you gave me a few days back when you stopped Mae and me from cleaning the outside of the house, remember? 'Leave it be,' you said, 'clean the inside if you have to clean something, but let the outside be.'"

"You know I don't think we should rub people's noses in it, Mother. Glass in all the windows, and clean glass at that."

"Yes, I remember Paul, and I thanked you for stopping us. Now why did you look at me like that this time?"

"I guess I figure our coming through safe ought to have some meaning. Maybe it doesn't mean anything by itself, but we can make it mean something."

The door bell jangles beside them, and Lavinia cries out loudly before she can clap a hand over her mouth.

Paul lays a hand firmly on Lavinia's shoulder, as if he's pressing her back down to the floor. She moves her hand from her mouth to her heart and nods, and then he goes to answer the door.

"Come on in, Bill," he says, shaking the man's hand, turning aside to pull him gently over the threshold.

"Oh, no, I won't stay. You're probably about ready to sit

down to dinner. I shouldn't have come, but I wanted to see you, to tell you how glad—" A sob erupts from him, the same bottomless sorrow folks all over town have been holding in their bellies until they break.

Lavinia steps around Paul. She knows a man doesn't like to be seen to be broken, even if he is. "Don't you be silly, Bill. We haven't even sat down yet." She keeps her voice bright and takes him by the arm. "You're not disturbing a thing."

He lets Lavinia lead him to the davenport, where they sit together politely, perched and jittery on the edge, both ready to get up if the other should rise. Paul draws up a chair to sit on, and waits.

"I heard your Ford got turned around, right where it was standing," Bill says.

Paul and Lavinia's eyes shoot up at each other's, then just as quickly return to Bill who is stuffing his handkerchief into a loose fist, like a magician setting up for a trick.

"That's right," Paul says quietly. He continues, unsure of the right thing to say. "Funny thing. I heard a two-by-four got itself driven through Myerson's oak, too. Kids looked at it for a while, sticking out there. Finally someone found some rope and a plank and hung a swing on it."

Bill nods, and says, "I guess you heard the storm picked up my car."

"I did," Paul says softly, as if he's been chastised.

"I suppose they drove over to see the new frame going up. They weren't even supposed to be there that day. I don't know why they would've been, except for Isaac's pestering. He was always after us to take him to see the new house going up, you see, and I reckon Clara thought she'd just satisfy him with a quick trip."

Bill worries his handkerchief, folding now it into smaller and smaller squares, pressing it between his palms, shaking it out again. Paul and Lavinia sit still, each knowing in their way that, however horrifying the story and however much dread they feel at the thought of hearing it, their role is simply to hear it, solemnly and reverently.

"I can hardly stand to sleep," Bill says. "I see them there every night, running back and forth, Clara holding onto Isaac, not knowing what to do. I call out to them, but the wind is too loud; they can't see, because of the dust that's driven into their eyes. Their clothes are flapping hard, the wind pushes at them so that they can't even stand in one place. And then they get into the car because there isn't any other shelter, and I'm shouting at them to get out, but they stay there in the backseat. Clara is bent over Isaac, and the car is rocking, lifting up on one side and then slamming down again. I know they must be screaming, but I can't hear them and I can't get to them. Then the storm lifts the car right off the ground, easy as you like, flips it over and smashes it down again."

Bill face breaks into a strange, dazed smile. "And once they're gone," he says, "the storm stops and it's just me standing there, seeing what I saw when I found them."

Paul sits, powerless and frowning, leaning forward on his knees with his hands clasped hard together. Lavinia daubs at her damp cheeks again and again.

"The thing I keep coming back to is the car. If I'd just taken it that morning, they'd have stayed at the old place and had a finished cellar to go to. But I didn't. I wanted them to be able to drive the car if they wanted to go somewhere."

"Of course you did," Lavinia says.

Paul exhales, wishing he could feel more resolute, instead of merely baffled. He straightens his arms, props himself up higher with his palms gripping his knees. "Look here, Bill," he says, "You and I have known each other a good long while now. You're a sensible man. I can hear what you would say if this weren't happening to you—you can't blame yourself. There's pain enough right now without adding blame to it."

The kitchen door slams at the other end of the house, and Mae's voice comes rising, shushing the children, sending them off to wash before dinner. Mae comes in with a stack of dinner plates, ready to lay the table. She hesitates, but only barely. "Hello, Bill," she says, smiling softly, with a fondness reserved for old friends, almost as if she had expected to find him sitting there. "Supper's ready. It's not much, but I hope you'll stay."

"No, no, I don't want to impose," Bill shakes his head adamantly and holds up a hand, to prevent further entreaty.

"It's not an imposition, and you know it," Lavinia says. "We'd all like you to stay."

She gets up from the davenport, smoothes her dress, and starts laying the table as if the matter has been decided. She lays the plates and cutlery quietly, though, so she can hear what the others are saying. It's up to Paul and Mae now to get Bill to stay; she'll only embarrass him into leaving if she says anything more.

Bill leans forward and drops his voice to speak to Paul. "I wanted to come to see for myself that you all were all right, but I won't stay. I'll get my supper down at the relief center, same as yesterday."

"Bill, I think you should stay, and not just for supper. We can make room for you, easy. You'd have a home with us while you decide what to do next." Paul's voice is earnest, but he speaks softly so that only Bill can hear him. "I mean it."

"I know you do," Bill says with a remorseful smile. "And I thank you for it. I hope you'll understand that I can't imagine myself living in a house with children. Not now, maybe not ever again."

Bill sees Little Homer over Paul's shoulder, standing in the doorway, watching the adults in the room. Grief bubbles up again from his belly, but he can't look away from the boy.

"Do you reckon you'll stay, or are you fixing to leave town?" Paul asks. He figures he might as well be frank, seeing as Bill has paid him the compliment of not disguising his grief.

"I couldn't say yet, although—" Bill rises to leave but crosses the room to Little Homer before going to the door. He lays a hand on top of the boy's head, feels the shape of his head that fills his hand, just so. Looking down at him, with his arm obscuring the boy's face, he could be any boy of five. "I do think it might be easier to start somewhere fresh. Maybe Carbondale. That's a big place. They'd surely have room for one more banker there."

He turns swiftly for the door muttering, "Good-bye, folks." They hear his footfalls, rapid on the steps, then the heels of his shoes striking the pavement, fading away.

Mae is watching the door, the forks still in her hand, ready to lay on the table.

"We won't be seeing him again," she says, frowning, distracted, as if she is really thinking about something else.

"Whatever do you mean, Mae?" Lavinia says, looking around as if the closed door will tell her something. "He only said good night!"

"He said good-bye."

"Well, yes, but he meant good night or good evening." Lavinia continues laying the table, speaking under her breath. "You two will both overthink a thing, won't you. Can't let a thing be what it is."

Paul looks out the window, but Bill is already out of sight. "I hope you're wrong," he says.

"You know I'm not." Mae looks down at the table, her mouth twisted into something between disappointment and resignation.

"Paul, will you please come away from that window!" Lavinia cries. "How can we have any peace at suppertime if you're standing there like a mannequin in a shop window, advertising that we're home to all callers? Children!" She bangs the table with the flat of her hand. "Supper!"

Lavinia is still frowning when everyone is seated and mumbling their way through grace, "Bless us, Oh Lord, and these thy gifts . . . "

"Peas again?" Ellis takes the serving bowl from Mae and slumps in his chair.

"Yes, and bread and potatoes and milk," Mae says evenly. "That other can turned out to be peaches, so you can have some dessert."

"You'll eat what your mother gives you, all of you," says Paul, "No one in town is eating any better than we are. Everybody gets the same food handed out every day. I'm just grateful there's milk for you kids and a stove to cook the potatoes on."

"Heaven knows there's enough kindling these days for the stove," Lavinia says sharply. "Nothing but kindling all around us."

"Mother, please! Don't you see, that's just it! We should set an example. I don't mean just here at the table. Sure we can rattle the cans of food and try to guess what's inside them, laugh that the roof of the store got blown off and all the canned goods got their labels soaked off in the rain. I mean I think we should be an example to the town. I believe we were spared for a reason."

"What reason could that be?" Mae's voice is cautious, but Paul goes on as if she hasn't spoken.

"Mother, you say you don't want me to try to find any meaning in all of this. But there is meaning! Why were we the only ones? Some families survived with body intact, but have no home; then there are others whose house is fine, but lost their families. And then there's the Graves family. What happened to the Graves family? Nothing! We got ourselves and our house muddied up is all!"

The children are wide-eyed. They hold their forks suspended, forgetting to pass the food into their mouths, and stare at their transported father.

"I wasn't sure before, but I'm getting surer. You saw how Bill came to us. You see how they're all coming to us. They want to see for themselves that we were spared. They don't want to trust the stories. They come here to see proof that while that one evil hand reached out of that cloud to smash everything up, another hand reached down to stop it."

"Paul, be careful, now. Think about what you're saying," Lavinia warns him. "Bill came here because he's your friend. The others are just gawkers, same kind as gather around to gape at a car wreck. Only this time it's in reverse; there's devastation all around, so they come to stare at the survivors, instead."

"You don't think it was providential that the lumberyard was spared?"

"Of course it was providential! It was providential for us! And if you're so determined to find meaning in all of this, maybe you should come with me to a church service or two, like you did when you were a boy."

Paul continues calmly, plainly trying to control his voice. "Mother, you of all people should be able to see this. The lumberyard is still there. All the lumber is still there for people to rebuild with."

"And to make coffins with," Mae says quietly.

"There! At least Mae sees sense. You have a care who you say these things to, Paul. If people cotton on that you think you were chosen somehow, well, you won't make any friends."

Lavinia shakes her head wretchedly, wishing her Homer were still alive to shake a finger in Paul's face and make him see reason.

"I'm certain that's not what he meant, Mother," Mae says, looking up tight-lipped at Paul.

"This house is acting like a beacon," Paul says. "It's a reminder of what they all had before the storm and what they have to work toward now they've lost it. I sold most of them the lumber they built with the first time, and I'm still here to do it again. Doesn't that give me a duty to act a certain way?"

Lavinia looks around at the children who seem content and have gone back to eating. When she looks at Mae, she sees the same worry she feels herself before Mae lowers her eyes. You can sell them all the boards in the world to rebuild their houses, Lavinia thinks, but you can't sell them arms and legs to build new children and husbands and wives.

"I'm sure you know best, Paul," she says instead.

18

Lavinia puts her hat on in front of the mirror while she waits for Mae to come downstairs again. Mae comes down slowly when she's ready, and Lavinia looks her over. "Much better," she says. "Somber, not funereal. We're going to visit the living, after all."

Mae stops before the bottom of the staircase, face and eyes turned down.

"You look like Ellis," Lavinia says. "You look exactly like he does when it's time to go to church."

"I think I feel like Ellis."

"I can see that. What's wrong?"

Mae looks up at Lavinia, but looks away just as quickly. "I don't see how this will help anyone, least of all Alice."

When Lavinia holds out Mae's hat, Mae comes the rest of the way down and puts it on distractedly. Lavinia lifts Mae's face up to look at her. She smoothes Mae's hair along the sides of her face and adjusts the hat. "You know we have to pay them a call. We really should have done it before the funeral."

"I won't know what to say."

Lavinia applies her lipstick, chin tilted toward the mirror, then frowns after she points to Mae's handbag and Mae shakes her head, refusing to do the same.

"We'll only make her feel worse," Mae says. "Think of the last two times we saw her."

Yes, Lavinia thinks, Alice was screaming for her baby both of those times, and she may be screaming still, and that's part of what we have to find out. She wants to tell Mae that the thing making her hesitate is only herself, that she's too young to have gone on many calls like this before, if she's gone on any at all. That what she's afraid of is feeling worse herself.

But Mae meets Lavinia's eyes in the mirror and says, "I hear her voice in my head. It wakes me up at night, and I think I must have woken myself with screaming, but it's Alice's scream I'm hearing, and it's only been a dream."

Lavinia has no answer to this. She's so easily undone by Mae's candor, which always comes so unexpectedly, so inopportunely. She can only respond with a truism: "The longer we wait, the worse it will be."

Lavinia knocks once, twice on the door of the house the Duttweilers have been staying in since the storm. Mae is looking down at the porch boards, holding her purse in front of her with both hands. Nash Duttweiler opens the door finally, but then he stands there without saying anything, looking puzzled as if he's neither sure who it is who's standing there or even why he's standing there, himself.

"Hello, Nash," Lavinia says. "I guess we found the right house."

Nash nods and says, "I guess you did."

Lavinia looks at him in consternation, resisting the urge to speak slowly and a little louder than usual, as if she were addressing an idiot. She prompts him, "May we come in? We hadn't planned to stay long."

"It's just Alice and me here today," Nash says. "No one else, just us."

"Well, that's fine, Nash. It was you and Alice we wanted to see," Lavinia says, in spite of feeling her stomach fall at the realization that the Duttweilers' hosts will not be there to relieve the mood, to force a superficial formality on the conversation.

Nash turns and walks away from them calling, "Company," up the stairs, and they follow him. He forgets himself again and leaves them standing there in the living room, and Lavinia and Mae stand there together, side by side in their coats and hats, throwing identical, kindly smiles up at the stairs at Alice, who slows coming down when she sees them, and frowns. She laughs then, a hollow, too-loud laugh that bounces back at them off the walls, forcing them all to hear it again.

"I didn't recognize you. I thought you were more ladies from church."

What little smile there is on Alice's face falls quickly away, and she gestures toward the davenport for them to sit down. Lavinia sees the indifferent look in Alice's eyes, as if Alice is both absent and yet somehow more fully present than any of them. Alice's expression unnerves her, even more than the frankly vacant look in Nash's eyes. Nash doesn't seem to be seeing much of anything, but Alice, Alice looks as if she sees them all quite clearly, even as she's looking right through them to something else.

"Have you had many visitors from your church?" Lavinia asks.

"Oh my, yes. Every day for a while there, telling us about God's plan and how we needed to come back to church."

Lavinia knows she can fill in the rest for herself and turns her eyes toward her lap as a signal to Alice that she won't be mentioning any of those things. She can imagine everything the ladies would have said, how they would have tried to vary it each day, thinking some days that simply sending a different set of women would render the message convincing and suddenly do the trick. And from the hardness that has overtaken Alice's face, she can also guess what Alice said to stop the visits: that they could keep their kindness and their God if he was the one who had sent the cloud that snatched her baby away and left her without a single bone to bury. Lavinia can well imagine the women stopped coming rather than face Alice again. She recognizes in Alice the same capacity Mae has for inconvenient candor, but fueled in Alice by rage and grief. She guesses that Alice has now more or less stopped being polite to people, decided on it one day as a policy, and if she had not yet behaved rudely towards them, she was prepared to do so if they gave her reason.

Lavinia supposes Alice might well be entitled to a little belligerence, if people are going to behave so clumsily. But how it will serve her in another month or even a year is another matter. She could easily enrage Alice herself right here if she wanted to. Tell her all the things she knows to be true about grief and youth and life and living. That neither she nor Nash have even hit thirty and that they will likely have another child and even children. That an enraged stupor is no mood for her to make her way through all the years remaining to her.

Alice turns to Mae and says, "I imagine you still have folks sheltering with you."

"No," Mae says. "The McKinney's were the last ones, and they're out in one of the tent cities now."

Alice nods. "We heard how your porch got used."

Lavinia knows then that Alice is still living freshly in the moment of the storm. That she hasn't moved forward in any meaningful way from that first terrifying night when they laid out the corpses on porches around town. This house has a good porch, too. Lavinia wonders if Alice and Nash arrived to shelter here before the bodies were laid out, if either one of them was then able to look among them for the baby or if they just waited to be told. And she wonders how in heaven a person moves forward from a thing like that, from baby to no baby. There isn't a word like widow for mothers who have lost a child, she thinks. There should be.

"What will you do now?" Mae asks. "Are you going to rebuild?"

"We can't stay here forever. There's insurance money coming on our house, but we can't even stand to look at the place, so I don't see how we can rebuild it."

Lavinia shakes her head. She wonders if either of them would remember the day last summer when she and Mae were out hanging laundry and they saw Alice leaning heavily on a tree in her yard. Lavinia had rushed over, seeing Alice hugging her belly with one arm and pushing against the tree with the other, thinking she was losing the baby, but Alice had only been looking down at something in the grass, working out the best way to get low enough to pick it up. Alice had laughed at her awkwardness, at her belly that made her ponderous and slow, and pointed to the remains of a robin's egg laying at the base of the tree. Lavinia had picked it up and put it in Alice's hand, and they had both stopped thinking whatever else they had been thinking; they had stopped entirely to marvel at its fineness and color.

Alice had laughed and closed her hand around the broken shell, and then opened it flat again and held it up higher. "I'd like a room painted that color," she had said.

"Well, you take that to Nash and tell him," Lavinia had said. "He'd paint the whole house that color if he thought you'd like it."

Alice's smile, the hot breeze in the green yard, the bright blue shell already saved in her pocket.

"I imagine he would."

19

Paul is standing in the upstairs hall looking at Ruby's and Ellis's bedroom doors, both closed against him. He hears Mae coming up the stairs and wonders how many minutes will pass before he's out here again and Mae is hiding behind a third closed door.

"You told them?" she says behind him when she's standing on the top stair. He nods without turning around, without saying anything more about it because he's got bad news for her, too. He'll keep this much to himself, he thinks, and spare Mae a description of Ellis sitting on his bed and refusing to look at him, fighting to control himself until Paul was out of the room and he could close the door. Or Ruby, who looked suddenly younger when he told her, her eyes and mouth gone wide open so that she looked as she had at two or three when she was caught up in listening to a story. But then her eyes darted with worry, and Paul could see her mind working, picturing her friends' faces and wondering how those people could be dead, how a father could promise that they would never come to the house again calling for her to come out to play, when she could still perfectly conjure their faces in her mind.

"Did you tell them there'll be more?" Mae asks in a low voice.

"No, I kept to the ones we know for sure."

Paul turns and holds out a hand to Mae. "Come with me," he says and leads her into their bedroom. Mae sits in the rocking chair by the window, and Paul sits on the edge of the bed, facing Mae and her mouth that's gone into a straight line and her hands that are ready to turn into fists.

"You know that we went to the World's Fair when I was twelve and Johnny was fourteen," he hears himself saying. "Mother and Dad had left Arthur Coffman to run the farm for a couple of days so we could go to St. Louis, and on the morning of our second day, when we were walking to the fair from our hotel, I saw an old man sitting on a city bench on a busy sidewalk, tearing at a piece of cooked chicken with his bare hands and stuffing his mouth with the meat.

"I suppose I'd seen beggars before that, but he wasn't a beggar. He wasn't a hobo, either; he was just an ancient, broken man who'd found a sunny spot on a busy sidewalk to eat his breakfast. I stopped cold in my tracks when I saw him. I don't think I could have moved or stopped staring if I'd tried. Not even if he'd looked up and stared back at me. I could see the grease on his fingers and the black around his nails, even from a distance. He had on a sour old suit that was this side of going to rags, and he sat there in plain sight of every passerby, watching those bones come clear as he tore away the meat.

"Mother and Dad got half a block away before they realized I wasn't with them, and when they turned back and found me there, they tried to comfort me. They thought I was frozen there in shock or pity. Dad laid a coin on the bench next to the man and mumbled something to him, and I remember Mother shaking her head and putting her arm around me to lead me away. They mistook me completely, and I was too young to put words to what I was feeling, so I didn't say anything. Years later, I understood that what I had felt that day was admiration, even envy, because that man had been so badly broken and had still decided that there was no need for shame, no need to hide himself—his real self—from anyone at all.

"Dad spent a whole quarter on a box of fairy floss that day at the fair, and we four stood there, pinching off wads of the stuff and holding it up so it trailed in the breeze. I remember the others were laughing and talking about what they still wanted to see before we left to go home, but I was stuck again, standing there staring at a pinch of spun sugar because it reminded me of that man and the way the breeze had lifted up his hair and floated it around his head."

"Why are you telling me this?"

"To tell you that I decided that day that I would never hide. I would never hide, no matter what happened to me when I was a man."

Mae's eyes close in a grimace and she shakes her head. "I don't understand you, Paul."

"To ask you not to hide."

"Just say it."

"They found Bess."

Mae's skin blazes red and then white in the space of an instant, and when she smothers her expression, even as it's taking shape on her face, Paul knows that this is what he will see from now on—this vanishing of emotion, a magician turning solid things to air.

"The hospital in Carbondale finally sent a list of people who got sent there on the first trains out after the storm. She was buried there last Sunday. They sent Stuart's coffin out on a train so they could be buried together, husband and wife."

Mae still won't look at him. Her breathing has gone quick and shallow. Paul feels reckless, continuing to speak words he knows Mae is struggling not to hear. He says, "Stuart died first. They pieced enough together to fill a coffin. They did their best."

He's on his knees in front of her, holding her fists in his hands. He feels as if all the heat and air have gone out of the room and that Mae is no more present than her image would be if he were looking at it projected up on a movie screen. He would shake her and shout that she cannot hide, that this is no way to be. He would say that he carries an image like a photograph of Bess as a child in his head, put there by the stories Mae has told him. That he sees her standing in the school yard in a sailor dress with her hair twisted into braids, smiling and crooking a finger at Mae, inviting her to play when the others thought Mae too quiet, too strange. He could say that he sees this as clearly as if it happened to him, that he has always been grateful to Bess, grateful for Bess. Paul would insist that Mae show herself to him, and he would take her face in his hands and tell her that exactly nothing will happen if she cries or even if she screams, but it's already too late and instead he says, "They say she died that first night," before he goes back into the hall and closes the door behind him.

20

A baseball cracks hard against wood, and someone whoops in answer. Faces turn up to follow the ball's flight, eyes screw up tight against the white spring sun. The ball is lost for a moment in the bright sky, and then a startled girl cries, *I got it! I got it!* Cheers and hollers and, *That's three!* The girl is swung up high by a Guardsman yelling *Atta girl!* and the teams change sides.

No one in the tent city can ignore the joyful din. Some, sitting on camp beds inside their tents or on kitchen chairs set out in the grass, purse their lips in irritation. Too much noise, they think. *Children should be schooled in the middle of the day, not let to swat at balls.* Others, who sit on blankets on the ground, watch the game with cautious smiles, grateful that the Guardsmen can abandon themselves, childlike, to the game.

The ruined town refashions itself in the tent cities. The rows of tents mimic the town's streets and makeshift signs appear at crossings: Illinois Avenue, 5th and Poplar, Hattie's Way. Paths wear into the grass. By day, washing strung out on ropes between the tents lifts and settles in the breeze. Women fetch water in pairs, carrying the sloshing washtubs between them. A man offers coffee, boiled fresh in an enameled pot, to his neighbors. In the afternoons, children clutching jam sandwiches shout promises to stay clean and dart away to the fields and the riverbanks to search for storm-borne treasures. And in the evenings, identical woodstoves in each tent send up identical curls of smoke, and people make a haphazard supper from the food they have been given in the day's relief boxes. Those who have kitchen chairs set them in the grass outside their tents to sit and watch the twilight a while before lighting their lanterns. Girls hoping to catch sight of a particular boy promenade arm in arm along the rows.

If the evening is fine, the men build a bonfire in the field beyond the tents and settle on crates and chairs in a ring around the fire to work out what will happen next.

Claims adjusters be coming through soon.

That's all right for them as had insurance.

Red Cross is coming, too.

Coming? They're already here!

No, I mean new ones coming with money. I heard they're gonna give out money to rebuild.

Rebuild? Huh.

Yeah, rebuild! You planning on staying in that tent forever? I say rebuild quick before another tornado gets us in these tents.

And if the next tornado gets us in our new houses, we're right back here in these tents.

Another one like that comes through, we're lucky if we end up back in these tents.

Maybe I don't want to rebuild here. Red Cross gonna give me money to go somewhere else?

Where the hell else would you go but here?

Someplace. I dunno.

You wait. You'll see. Any time now, the whole town'll be crawling with claims adjusters and insurance men and contractors just begging you to let them put up a new house for you.

Place'll be hoppin' then.

Hoppin', sure. It won't ever be what it was.

They kick dirt over the dwindling fire and go early to their beds. The dawn comes quicker here, with nothing but canvas walls to shut out the birdsong. A widowed man lies on his cot, still dumbfounded that he is sleeping alone. A woman chafes her hands against her blanket to stop them remembering the warm feel of a child's head. In the morning, the children will be the first out of the tents, running to the latrines and then among the tents to pluck at the guy ropes and snap them free of the night's accumulated dew. Women will linger to look at the dawn before calling the children to their breakfasts of bread and cold potatoes. Faces will be washed, necks scrubbed, nails scraped clean with paring knives. Wheelbarrows and wagons will be taken again into town to collect food staples and gather firewood from the wreckage of the houses. The children will set off into the fields and forget the day's new promises to stay clean. Smoke will issue again from the chimneys, plates will be wiped after the evening meal, and lanterns will be lit one by one along the rows of tents.

The men and women will settle again on their crates and chairs around the evening's bonfire. They will be unable to stare impassively at the fire, made as it is of their own broken clapboards and chair spindles and other junk that hisses and pops as it crumbles. Their mouths will tighten and resentment will steal over their tired faces. The children, seeing the adults' faces, will find themselves compelled to goad them, to test their mood and see if it will spill over on to them. A small boy will leap out behind a man seated on a crate, roar a lion's roar, and dart back to safety among the other children. When the next boy jumps out with a roar, the man will turn quickly and catch him by the shirttail. He'll pull the boy toward himself to thrill the children who wait wide-eyed for the walloping, then he'll bare his own teeth, growl, and make a lunge for them, sending them gleeful and shrieking back toward the tents.

There will be soft laughter around the fire and then a woman's sigh. *Will you look at that,* she'll say looking toward the glowing rows of tents, incandescent with light like strings of Chinese lanterns. *If that isn't a pretty sight.*

BOOK TWO

21

Miss Schuster and Miss Williams are the only two teachers in the makeshift school in the church; the others are either dead or lie injured in hospitals in St. Louis and Carbondale. The children sit unnaturally still in the pews. They look only at the teachers or at the books they hold in their laps, old McGuffey's Readers brought from home because it is too dangerous to try to salvage any books from the remains of the school building. They dare not look at each other; each glance at a pew mate is a reminder of the children who are no longer there. Instead, the children look imploringly at the teachers for help in understanding how they should act.

The teachers try to take a proper attendance, certain that behaving as normally as possible and following routine will be best for the children. A sense of the familiar will reassure everyone and establish order. They have no class lists to proceed from and call what names they can from memory, asking by surname who is present and who is absent, knowing that some of the children are simply truant, kept back in the tent cities by parents still too frightened to let them go into town. But the children become increasingly upset when they hear the names and must answer again and again, "No, ma'am. Not injured, dead."

When Miss Schuster calls "Graves?" heads in every pew turn toward Ruby and Ellis.

"Here, ma'am," Ruby answers.

Miss Schuster looks at them both, uncertain of how to proceed. She should look at the other children's faces and try to recall other names and proceed with the roll, but she can't seem to look away from these two.

"You're both here," she says. "And your little brother is home?"

"Yes, ma'am."

"Is it true then, what they're saying? Didn't anyone in your family get hurt?"

"No, ma'am."

"No one at all?" she repeats, and Ruby shakes her head.

"Well, I'll be. Your house, too, and your daddy's business? All just the way it was?"

"I suppose so, ma'am."

The children in the pews ahead of Ruby and Ellis are still turned around to look at them, elbows hanging over the pew backs, chins resting on hands. A stranger might judge their faces to be impassive, except that they wear the same expressions they would in the school yard if they were standing circled to gawk at a child who had soiled himself.

"You two can be an example to everyone else," Miss Schuster says with her arms folded across her chest, looking down at them. She continues, addressing the rest of the children, "You all can look to Ruby and Ellis to see how to conduct yourselves now. They didn't lose a thing, they weren't even at the school when it collapsed, so they can be expected to behave normally and lead you all by their example."

She looks again at Ruby, but Ruby doesn't reply.

The children then take turns standing at the front and reading lessons aloud from the few primers they brought along to share, an arrangement that puts both Miss Schuster and Miss Williams in mind of their own girlhoods spent in one-room schoolhouses. There is no blackboard in the church, however, and since no one has brought a slate, they try to drill the children in mental arithmetic and even hold a spelling bee, standing the children in two groups on either side of the aisle, the youngest and the oldest divided equally between them, and the children try hard at first but soon grow too weary even to try and simply begin to take their seats rather than answer, too distressed to spell the words.

Both teachers know they are floundering. Miss Williams looks at Miss Schuster hoping for some sign of how to proceed but finds that Miss Schuster is looking at her the same way. They understand that they have somehow gotten things wrong, every last thing, and also that it is too late to set it right again.

They dismiss the school early. Miss Schuster calls out, "I hope everyone will be less upset tomorrow," looking at the girls who are weeping openly and at the boys who are stone-faced, trying to control themselves. She and Miss Williams stand in the church door, bewildered, watching the children file down the church steps and into the street.

22

Mae takes Ruby onto her lap and rocks her as best she can, sitting there on the davenport. How many times Mae has held a child on her lap, sitting on that end of the davenport, Paul can't imagine. It's hard to reconcile his memory of Ruby as a small child with this long-legged creature who is sobbing and gulping, clinging to Mae.

Ruby has turned her face against the front of Mae's dress, but Paul can still see her mouth, lips pulled back in a howl like a wide smile. Ellis stands beside Paul, taciturn and staring at Ruby. His fists jerk now and then, and Paul suspects that, given an invitation, he'd climb right on top of Ruby to get near Mae. It's clear that Ellis doesn't trust himself to talk, doesn't trust himself not to lose control. Paul lays his hand on the small of the boy's back and looks across at Little Homer who is watching everything from Lavinia's lap in one of the wing chairs by the fireplace.

"Ruby, sweetheart," Mae says, smoothing the girl's hair. "I couldn't understand you. Can you tell us again?"

Ruby shakes her head. She has stopped crying but is still shuddering each time she draws breath. Paul shakes out his handkerchief, still in an ironed square, and hands it to her.

"Was it the teachers who said something to you, or one of the children?" he asks.

"Both," Ellis says, still not looking away from Ruby.

"What was it the teachers said?"

"That nothing happened to us so we should act normal."

Paul catches Mae's eyes before she looks down again at Ruby. He asks Ellis, "What did the children say?"

"It was just a couple boys. They followed us part way home, out of their way, and yelled stuff."

Paul looks up at Ellis standing there next to him and waits.

"How maybe they should show us what it felt like when a school falls on top of you."

Mae starts to cry at that, lips and eyes squeezed shut tight. The sight of her, blindingly angry and struggling to control herself, is too much for Little Homer, who throws himself off Lavinia's lap and onto the floor and lies there crying with his face in his hands as if he'd done himself an injury. Lavinia tries to pick him up again but isn't strong enough, and Homer crawls away from her across the rug to Mae and presses himself under Mae's arm so that she's holding him and Ruby, both.

"One of them threw some rocks at Ruby. Just a handful of gravel or something. He missed and I grabbed some gravel where I was standing and jumped out in front of her. I didn't have to throw it or nothin'. Just show him I meant it."

Paul takes hold of Ellis's fist and opens it. Ellis raises his other hand and opens it, palm up, next to the other to show Paul the gravel he has been clutching.

"You want to tell me who these boys were, son?"

Ellis looks back at Paul, unblinking, and says, "No, sir."

Paul brushes the gravel off onto the floor and rubs the red marks on Ellis's palms with his thumbs. He pulls Ellis to himself hard and stares across the room. Eyes stinging and mouth tight, he kisses the top of his boy's head.

23

Y ou'll wear that letter out inside a week if you don't let it alone," Lavinia says, sitting across the breakfast table from Paul. He can't stop reading it, won't stop reading it, and every time he manages to put it back in its envelope, it's out again just a few minutes later and he's sitting with that same smile on his face, reading it again.

"You'd think it was a love letter, the way you're grinning at that paper," Lavinia teases him.

"Well, Mother, it is, after a fashion. Things haven't been right between Johnny and me for a long time now, but this letter sets it all right."

"I think it was your letter to him that set things right."

"Could be," Paul says. "Could be."

Lavinia laughs aloud, "Lord, you sound just like Homer. You look like him, too, sitting there with your coffee cup in one hand and that letter in the other. Only he would have been mooning over the newspaper."

"Homer doesn't read newspapers!" Ellis protests and makes Lavinia laugh again.

"No, snookie, I meant Grandpa Homer, not Little Homer."

"I could read a newspaper if I wanted to!" Little Homer says. Mae puts the coffeepot back on the stove and walks around the table to smooth Homer's hair and kiss the top of his head.

"Next one we get, you can read me the headlines," she says. "Right now it's time to finish up your breakfast. Ellis, eat up.

Ruby, take your plate to the sink, please, and go brush your teeth."

"Aw, Mama, can't we stay home today?"

"Please don't start that again, Ellis. You know you have to go to school."

"But not all the kids go. Some of them in the tent cities don't go."

"That's a problem for their parents and the teachers, not us." Paul says. "There's nothing wrong with either you or Ruby, so you're going to school today, tomorrow, and the day after that."

"It's not even real school. We have to sit in pews in the church!"

"Well, you don't have to sit any stiller in the church than you did in school. There'll be a new school building soon enough, if you're missing it so badly."

"Homer doesn't have to go to school."

"Homer's five."

"Maybe Homer could go instead of me and I could stay home. People say we look just alike."

"Nice try. Now get upstairs and brush your teeth."

Ellis pushes his chair back and mutters, "I wish I lived in a tent."

"What was that?" Mae stops him on his way to the sink with her fingers against his chest. "What did you just say?"

"I said I wished I lived in a tent."

"What is it you think they're doing out there, camping? Do you think it's fun, having to live in those tents? Tell me why all those people are living out there in tents."

"Mae—" Paul wants to stop her, but it's too late.

"Go on, Ellis," Mae says. "Tell me why they're living in those tents."

"Because the storm knocked down their houses."

"What else?"

"It wrecked all their stuff."

"And did your house get knocked down?"

"No, ma'am."

"That's why you don't live in a tent. Your house is standing, so you live in your house. And school in is a church for the time being, so you go to church for school."

"Yes, ma'am." Ellis is looking down at Mae's apron, waiting to bolt.

"Go on," Mae says, shaking her head. "Go brush your teeth."

Paul waits till Ellis has pounded his way up all the stairs before he says, "He's only seven. He didn't mean anything by it."

Mae is staring out the window. She won't meet anyone's eye. "He has to be made to understand," she says. "What would happen if he said something like that while he was at school? What if he said that to a child who is living in a tent? You're the one who's wanted to be so careful, Paul. How we appear, what we say, what we do in town. That means the children have to be careful, too."

"Yes, they do. Why couldn't you have said that to him instead?"

"Because I didn't. I just didn't, that's why."

Paul gets up from the table and tries to go around to touch her, to stop her trembling, but she turns quickly toward the sink, wiping her eyes. "I have to get ready if I'm walking them to school."

Lavinia hands John's letter, back in its envelope, out to Paul. "You might want this today," she says, and when Paul leans down to kiss her cheek, she nods toward Mae and gives him a shove.

"I'll take them," Paul says, dropping his hands. "You stay here."

He's afraid Mae will move away from him again, find some excuse to turn.

Mae lowers the plate she's washing and even turns to kiss him. The corners of her mouth twitch into a tiny smile. She lowers her eyes again and begins to rinse the plate. There she is, he thinks. He hooks her around the waist and kisses her cheek. "Whose pretty girl are you?" he says and laughs when she shakes a wet hand at him to get him to stop.

That Little Homer laughs the loudest of any of them, as if it were his job to finally dispel the mood, weighs heavily on Paul the rest of the day.

Small wonder Ellis wishes he could live in a tent, Paul thinks on his way to the lumberyard after taking the children to school. He had promised them that school wouldn't be so bad again after that first day, but he had been wrong. Wouldn't Ellis or Ruby wish away the house or the lumberyard if it meant all the staring and the whispering would dry up and they could look their schoolmates in the eye? If Paul himself can't figure how to prevent people from thinking that they alone in all the town are living it up like a bunch of swells, living life in a bubble like it's still the day before the storm, how on earth are his children supposed to manage it? People in town haven't stopped staring at him, why on earth would they stop staring at his children?

It's easier for him, he knows. If Ruby and Ellis feel eyes upon them they have no recourse other than to stare harder at their primer or look at the street ahead of them and quicken their pace. If Paul feels he is being watched, he does what he has always done when he meets people out somewhere in town—simply greets them by name and stretches out his hand. Usually, that causes a person to blink and seem to wake up in an odd sort of way. They smile back then, and shake his hand, fully aware that he is only Paul Graves after all, and not the ghost of a man they once knew.

Other men and women who stare at him seem shamed by

his greeting them. Paul sees that, and although it unnerves him, he continues to greet them anyway, figuring that he won't have to do it a second time. Still others frown at him like they're figuring something out and are then embarrassed by his walking over and shaking their hand. It's as if they're trying to work out a trick he's played on them and if they just watch him long enough without his looking back they'll figure it out.

Now and then Paul meets a man who seems to want to pin blame on him. He shakes the man's hand and asks how he's been keeping himself, and when no shadow of compunction, no trace of remorse or recognition that he's been rude crosses the man's face, Paul begins to shiver. He finds a reason he has to be going then, wishes the man a good afternoon, and sets off back in the direction he was headed, all the while feeling the man's frowning eyes as if they are raining blows upon his back.

Such a man stands in his path now, ten yards or so between him and the front door of the lumberyard. Old man Rittger, bent over his cane, scowling unashamedly at Paul as if Paul is blind and can have no notion that he's been watched.

"Morning, Mr. Rittger," Paul says as he nears him. "How are you today?"

"Fair," says Rittger, who leans on his cane now with both hands, to prevent himself from shaking hands with Paul. "Come to work have you?"

Paul nods, "Just took my kids over to the church for school."

"Is that right."

"Yes, sir."

"How many teachers they got left over there?"

"Just the two. A few of the others are injured and might come back later."

"Two, you say?"

"I hear there's a few more over at the high school, although that's still not enough. School board's got its work cut out for them."

"That's a fact."

Paul hears that he's chattering and is amazed that he feels powerless to simply make his way around this frail old man. Rittger is still glowering at him, as if Paul owes him an explanation for standing before him there on the sidewalk.

"Be needing a new principal, too," Rittger says.

Paul frowns. "What happened to Claude Frayley?"

"Frayley?" Rittger snorts, "Nerves got so bad he up and left town. Went to live with an old aunt somewhere around St. Louis. Just as well, man hasn't any more backbone than that."

Paul has never been one to think badly of anyone, but the image of Rittger as a rank, ancient bulldog enters his mind and he does nothing to shake it off.

Rittger squints up at Paul. "I heard they're set on building the grammar school even bigger than it was," he says.

"I couldn't say," Paul says. "I haven't heard a thing about it."

"Course you have. Who else will they be coming to for the lumber to frame it?"

Paul knows that Rittger has been a crank as long as anyone can remember. Back before the storm it had been possible to smile at him and laugh as if everything he said was just a put-on. No one could be so truly cantankerous all the time. Back then, it hadn't been unheard of for some of the older ladies in town to shake their heads at him and tell him he was just a cheerful dreamer as he railed on about something or other in the street. But Rittger had grown more ill-humored with every passing year, even as his body had become more wizened and bent. If his moods seemed more sour, Paul thought, perhaps it was only because they'd been magnified somehow as he'd shrunk. Now Rittger is acting like nothing more than a bully, calling Paul to account for some imagined wrong and daring him to walk away before he's through with him.

"Everyone's in a hurry, what with everything that wants building around here. You're sittin' pretty good, though. Don't have to rebuild a thing."

Paul stops talking and resolves to say nothing more, not even yes or no, until Rittger has finished his raving. He has even abandoned his customary propriety and is scowling right back at him.

"I heard talk they want the grammar school even bigger than it was," Rittger repeats. "Doesn't seem to bother anyone that there won't be enough children to fill it. Suppose you'll make out all right, either way."

Rittger looks past Paul, as if he sees something down the street. "That'll be a sight," he says, finally. "Graves's lumber going up all over town."

24

Magnolia blossoms open into pink-veined cups on ivory saucers. Pale green leaves jut on rain-blackened branches. A torn oak stump weeps its sap.

The smell of freshly cut lumber hangs in the air; sweeter than the few apple blossoms in the ruined orchards, though not so sweet as to crowd out the remembered stench of corpses. The wreckage is gone, hauled off and burned. Trains roll unimpeded in and out of town. Power lines and telegraph lines stretch again between their poles. Convalescents begin to return, aghast at the razed town. *It's gone, all gone. They tried to tell me.*

Contractors armed with their ready-drawn blueprints and assurances descend upon the town to nose out men expecting insurance settlements or Red Cross money. *A bigger, better house, that's what you can have. What do you need time to think for? You want to be under a solid roof again, don't you? A man who waits, well, he might not have a finished home before the cold sets in.*

Footings are poured, foundations laid. Resentment creeps in. A man perceives that he has received less somehow than others and allows himself a furtive bitterness. He is silent at first because he knows his bitterness is a shameful thing, but once he realizes that his rancor makes him feel more alive, once he accepts it, he must begin to feed it. He broadcasts his bitterness in open conversation hoping to find companionship, hoping to foster that same feeling in his neighbors.

Did you hear about Schedler? All he had was a shack, just

that three-room shack. I'll be damned if the Red Cross isn't giving him a five-room house.

Is that right?

Won't cost him a penny. Makes a body wish they never had insurance in the first place.

A man makes himself important, clothed in false dignity, by passing judgment on those made suddenly more fortunate than himself. He'll persuade himself that he is performing a kind of service this way, alerting his neighbors to the unevenness of it all, and imagine himself justified when he begins to hear similar things in return.

I heard there was a couple brothers got themselves a new truck. Said they needed a truck for their business and that committee gave 'em a truck, free and clear.

Another man consoles himself with sneering, pointing out foolhardiness where he sees it as a salve to his imagined wounds.

Jess Meagher up and left town, damn harebrained fool. Figured he'd take his relief money and start somewhere fresh. Cleared his lot and hammered a "For Sale" sign into the ground. Who in all creation he thinks is gonna buy that lot is beyond me.

Resentful men, brooding men. Dissatisfied and restless because everything has been spoiled, persuaded they are seething because those who had little now have more.

Sure is a lot of money floating around. Wish some of it would land on me. I got insurance money coming on the house, but nothing on my furniture. What am I gonna do with a brand new house and not a stick of furniture to put in it? Got to wonder why I always worked so hard. Seems like a man's better off these days without a job.

A woman will feel a bottomless rage and think herself powerless to escape it. Terrified of her anger and unable to see that it is only fear, she will imagine a purpose in it and allow herself to spoil for a fight. *You go right back down there and tell them,* she'll say to her already defeated husband. *Tell them the insur-*

ance isn't enough. Baffled, bitter, and foundering, the men and women sink into a shriveling kind of loneliness. They begin to believe that they have failed somehow. They watch the contractors and their crews at work, they see the good foundations laid over the scars of their old houses and the wood frames beginning to rise out of them and can think only of the storm. How long before they can rest easy again? How long before a house can be a strong thing of bricks and mortar and not a stack of cards? How long before they're done being angry?

A tornado is a spasm in a thundercloud, a thing of chance arising out of nature. It might touch down, and it might not. A tornado is a ravenous thing, untroubled by the distinction in tearing one man apart and gently setting another down a little distance away. It is resolute and makes its unheeding progress until, bloated and replete, it dissipates. A tornado is a dead thing and cannot acknowledge blame. If a tornado smashes your house or takes your child, it does no good to blame it. You can even rail against God, and it will be no use. The tornado is gone, used up. You can't throw it into reverse and resurrect your house and your child by laying blame. And even after you've yanked up another house in the place the old one stood and planted flowers in the dirt where you laid your child, your fury remains as well your desire to lay blame.

Funny we got to give our money to Graves. Built with his lumber first time around.

No one else to give it to. 'Sides, there wasn't much left standing after the storm but stuff he'd built. I guess I'll buy me some of that luck.

Can't buy luck.

Who says? Anyway, he's the only game in town.

You can say that again. Goddamn! How lucky can one man get. He's still got everything he started out the year with, and now he's getting more.

More what?

Money, our money.

Red Cross money, you mean.

Doesn't matter. That lumberyard is a land-office business now.

So ask the man for a job.

A job? Hell, I got a job!

Well, he's got lumber and we need it. Can't hardly begrudge a man making an honest living.

Profiteering's more like it.

Guess he is making out best of everybody.

Almost like he struck a deal with someone.

What do you mean, downstairs? Aw, come on, you don't mean that. Anyway, any man strikes a deal like that's supposed to come out with something better than just his same old lumberyard.

All right then, upstairs. 'Sweet Jesus, send me a way to make more money, 'cause my house, my business, and my pretty wife just ain't enough!'

Careful, now. Somebody might think you mean that.

I don't give a good God damn. I'm worn out. I'm just plain worn out by the whole thing.

25

Midmorning and the breeze is blowing hot. The children are racing up and down along the clothesline, slapping at each other's shadows through the white sheets, squealing when the shadow of a hand almost touches them and then slapping back at the sheet to push it away. Mae swats at the seat of Ellis's pants and tells him, "Scoot," and pulls off the clothespins holding the first sheet to the line. The children obey and begin to chase each other in a circle around the second sheet.

"Are you taking them all down, Mama?"

"No, we'll leave you one for now," Mae says. She drops the clothes pins into their bag and looks across the street to see if the woman is still there. Catty-corner from the house, standing there on the corner like she's waiting for something to happen, a woman is staring at them. Whether she's staring at the house or at Mae or at all of them is impossible to say, but she is staring. She's not holding anything like a handbag or even a paper sack, she's just a statue in a summer hat with her arms hanging at her sides. Mae squints back at the woman, standing stock-still herself now with her arms raised, ready to take down the end of the next sheet. Lavinia unpins her end and gathers the sheet in folds, walking toward Mae.

"Whatever are you looking at?" Lavinia says, squinting quickly in the direction Mae's eyes are fixed.

"Who is that?" Mae says. "Over there, across the street."

"I don't know. I can't see a thing from here," says Lavinia.

She moves Mae's hand and pulls the other clothespin off the line. "We can't stand here staring all day," she says, turning. "Here, take this end, will you?"

"I don't see why not. She's stared long enough at us."

"Well, you look, then. My glasses are inside."

Mae feels the sheet stretch out as Lavinia walks backward away from her and then feels it slacken again as Lavinia walks toward her to make the first fold. Lavinia has positioned herself in such a way that Mae can look past her at the woman without appearing to be staring. Whoever this woman is, she isn't a gawker like the others. Mae's seen enough of them the last few months to know by the quick little leap in her gut that she's being watched and why. When it's people walking past the front of the house and you catch them slowing out of the corner of your eye, you simply turn away from the window and go deeper into the house, where you can't be seen while they make their survey of your good fortune. You find work to do in another room; you leave your straightening or your dusting and you go into the kitchen and wipe the table again with the wrung-out cloth, and when you see another passerby coming, because the house is on the corner and they come at you from behind, too, you go upstairs where no one can see you unless you stand at one of the windows and look right back at them.

But this isn't gawking. Gawkers only slow down some and point before they move on. This woman is looking hard, like she's looking for something, like if she just stares hard enough Mae will go inside and get whatever it is and give it back. She knows what Paul would do, but can't do that herself. Can't walk across the street with a real smile on her face and ask neighborly questions until the woman goes away appeased, thinking it was her own idea to leave. I'd just drop this sheet, Mae thinks. Send the others inside and stand here like a mirror to show her how she looks, no business being there but planted there anyway. Shame her into going away. But then Lavinia or one of the children would let something slip at dinner and next thing Paul would be telling her to remember how different a thing can look if you stand next to a person and look at it with them. Mae could speak Paul's words for him now. *Don't let her be a stranger hiding under a hat.* But Paul's eagerness to see things as others see them does not always extend to Mae. He'd tell her all day long to cross that street without stopping first to imagine himself making that walk inside her skin, without stopping to understand that what Mae wants is not to know who the woman is or what happened to her in the storm that's making her stand there in particular, but only that she wants the woman to go away, to never have been there in the first place. Finding out who means taking on *why* and *what*, and Mae has no room for any of it. She can already see the only thing worth knowing without having to pretend to be Paul, and that is that this woman isn't really staring at the house or even at any of them but at some imagined or remembered thing she's laid on top of them.

Mae and Lavinia are folding in movements so practiced Mae is only barely aware of what she is doing. They could fold a double sheet together in total darkness, moving all the while away from and toward each other as if they were dancing. Paul said as much once, that they looked like they were dancing, but that had been inside the house last winter when they'd been folding bed linens dried on the lines in the basement. Lavinia had begun to hum a waltz then and Mae had risen up on the balls of her feet and begun to dance as she and Lavinia had moved back toward each other holding up the corners of the sheet they'd just started to fold. They had sung aloud together and danced and they'd waltzed that sheet into a tight square. It was only last winter, but it might as well have been a hundred years ago, for all that it was possible now. Neither of them would do that outside for all the neighborhood to see, but then neither would it occur to either of them these days to hum that waltz, if only to make the other smile.

"It's just Mittie Hoyt, isn't it?" Lavinia asks and puts the folded sheet in the basket.

"It's not. I might understand if it were Mittie standing there on her own property, but that's not her."

The children are still racing and dodging each other, running in circles around the last sheet that's hanging half off the line now, trailing in the grass.

"Whoever she is, she might be staring because of the noise as much as anything else," Lavinia says. "There aren't any other children outside anywhere."

Mae shakes her head, biting her lip and frowning, as much provoked by Paul's voice in her head telling her what to do as by the woman's staring.

"She was there before we all came outside," Mae says, turning on her heel. "She's been just standing there the whole time." She yanks at the last sheet until it comes free of the line and the clothes pins fly into the grass. She balls up the sheet, stuffs it into the clothes basket, and snaps at the children, "Everybody inside now!"

"Land's sake, control yourself!" Lavinia says, but Mae is only listening for the sound of their feet in the grass, following her inside.

More and more, it's easier not to leave the house. Easier to keep the children inside and tell them it's too hot out, that they'll boil their brains if they play in the yard. Do the baking in the early morning—pies, bread, and cookies—when the windows and doors are still standing open to let in the last of the night air. Close up the house well before noon each day to keep the air inside cool. Say, "Nonsense," when someone complains things are getting closed up earlier in the day than they used to last summer, earlier than the day before. Doors shut tight, curtains drawn, and blinds pulled down, the only light that gets in downstairs comes through the lace curtains on the windows looking on to the porch. Lavinia lets her, since she relishes people looking in as little as Mae and hasn't yet understood that when Mae pulls down each shade she's behaving no differently than a frightened turtle winching its legs and head inside its shell.

Mae lets the children spread out their games on the floor to keep them content inside and doesn't yell even if one of them bounces a rubber ball in the living room. When the kitchen is hottest at the end of the day, when she's given in and started opening up the house again and they're waiting for the evening breezes or the cold air following a rainstorm to shift the heavy air inside, she'll put the ice cream maker on a folded towel on the living room floor and let them crank themselves a cold dessert. "No, not out on the porch," she says when they protest. "It's not so bad in here. Let Homer have a turn." When they protest again and ask why they can't at least eat the ice cream on the porch, she says, "Same reason I told you before, same reason the porch swing is still in the garage." She can see that Paul is rattled every time she has to remind the children, even though it was his idea in the first place to limit what they were seen to do outside the house. She sees that he's more rattled every day, rattled and baffled and unable to concede that his consideration and restraint have not been enough, that if anything people around town have begun to stare and talk as if they've taken a vote and decided somehow it's their right to do so.

Try not to mind the cracking paint on the porch railings. Mulch the vegetables so all they want is water. Ignore that loose shingle on the roof and grab quickly if you must at the grass growing between the bricks on the front walk. Silence the children when they become too boisterous or better yet, just shoo them inside.

It's her mother Mae is thinking about, more and more every day. Her mother she's reminded of when she pulls a blind down over a window or shuts a door. Her mother whose odd behavior they always seemed to need to hide with excuses. Mama who's been a little under the weather lately, thank you for asking. Mama who can't leave that cup until she's washed it twice. Mama who can't come downstairs, can't go to church today. Can't come to the door, she hasn't been well. Not quite herself these last few days. She'll be there next time, I'm sure. She'll be so glad you asked. Mama, always so busy, washing and rewashing every cup. Mama leave it, that's enough. Mama no one's looking in, let the curtains be.

They'd been so glad when Mae had found Paul. So glad, both her mother and father, when she'd married him. But more than that, they'd been relieved because it meant she could leave their house and her half-life of excuses. Mae married would be safe, they'd reasoned. Mae with a home and a family of her own would be Mae who'd escaped, whose life would never become a series of constraints. Mae had also felt a kind of relief, as if it had proved that she'd been right all along when she'd married Paul, that there'd been no need to fret, no need to worry that she'd be unable by degrees to see that a washed thing was clean, unable to make a bed just once or see a window without wishing it were wall.

It's not the same, she tells herself now. It's not shame or fear that makes her stay inside, although it amounts to the same thing if she's unwilling to pass an open window. Things would go back to normal, she and Paul had told themselves, or as close to it as circumstances would allow. The houses around them would get rebuilt and once folks had grass to cut again, porches to sweep, and work and school taking them downtown each day, things would be different. She and Paul could open the box they'd shut themselves in inch by inch and reassume their lives. But the box got shut tighter than they'd meant, and everything outside it has gone strange. A frightening truth has begun to enter Mae's head that Paul will never admit: that although they willingly withdrew and boxed themselves in, the town now means to keep them there. If she pushed to get out again, to claim her place among the survivors, it would be like being trapped again in the storm cellar in those first moments after the storm, but now with the weight of a hundred trees fallen across the doors to prevent her climbing out.

Mae moves close enough to the lace curtains on the windows at the front of the house to see that the woman is there again across the street, in the same spot she's been standing every day this week. There's no foot or automobile traffic, no one to see the woman but Mae, and it wouldn't matter if there were; she'd look through any car or person that got in her way, straight through to whatever it is she thinks she's seeing. What is it exactly that you're heaping on us? Mae wonders. How much more will it be? How big a house and how many coffins are you tossing up on the pile?

Mae is trembling now. It's the same woman she saw the first day when she was folding sheets with Lavinia in the yard, but it could be another. It could be one of any number of women each day, coming to take up the post and stare in turn. She hasn't told Paul and won't, and although Lavinia must know the woman keeps coming back, they've agreed somehow not to talk about it. Mae can feel her heart's beating turning to a throb, the reliable swell and collapse of her ribs shifting into jabs. "Yes, I see you. I see you," she mutters. "Where were you a year ago?" she asks. "What were you doing? Not standing there, anyway." Mae feels it then, for the briefest of moments she feels herself wanting to know who this woman is and who she has buried. How many places she set for breakfast the morning of the storm, how many eggs she cracked, how many chairs scraped her kitchen floor in turn when the food was hot and she'd called them all to sit and eat.

It's the sounds, Mae thinks, all the remembered sounds that are weighing on the woman. A screen door cracking shut. A fork dropping on an emptied plate. A toppled glass slopping milk on a tablecloth. It would be easier to bear somehow if it were gall or effrontery that made the woman stand there, but it's only anguish that has led her to Mae's house and let her imagine her dead children thumping down Mae's stairs and sitting at Mae's table. And now Mae is shaking and she's squeezing fistfuls of her dress so hard her knuckles have gone white. She should have gone over to the woman like she'd wanted to that first day out in the yard, just crossed the street and told her, "What you want is not here," because it turns out that leaving her to stand there every day was the same as opening her door to ghosts.

Mae moves suddenly and snatches open the front door. She stands at the top of the porch stairs looking across the street at the woman, and when the woman doesn't move, Mae goes quickly down the steps, wondering what it is she is doing. She goes down the front walk and then along the sidewalk to the corner and stands there, opposite the woman, still wondering. The woman is not wearing a hat today and, at this distance, even in the bright sun light, they can see each other's faces clearly. Mae is about to call out to her when she hears Little Homer's voice calling, "Mama?" from the porch behind her. The woman's face changes then and she's staring hungrily past Mae at the porch, at Homer.

Mae hears Lavinia's voice then, saying, "Let your mama be. Come on inside."

Mae can't move from where she is standing. She is ashamed and crying. "No, Homer," she manages to call. "Go get your brother and sister and play outside in the yard a while."

26

Here is Mae, before the children, before they were married, handing him an apple she has just twisted off its branch and saying, "This one." Paul is taking her in, hardly breathing because he can't believe his luck. He can't quite believe that this creature in her swaying summer dress is smiling up at him that way. She's tilted her head just so and all he can see is one blue eye under her hat's straw brim. He's forgotten to reach for the apple and she's laughing at him, biting into it now herself. Here's Paul, all of twenty years to Mae's nineteen, following her around an orchard and panting for the joy of it because he knows this girl will be his. He could kiss her now, but he won't. Not just yet. He'll watch her a little longer instead and let her see it, let her see that she's made his breathing go shallow and quick, that he's barely blinking.

And here is Paul in his good suit, shoving his hands deep in his pockets and letting his heels strike the pavement hard so he can feel the jolt of each step in his spine. He wants to run, he wants to laugh. He pulls his hat down a bit more and lowers his face to hide his grinning because he knows he needs to keep this bubble inside until he reaches the lumberyard and can shout, "I got the loan, Johnny! I'm gonna build her a house!" And here he is, running now because John took hold of him by the arms and looked at him hard with something that was both loss and pride before spinning him around and shoving him back out onto the pavement, sending him running toward Mae and yelling after him, "I know a good lumber-yard!"

Here is Mae, lying on the bed to feed the baby, and Paul watching from the edge of the bed unable, suddenly, to remember how they were before. The baby's jaw works, then slows, the red fist unfurls, and Mae takes her hand from the baby's back to reach for him. This is how they will be. And here they are locked together in the bed, barely moving because it's different for Mae now after three babies and Paul must wait first and hold her face till the moment her lips will open and she'll exhale against his mouth and her hips will begin to toss. "Who's my girl?" he says afterward, when she's laughing and pushing him away because they're both sweaty and he's kissing away the salt above her lips.

Here is the town, exploded and drifting back to earth, and Paul running toward Mae through the debris, desperate to reach Mae, who is core and substance and marrow lining bone. Mae who sees it's him through the muck he's been soaked in. Mae who is still standing, who for all that she's sobbing is fierce and is the reason the children are there to hug his legs.

And here is Paul now, watching Mae at the kitchen sink, thinking that she's slipped still farther away from him than she did yesterday and the day before. He's afraid to look at her much these days, or for very long at a time, because he knows she won't like it, that she'll feel she's being observed. The worst of it is that he can't say precisely what has happened. He thought at first that he was afraid of what he might see in her face, that she'd be angry or irritated or struggling to keep from crying. Then all that shifted somehow, and he realized he wasn't seeing anything at all. As if she were standing right in front of him but wasn't really there, like she'd managed somehow to crawl outside herself and all that remained was a shell in her exact likeness, left there as a diversion to give her time to get away.

He'd blamed it on the storm of course, but even if the storm was initially to blame it isn't anymore and he's grown anxious, casting about for something to hold onto, for a way to understand. They have been married enough years now that everything between them has changed and changed again. The children coming one by one, his father dying, John and Dora moving their family out to California. People moving in and out of a room he'd thought only he and Mae would occupy. He's carried the same image of Mae in his head through it all; that image of the girl in the orchard he's about to kiss for the first time with her eyes wide open and the scent of apples on her mouth, and now, sitting at the kitchen table, he finds he cannot conjure it. Or perhaps it's only that he's unwilling to try, afraid that the girl in his head will be closing her eyes and turning down her face, or worse yet, that she'll already have walked away.

He looks at his mother sitting across from him, entering sums with the stub of a pencil in her book of household accounts. She's thumbing back and forth, looking down her nose through her reading glasses, checking last month or last year against this one. She looks for all the world like she's still at the farm, sitting as she did when he was a child after supper at the kitchen table with one of these books that she'd bought through the years at the stationer's in town. The same books she kept rubber-banded together in the kitchen drawer at the farm that now lie rubber-banded together here in a drawer in his kitchen. For all he knows the pencil in her hand is the same one he watched her write in those books with when he was a child.

The same pencil writing in the same book spread out on the round kitchen table his mother brought along with her when she moved to town from the farm. Paul wants Lavinia to look up from her book and ask him something, ask him anything about his day. Who he saw and talked to in town, whether he'd liked the wilted lettuce salad they'd had with dinner because she'd made it with him in mind. If Johnny came through the door then, he'd sit in that chair there and say, "I believe I will," when Mae asked if he'd have a slice of cake. Johnny, who fills a kitchen by himself. Johnny, whose legs steal all the room for stretching out under the table. Their father would laugh at him, slouched like that in his chair. He'd reach down and clap Johnny's leg like an old dog's haunch and tell him, "Sit up straight!" Their father, forever chewing a duck call the way other men chewed cigars, watching John fork the tender cake into his mouth, spreading out his hands and saying, "How about me?"

Paul drinks the last of his coffee and clatters his cup back so loudly onto its saucer that it makes Lavinia look up. He clasps his hands quickly under the table and squeezes them together hard to control their trembling. A moment later, Lavinia has looked back down at her book and Mae is taking his cup and saucer to the sink to wash them. Silence prevails, despite his having clattered the cup, despite Mae's sloshing it through the dishwater and setting it *chink* in with the rest of the dripping dishes, and despite the scratch of his mother's pencil in her book. He can't hear the children anywhere and doesn't remember where they are. He wants to ask, "Where are the children?" but he thinks he might shout it or that his voice will sound desperate, as if they truly are lost, and then Lavinia or Mae will look at him in astonished disbelief because he should know that, he should remember, because they just told him.

Then the children are there racing through the kitchen, letting the back door slam behind them. They pound up the stairs to one bedroom or another and stay there. They were quiet outside and they're quiet now upstairs; the only noise they made was in getting from place to place. No one stopped to cadge just one more cookie. No one needed or wanted a thing.

No child's voice yelled, "Look!" with a half-dead worm or snail or a misshapen rock held out on a grubby palm. No adult voice ordered, "Put that back outside and wash your hands." There were no voices at all.

They don't seem to understand how it wears at him, this eroding life without voices. "I didn't speak to anyone today, Mother," he could say if she asked, and it would be true enough. He'd hardly spoken at all, he'd just stayed in the office or been out back at the saws all day because it had gotten easier if Clarence or Lon were out front instead of him when the bell rang over the door. People had started writing their orders on bits of paper and sliding them at him across the counter, and he'd already had about as much of it as he could take. They'd wait for him to write the order up, to say when it would be ready, and then they'd give him their perfunctory nods and walk right out again, having spared everyone the trouble of actual conversation.

Still worse was when they came back to pick up finished orders, when the thing they were shoving at him was their money, which didn't move easily from hand to hand anymore but was counted out with slow fingers and then pushed deliberately, indignantly across the counter as if to goad him. And before they went around back to have their lumber loaded, they'd look at him once more to make sure he saw the bitter twist their mouths were in and the contempt they wore for him in their eyes because he had one hell of a nerve.

Here is Paul sitting with his mother at the kitchen table, bewildered and diminished after another day without voices, watching Mae swat at a fly the children let in with them through the kitchen door. She misses again and again and Lavinia is straining, turning right and left in her chair to follow the fly's haphazard path. The crack of a fly swatter is really no different than a whining saw when it bites into wood. No different than the scratch of broom bristles in a room without voices. It's all louder than it's supposed to be. And now the fly is refusing to be hit and Mae is refusing to stop trying to hit it and Paul sees Mae's furious lunging and he wonders if Mae even knows how she ended up so trapped.

27

A mindless Friday spent plodding forward, forward, ticking off the unvarying tasks that, once done, will simply reemerge, thankless and undone, the next day. That laundry will just have to get itself upstairs somehow, Lavinia thinks. She knows that either she or Mae will eventually carry the basket upstairs and empty it onto closet shelves, but for now she leaves the folded whites to stand on the kitchen table, unties her apron and hangs it next to Mae's on the back of the kitchen door. It's not weariness that's made her leave the last of her work for later, it's restlessness. She's distracted, even edgy tonight. There's something else that wants doing. Not something she's forgotten, but a thing she hasn't thought of yet. She's never been given to nerves, she thinks, and she won't let herself be now. Best to just put this feeling right out of her head.

Paul, Mae, and the children are already all in the living room. Lavinia goes in cautiously, and is grateful when she sees that everyone is occupied. She doesn't much feel like talking tonight, or explaining her fretful mood. There's plenty to talk about, of course—not least the business of watching the town being built for the second time in her life, from the ground up this time instead of simply outward—but there are fewer times she feels like talking lately. There's less and less reason to walk downtown now, too. Not for lack of things to do, but for the want of conversation. People will sometimes still nod in her direction, mutter, "Morning," as they pass on the sidewalk, but only because it is still less awkward than saying nothing at all. These days Paul's dinners are still warm in the pail when she reaches the lumberyard. "Why don't you just call it a walk, Mother, and let me eat a sandwich at noon?" Paul used to joke. "Because I can't just go visiting in the middle of each day. If I'm out on an errand and stop to talk, that's another thing altogether," she'd say.

It's baffling that people she has known for decades, some her old schoolmates, can be so discourteous. It began with people neglecting to inquire after her and her family. Oh, they'd smile some and nod when they met each other walking, they'd answer her questions about their own families, but then they'd make like they had somewhere to be, leaving Lavinia alone and perplexed in the middle of the sidewalk. Then the same people began to give her only tiny nods, barely meeting her eyes and muttering, "Hello", as they rushed past. No one had yet ever gone so far as to cross to the other side of the street when they'd seen her coming, but plenty had ducked under umbrellas or the brims of their hats, feigning that they'd never noticed her there in the first place, coming down the street at the same time she always came with Paul's dinner.

It's not right, she thinks. I doubt Homer would ever have believed it was possible. Our people have been here longer than most of the rest of them. The farm was here before the town, before the land was even cleared. Maybe people don't want to remember that, since we sold out and moved to town. Maybe they'd rather only see the new headstones in the cemetery, not the old plots under the old trees with our names on them. It's a pity to think that people can forget so willfully, so easily. But if they decide to do a thing, who can stop them? And if people can decide to do such a thing, why, what kind of friends were they to begin with?

Paul is sitting deep in the davenport, the newspaper stretched out in his hands. How can he be so comfortable,

Lavinia wonders. He looks the same as ever, legs crossed at the knee, newspaper held up high to catch the lamplight. Lavinia goes to the sideboard, trailing a fingertip along the hard, silky wood. She takes up the photograph of her and Homer, taken on their thirtieth wedding anniversary. They had posed for it on the porch steps of the old farmhouse before going down into the yard for the big picnic supper. They were all there in the yard, the whole family, while John took this picture. John and Dora hadn't yet moved out West; everyone was there, smiling and laughing up at her and Homer while they posed, squinting in the early summer light.

Homer would have understood Paul, she thinks. He would have understood Paul's desire to mollify people lately, and his saying, "Wait for them to come around, they'll all come around soon enough." Homer would probably have behaved the same way. But somehow knowing that husband and son would have been like-minded in this, knowing that she might even guess at what her son will do next, having known her husband so well and long, is little help in understanding.

Lavinia replaces the photograph and looks up at herself in the mirror hanging above the sideboard. She turns her head, lifts her chin slightly to look at the line of her jaw. She runs the backs of her fingers along her jowl, dips her chin again and pats at the back of her hair, as she does habitually, as if her hair pins might have fallen out without her noticing. Her hair is soft, half snow-colored, half steel, and not much thinner than it ever was. She sees Paul in profile in the wide mirror, where he is sitting on the davenport, wearing her nose and chin on his face. She had wondered, when he was small, what that would look like when he was grown. She had always been pretty, she was pretty still, and on Paul's face her fine features had made a boyish, handsome man.

They're a fine-looking couple, Paul and Mae. Lavinia takes a step to the side, so that she can see Mae reflected in the mirror. Mae's hair is walnut brown, just the color of the sideboard in the lamplight. It almost looks marcelled, except that Mae would never bother with the hairdresser's. Neither she nor Lavinia would bother. Not because of the expense—they could bear that, she supposes—but because neither needed or wanted to gild the lily. Lavinia is used to Mae's bob now, even amused by it. Funny to think of Mae and Paul taking turns to sit in the same barber's chair. Homer wouldn't have approved. *They're both so pretty with their short hair, who can tell them apart?* he might have said in private.

Mae and I would have been friends, Lavinia thinks, if we'd been the same age. She had felt she recognized something in Mae when Paul first brought her home to the farm. She'd known who Mae was, of course, but Mae and her parents always seemed to keep to themselves; they were town folks she rarely saw and knew only a little. When Paul had first walked through the kitchen door with Mae beside him, they were both beaming. So happy, so happy. Lavinia had felt certain they had just dropped each other's hands before they came in, and then felt as if they were always touching, somehow, even when they were not. "I believe we've just met our daughter-in-law," she'd said to Homer that night, when Paul had gone to take Mae home. "Could be, could be," Homer had said from behind his newspaper, and Lavinia had swatted the paper and said, "You know I'm right." She had been touched by Paul's choice, because she saw that she and Mae were of a kind, and understood in a quiet way that Paul's loving Mae had something to do with his regard for her.

Perhaps she could have been more of a comfort to Mae if they had met as girls of the same age. As quickly as Lavinia had felt her mood lifting, watching Paul and Mae in the mirror, she feels it shift again as she considers Mae alone. How ever can she stand it, Lavinia wonders. How can she have allowed herself to become this way, to let that part of her that Paul fell so quickly in love with be clouded over like this? She might understand it if Mae were unloved, of if she had been unable to bear children, but Mae had always had family around her, and had never wanted for anything. Lavinia cannot fathom why Mae can't just look across the room and see, truly see, her husband and children who adore her; why she can't just look at her pretty, comfortable house and let her good fortune buoy her up.

Of course, the unevenness of it all is as troubling as the fact of Mae's unhappiness. Paul's having to come home each day from the lumberyard, not knowing what he'll find when he comes through the door; whether Mae will smile and greet him, or just turn away, trying not to cry. The children all cling to her in their own ways, unwilling to let her out of their sight, even on days they dare not approach her.

And yet Mae has never taken to her bed, like others you hear about. Her work is always done. She and Lavinia work together, inside and out and, no matter Mae's mood, the house and the children are clean, and the yard is tidy. Lavinia is grateful for this: for Mae's freeing her of the need to feign that all is well because, to anyone else's eyes, it seems that it is. When Mae's moods descend on her, she simply retreats, does not seek out people, so there is little to hide from others.

If Mae and I were friends, Lavinia thinks, perhaps she'd trust me. Her own parents are gone, she has no brothers or sisters, and though she might have trusted Paul, he won't face her, not properly.

If she thought Paul would listen, Lavinia could tell him what she sees: that he's utterly lost when Mae sinks into her moods; that when he's most wary of her, clinging to her as the children do, he should instead leave her alone; that when he holds Mae's face in his hands and whispers, "How's my girl?" she will always keep her eyes lowered, and she will never accept his sympathy. She could tell Mae a few things, too; that she has overcomplicated Paul and missed her opportunity to understand him. It had been a great disappointment to Lavinia, seeing an uncomprehending Mae decide to give up her habit of asking Paul what he thought of this or that for dinner over the breakfast table, having mistaken Paul's desire to submit to her for a lack of opinion.

Lavinia watches Mae bent over a skirt hem she has been mending. A wry little smile twists up the corner of Lavinia's mouth. Oh, darling girl, she thinks, I can love you all I want, but you'll never trust me. You'll never let me be another mother to you. You think you can only ever be my daughter-in-law, but you're my child as surely as if I bore you myself. My willful child. It is surely willfulness that keeps you this way. And if you can will yourself into it, you can will yourself out of it, too.

How ever did we get this way? Lavinia thinks. Mae staring out of windows with that desperate look, staring, always staring, no matter what is going on around her. Paul, baffled and loyal, smothering Mae with concern. The children, well, they were all changed, too. Ellis had just gone and crawled inside himself. He kept busy and did what he was told, mostly so he wouldn't have to meet anyone's eye. His head was usually bent down over whatever it was he was doing, not out of concentration, but in order to hide his frown. He'd gotten tired, like his mother, of constantly being asked was he okay. All at the grand age of seven.

Ruby had gone the opposite way. She was like a pocket turned inside out. Everything that should have been hidden was there for anyone to see. She kept busy, too. Often as not, she had a book in one hand. It was whatever she was doing with her free hand that was trying. If her nails were bitten all the way down, she'd bite some more, down into the painful quick. Then she'd chew the ends of her hair, till the strands of hair in front, the longest parts of her bob, were either perpetually wet or tucked into the corners of her mouth. And if she'd been told to give her nails and hair a rest, she'd start in tugging at her dress front. She'd wiggle her shoulders and her head would twitch like she needed to adjust the fit of her clothes. But then she'd tug at her dress again and twitch some more and sometimes, if she was standing, the neck of it would get pulled down so far in front you could see the top of her chest, and at the back, the hem would be hoisted indecently high.

And Little Homer. He seemed the most like his old self of any of the children, but that was perhaps only because he wasn't all that old to begin with. Somehow he was the one who could still cheer Mae, if only because he hadn't stopped trying. He was the baby, and Mae knew he still needed her most. She was dependent on Ellis and Ruby's being older, on their needing her less. It hadn't yet occurred to Mae that her moods had actually made the children younger than they were.

No, it wasn't the storm that got us here, Lavinia thinks; the storm just blew us here quicker. Maybe things wouldn't have been so bad if the town hadn't been knocked down around us. Maybe I shouldn't have sold the farm so quick after Homer died. We could have hired help until Ellis and Little Homer were old enough to work it. Paul could have kept at the lumberyard, and driven into town instead. Maybe if John hadn't moved, that's what we would have done. The lumberyard was too much for Paul alone, living out on the farm. Maybe if John hadn't moved. But if you go that far back for blame, shouldn't you go further? Lavinia wonders. What if our people had never been farmers, what if they'd settled right away in a town? Someone two generations back could have started a lumberyard in Marah, for that matter, and John and Paul could have inherited something they wanted to work at, instead of inheriting a farm.

But if we hadn't sold out, we'd have been flattened with the rest of them, Lavinia thinks. The farm house and all the outbuildings went as flat as the fields around them during the storm.

Lavinia's house. It wasn't the first house that had ever stood on the farm. It was Lavinia's father who'd torn down the small house he'd been born in and built a new one entirely of materials available on the farm. We could have done the same, she thinks. The storm didn't destroy any crops, coming so early in the year. We could have lived on everything we'd stored in the cellar, and Paul's a fair shot. We would have eaten. Then we could have rebuilt like they did before me, right over the old cellar. We could have fended for ourselves. It's not John's fault any more than it's the storm's, nor is it my Homer's for dying. Maybe it's just my fault, she thinks. I should have held out. But neither Paul nor John wanted to farm; they'd bolted as soon as they could and worked hard after they'd set up, so hard they'd paid Homer back his start money inside two years. It had seemed best to let go. And if they were busy rebuilding like the rest of the town, Mae wouldn't have time to stare out of windows. They'd all have been kept busy, even the children, with no time for reflection or self-pity or whatever it was they had all sunk into. They could have kept themselves focused on rebuilding, on making something out of nothing.

Lavinia is worn out, not least by Mae and Paul's stubbornness: Mae, in her withdrawal, and Paul, in surrendering to it. She realizes that not one of them has looked up since she entered the room, and turns away from the mirror to face them. They're not just occupied, she thinks, they're all pretending they're alone, even the children, hoping that no one will want to talk. She frowns, provoked and suddenly childish. Paul's not even reading behind that paper, she thinks. Wouldn't I just love to snatch it away from him right now. She looks at Ellis on the floor, concentrating, lost in making holes in his wood scraps with the hand drill.

"Take care you don't go through to the floor, now," she says, watching Paul, who lowers his paper to see for himself, then raises it again and says, "Keep that wood on the cookie sheet."

"I am!" Ellis cries, stung.

Lavinia takes her wing chair opposite Mae's. The fireplace behind the wing chairs is cold. They could do with a fire right now, for its cheer as much as any warmth, but they've all had enough of fires, she supposes. Little Homer has given up waiting for a turn with the hand drill and is jabbing a finger rhythmically into the repeats of the carpet pattern. Ruby is on the far end of the davenport, a book in her lap, chewing again on a lock of her hair.

"You don't have enough light there," Lavinia says. Ruby replies, "Yes, I do, Gran," without looking up. Well, no you don't, Lavinia thinks. The sun is down and the light outside is failing, but she won't be bothered to get up to switch on another light if no one else will. What on earth would Homer, her Homer, have made of this nonsense? Certainly, Lavinia can imagine him sitting there, looking around the room, taking their measure. She can imagine mild disgust crossing his face, his slippered feet flat on the floor and his hands on the ends of his chair's armrests, ready to haul himself up and tell everyone how things were going to be. She could do it herself, assume Homer's authority, make the pronouncements he would have made and expect them to be heard, but she's prevented by peevishness; a blazing indignation at having been left with both a widow's clarity and a matriarch's obligation.

Lavinia is distracted again, and agitated. Something has come into her head—she doesn't know from where or why—and she is thinking about the town's name. How many years has it been since she considered it? "Homer," she says, "Get my Bible, please." Little Homer looks up, startled to hear his name, as if she's suddenly appeared in the room. "My Bible. It's right there on the bookshelf." She takes the Bible from him. Exodus, she thinks. The onionskin crackles, gilt-edged pages sliding in slabs under her finger tip. Lavinia skims and then reads when she finds it. She laughs resignedly, and shakes her head with a "what did you expect" finality. They all look up at her.

"What are you reading, Mother?" Paul asks.

"It comes after the plagues," she says, "When they're wandering in the desert."

Paul and Mae look at her silently, waiting for her to explain, and Lavinia begins to read aloud: "'So Moses brought Israel from the Red Sea, and they went out into the wilderness of Shur; and they went three days in the wilderness, and found no water. And when they came to Marah, they could not drink of the waters of Marah, for they were bitter: therefore the name of it was called Marah. And the people murmured against Moses, saying, What shall we drink? And he cried unto the LORD; and the LORD shewed him a tree, which when he had cast into the waters, the waters were made sweet.'"

Lavinia slaps the open pages on her lap and shakes her head. Paul lays his newspaper on his lap and exhales loudly. He looks quickly at Mae, then at Lavinia, and says quietly, "Well, what about it, Mother?"

"They named this town Marah because of the stream that runs through it. When settlers first came through here, no horse would drink from it. Finally someone tasted it and said, sure enough, it was bitter. Of course, that didn't matter so much once they got settled and started digging wells. They knew their Bible back then, I tell you."

"Mother, please," Paul says softly. The children watch Lavinia, waiting for her response.

"Paul, I am simply talking about how the town got its name. There can't be any harm in that."

"But that's not what you're talking about."

"Well, of course it is. What did you think I meant?"

"Marah means bitter, Mother. I remember you read me that passage back when John and I started up the business. I don't think we should dwell on it. It's upsetting."

Oh, go on and say it, Lavinia thinks. Say you mean it's upsetting to Mae. That I'm upsetting Mae. And then I can say that everything is upsetting to Mae these days, and that coddling her isn't making it any better and maybe you should stop coddling her. Life here is bitter, even though it didn't used to be. It's a fact, and pretending otherwise won't make it so. How much more of this is a body meant to cope with, she wonders? Prodding the children toward adulthood should be a pleasure. Waking each morning to find herself not only another day older but still spared the worst humiliations of old age should be another. But this evasion and pretense, the elaborate politeness their life together now required was suffocating. If the telephone were to ring right now, they'd all come clean out of their skins, they're wound so tight.

"All right," she says instead. "I'm sorry."

Little Homer has gone to stand by Mae, who has set her mending on the marble-topped table beside her. She's staring at the carpet, jiggling an agitated foot. Homer pulls apart Mae's clasped hands and climbs up into her lap. Mae sits with her arms loosely around him, never moving her head, staring off at the same spot on the carpet. Homer perches there, not daring to relax against her, but unwilling to leave her. He takes her hand on his lap, pulling up her fingers one by one, then letting them go so that they thump against his leg.

Lavinia sees that Mae is struggling to control herself, and says, "Come, leave your Mama be, Homer. She's tired. Come sit with me." Little Homer keeps hold of his mother's hand and looks into her face, defiant. Oh, look at him, Lavinia thinks. Look at your child! Ruby and Ellis know better than to try most times, and wait for their mother to come to them before they'll touch her. Mae's eyes are more focused now, but still staring at the carpet. "Come on now, Homer. Come sit here. Your mama's tired is all." Lavinia gets out of her chair just enough to lean over and catch Homer's free hand.

"Let go, Homer. Listen to your grandma," Paul intervenes, and Homer drops Mae's hand to go sit limply on Lavinia's lap, still looking sullenly at his mother. He leans against Lavinia as he dared not with Mae, resting his head against the side of her neck. Now Mae's breathing quickens, her chest and stomach rising and falling in little stabs. She shakes her head slowly in the tiniest movement, still staring at the carpet. Ruby turns a page of her book, Ellis drills his slow holes. Paul looks up once from his newspaper, across the top of it to Mae, purses his lips almost imperceptibly, and looks down again. Mae's eyes close and her head sinks in remorse. She looks up at Paul with her eyes wide and blinking as if she is waking up, then she looks at Homer with a tender, sorrowful look and holds out her hand. He rushes to her and she takes him on her lap, rocking him.

"I'm sorry, I'm sorry," she murmurs. "Mama loves you." Homer pulls Mae's face close to his, "Mama," he says. She kisses his hair.

"Why are you always tired, Mama?"

"I don't know, Homer, I just am."

Their faces are hidden from her, so Lavinia watches them openly, a sad sort of smile pulling at her mouth, somewhere between appeasement and contentment. Paul is watching, too, hungry and relieved. Lavinia wonders that the intensity of his gaze alone doesn't make Mae look up at him, but she's still rocking Little Homer, kissing him, her body bent around her rangy son, as soft now as it had been brittle moments ago. When Mae does look up at Paul, her face is timid and remorseful, but Paul sinks back against the corner of the davenport, leans his head on his hand, and he smiles.

There, Lavinia thinks. Isn't that better.

28

The town resurrects itself. It should be a joyful thing—hammers flashing and striking home, the wood skeletons of houses in their yellow rows, lustrous as sheaves of wheat—but there can be no contentment so long as the men and women bear the suspicion that each stud and beam is no better than a filament of straw, stacked by a clever child. It's no good trying to reason that it can't happen again, no good arguing that the tornado season has passed, because the next one will be upon them soon enough when the winter is over and the question that no one can manage to dispel is, "How long?"

A woman walks through the frame of her new house and manages to allow herself to imagine it plastered and painted inside, ready for living in and even in need of its first cleaning. She walks between the rooms and thinks, How happy this would have made me before. But when she stands between the studs where a wall will soon be built, she sees only the wreckage of her former house, the snapped beams and splintered glass the storm left in the very place she is standing.

A man at work building the frame of his new house knows that the lumber he's bought and the clapboards and window glass he has coming are just flimsy, brittle things, for all that they are new. He holds a stud and hits it hard with his hammer, though the head of the nail he has just driven in already lies flush. He sees the slight depression the hammer's head has made in the wood, points to it and says, *See that?* speaking aloud as he still sometimes does to the son he lost in the storm.

He strikes again, as if to show the boy how soft the wood really is. He hears the boy's voice in his head, saying, *Can I have a try?* and he strikes harder, denting and pitting the wood until finally he strikes so wildly he smashes its milled edge. *There!* he cries out, as if he has proven something.

He finds that he is weeping and kicks the stud. He kicks it again and again until his foot hurts and then he throws his hammer away from him into the grass and picks up the crowbar lying there beside the stacked lumber and lath. It slaps back heavily against his palms when he gives it a toss, and then his thick hands choke the straight end and his arms raise up high and he's swinging it like a bat. It's disjointed, somehow; the sound of each blow comes well after the reverberation jarring his arms and neck. He keeps swinging, waiting for them to match up but they never do, and he finally has to stop and sit for a while. It's funny that he's ruined the one stud without attracting any attention on the street, but then the sound of metal hitting wood is just the sound of building, and common enough these days.

The thought, when it comes to him, is simple and seems, in its way, pure. Still, he's shocked that he thought of it so quickly—that he thought of it at all—and now he's stacked his unused lumber and lath in the bed of his truck and he's driving it all out to the burn site on the edge of town.

Nothing is growing yet in the place they burned the wreckage from the storm; a little grass and some weeds poke up around the edges of a large circle of scorched earth. He stacks the lath there in a teepee, splashes it with gasoline, and leans a few boards together around that. He stands upwind a ways to light the end of a rolled up newspaper with a match, and when he tosses it into an opening he's left, the lath goes up like paper.

A car passing the burn site slows, reverses a ways and then stops. The driver gets out slowly, and as he walks toward the solitary man he'd seen from the car who had seemed to be jumping up and down beside the fire there, he sees that what the man is doing is stomping on a board, breaking it with the heel of his boot. The board broken, the pieces thrown on the fire, the man stands silently now watching it smoke. The driver of the car does little more at first than stand there, too. He puts his hands into his pockets and cocks his head a little to signal that he is at ease, that he'd stopped because the plume of smoke had been interesting and nothing more.

What's burning today?

Graves's lumber.

You gotta be joking. New lumber? Paid for?

Yeah.

Well, then why the hell burn it?

Don't want it. Don't want to use it. Figured I'd drive over to Johnsboro and buy my lumber there. Truck it back myself.

Well now, that's a curious thing.

Think so?

Yes, I do. I guess a man'd have to have a pretty good reason to do such a thing.

I guess you'd be right.

Word gets around and triggers something in the town. Some of the men are roused to action; to what they can do now, if they choose it. They are few at first, the ones who broadcast the slanders, telling anyone who will listen that Graves Lumber is profiting from their misfortunes. Is, has, and will continue to profit so long as anything in town needs rebuilding. These men feel a twinge of misgiving when they first issue their calumnies, a twist in the belly that comes as they say the words *Paul Graves himself figured it this way,* but their words spread like a blight, and in other people's mouths begin to sound like truth.

Didn't want to see people using scavenged lumber, is what he said. Folks should rebuild with new lumber.

I heard that. Said he didn't think it was safe.

Scavenged? Hell, we called it used in my day. My daddy gave me a hammer and taught me to straighten bent nails when I was five years old. We didn't throw out a thing then if it still had some use in it.

I thought he said folks might as well buy new, seeing as how the money was coming from the insurance or the Red Cross.

Sounded like an okay idea at the time. Now every time I see those goddamn new boards stacked up at home I think of everything I carted off to burn.

I did it, too, and I sure wasn't brought up to waste. I guess it seemed like too much trouble to sort through it all then. Seemed easier to just haul it all off and start fresh.

Graves said that, too. Start fresh.

Like he'd know a thing about that.

The evening the men make their pyre is unusually fine; clear and unseasonably balmy. These are the men who labored together side by side to burn the wreckage after the storm. But this fire is a different sort of fire and the expressions on the faces ringing it have changed. And unlike those nights last spring, there are no women or children present here. Only men with their fixed, stony faces; only men bent on doing a kind of murder.

29

S ay that again, Ellis," Lavinia says slowly. "Tell your daddy exactly what you told me."

"They said their daddies burned it, every scrap."

Lavinia looks to Paul, unable to keep an impassive expression on her face. "Why ever would they say such a thing?"

"Because it's probably true," Paul says. He's holding Ellis's arm, though he'd take him on his lap if he thought the boy would let him. "Did they say anything else?"

"Willie Starks said his daddy said he wished he could take his frame down and burn that, too."

Paul stands and takes Ellis by the shoulders. "You tell me if they say anything else like that to you. You hear?" Ellis nods. "Don't tell Ruby or Homer about this."

"They already know, Daddy. They were standing right there with me."

Paul squeezes Ellis's shoulders, gives him a nod to say that they are done, and then catches him by the hand as he's turning to run upstairs and says in a low voice, "Don't tell your mama."

Once Ellis has gone, Paul sits on the davenport looking at his hands. He'll have to say something in a minute to reassure his mother. It's a mistake, she'll want him to say. Children can be so cruel, but it will certainly all blow over. She'll make him promise to find out about it somehow, wait for him to report that it was just a misunderstanding, and all this without letting Mae know that something might be wrong. And then there's his gut that knows it's true, his gut that has gone cold and is waiting for him to simply look up at his mother and say, "They did it."

There's no one left he could possibly ask, although he reckons there are those who would relish telling him the truth of it. He'll have to say something about it down at the lumberyard of course, and then he'll have to stand there and see in their faces that they knew about it before he told them, that they weren't a bit surprised, even that they'd seen it coming. In truth, Paul can't imagine anyone being shocked by it, anyone except his mother, of course, who, agitated as she is, would go on dismissing the story as malicious nonsense until he forced a piece of the charred lumber into her hand.

It's confounding, the completeness of the transformation in the town. Just six months have passed since the storm; half of one year and two seasons behind them and every last thing has been made unrecognizable. Paul sees now that it was foolish of him to have thought that anything would stay the same, although a person could be forgiven for having wished it could be true. There were things that had only wanted washing, after all. Washing or changing, nothing more. A person who was left unhurt by the storm could clean off the mud and look just as he had before. A person whose home was still standing could wash the windows and look through the glass just the same and sit in the same chair on the same patch of floor as he had only the day before. A person could be forgiven for never having dreamed that the storm would leave other men willing to maim.

There's a knock at the back door after dinner. Paul knows somehow that it's for him and he shoos the children out of the kitchen before he opens the door.

"Scoot," he says. "Go find your mama." He opens the door to a man at the bottom of the stoop standing half turned around and looking at the street behind him.

"Hello, Ben," Paul says.

"I have to talk to you. In private," Ben Eavers says, looking over Paul's shoulder into the house.

Paul closes the door softly behind him and follows Ben into the dark yard. The children are telling Mae and his mother now that Mr. Eavers has come to the back door to talk to Daddy. They will know better, all of them, than to come back into the bright kitchen where they can be seen from outside, but likely enough that will only drive them upstairs to one of the back bedrooms to listen there, instead. Paul glances up and wonders which bedroom they're all standing in now. It could be either the boys' room or Lavinia's; the windows are raised in both.

"You heard what's been happening?" Ben asks him.

"Yes," Paul frowns at him. He can see that Ben is standing there like a child who has just admitted to some misdeed, his hands shoved deep in his pockets and his eyes flitting about.

"Well, it's not over yet."

"What do you mean? What else can they burn?"

Ben shakes his head. "They've burned all they're gonna burn."

"What then?"

"Folks aren't gonna buy from you anymore. They're planning to buy in Johnsboro from now on. They mean to put you out of business."

Paul wonders whether his mother is the one listening to this upstairs through an open window, or if it's Mae. He could easily force Ben to speak to him in a whisper or make him walk further away from the house into the yard, but he feels rooted to the spot he's standing on, determined to speak in a normal voice.

"I figured that much out for myself already," Paul says. "What I can't figure out is why."

Ben looks up into the branches of the mulberry tree above

them. His arms are folded across his stomach. Paul watches him pulling at the hairs on his forearm like he's plucking a chicken.

"If you know what they're doing, you know why," Paul says.

"I can't answer for all of them."

"But you could make a pretty good guess."

"Have you tried to see this thing from the other side?" Ben whispers harshly.

"You know me better than that. That's just about all I've done!"

"Then you should know it's just too much. You can't expect folks to come dancing into your store, hand you their money, and thank you for the privilege. You're the only one who didn't get hit, Paul. The only one."

"I can't help that! I can't do a damn thing about it!"

"They know that, they just can't stand being reminded of it every day. They're saying you fixed things this way, so people would have to buy from you."

Paul's eyes narrow in warning. "I know you don't mean to say folks think I arranged the storm."

"Did you or did you not tell people that they shouldn't rebuild with anything from the wreckage?"

Paul stares at Ben, silent and breathless. "I did," he finally says.

"They're saying you set out to make a better profit that way, that you knew you'd sell more if you told folks it was only safe to build with new lumber."

"I told them that because it is safer! Because there was hardly anything left in the wreckage they could have built with, anyway! I was all over town, Ben. I saw it for myself."

"That's what they're saying. I don't necessarily think it's what everyone believes. It's just got to where folks can hardly stand to look at you."

"What about you?" Paul says, surprised by his own composure. "What do you see when you look at me?"

Paul sees a flicker of something in Ben's face. Was it shame, he wonders, or regret? It doesn't matter; he's losing another friend and being made to watch it this time.

Ben answers, "I see my old friend, Paul Graves."

"Is that so."

Ben's eyes are pleading. "That's why I'm here. That's why I wanted to warn you."

"Then can't you tell them? Can't you say I never wanted this?"

"They wouldn't listen."

Paul sees that his old friend is agitated and itching to leave. "Does Frances know you're here?" he asks.

Ben looks back at Paul hard, without flinching. "No."

"And you're not planning on telling her." Paul exhales and gives him a rueful smile. "I expect she'll want you to drive to Johnsboro from now on," he says, and Ben nods. "Tell me, Ben, did Frances tell you to burn your lumber, or did you decide that all by yourself?"

"Please, Paul, she's my wife—"

Paul looks up at the row of bedroom windows. "I understand," he says. "Loyalty should be an abiding thing." He turns his eyes toward the ground, unable to look back at Ben who is waiting now for Paul to be the one to walk away as a last courtesy to an old friend.

"I wonder where that bit about the scapegoat is," Paul says. "Maybe Genesis."

"What?"

Paul smiles and his eyes flick up at Ben's before he turns to go inside. "Never mind," he says. "Mother will know."

He finds them upstairs sitting in the dark on the boy's beds, all of them there together by the open window, just as he'd worried. Now, suddenly, he wants to shout and kick the dresser and punch his fist right through the wall, but he leans against the door jamb instead and manages to say in a calm voice, "Bedtime. Please go brush your teeth." He touches each of the children's heads as they pass him in the doorway, then says, "I'll be downstairs," to Mae and Lavinia, and turns out of the dark bedroom into the light of the hall.

He can hear them from the kitchen. Bare feet thumping on floorboards, the toilet flushed, then flushed again, the medicine cabinet opened and slammed shut. The voices are hushed, though, and he can guess at what they're whispering. He should go upstairs again, he knows it. He should tuck the children in, let them see his face, but he tells himself it's their mother they'll want now, not him, and he stays where he is at the kitchen table, searching in his mother's Bible.

Lavinia comes into the kitchen first, rubbing her palms on her dress and avoiding his eye.

"Before you start, Paul, we had no idea of what Ben would say."

"Didn't you?"

"No! How could we? You didn't know, either."

"I knew he wasn't here to ask me what I'd like for my birthday."

"Don't you sass me. You know what I mean."

"Mother, Ben Eavers and I have been friends since high school. He just came to my back door after dark. He didn't want anyone to see him. He didn't even tell his wife where he was going."

Paul continues to leaf blindly, flipping pages back and forth, no longer able to read the words. He shoves the Bible across the table to Lavinia. "Help me find it, Mother. The part about the scapegoat."

Lavinia takes hold of the Bible slowly. "Whatever for?"

"I'll never find it. Please, just help me."

Lavinia smoothes her palms out across the pages. "It's in Leviticus," she says and places her thumb on the gold tab that reads "Lev". She looks up when she has found it and Paul says, "Read it."

She reads in a quiet steady voice, even though Paul's insistence has made her afraid of the words.

"'But the goat, on which the lot fell to be the scapegoat, shall be presented alive before the Lord, to make an atonement with him, and to let him go for a scapegoat into the wilderness.'"

"Keep going."

"There isn't any more. The rest is about sacrifice and burnt offerings."

Paul reaches across the table for the Bible, turns the page, trails his finger down the first column, and reads, "'And the goat shall bear upon him all their iniquities unto a land not inhabited: and he shall let go the goat in the wilderness.'"

Paul stares with blank resignation at the book in his hands, worrying the soft black cover with his thumbs. "Well, that's some comfort," he says. "They don't actually blame the goat. They just need the goat to carry off their sins."

Lavinia shakes her head. "I don't understand."

"It's just something that's been bothering me, Mother. I'm not sure I understand it, myself."

Mae comes in and Paul pushes out a chair for her at the table, but she shakes her head and leans against the stove instead with her arms crossed tight and her eyes fixed on the floor.

"They're not asleep yet. I had to leave the light on in Ruby's room," she says. "Please don't tell the children to keep things from me," she says, looking up at Paul. "I can either hear things from my family or I can overhear them when people slink into our yard at night."

"I wanted to spare you hearing it at all."

"People are burning your lumber rather than use it! How were you going to keep me from finding that out?"

Paul shakes his head. "I hadn't thought that far." How much of the evening is left, he wonders. How long before he can walk away from everybody talking at him and lie in the dark bed.

"How much did the children hear?" he asks.

"They heard what we heard," Lavinia says. She gets up to shut the curtains over the sink and then those on the window by the back door before she sits back down at the table. "I don't know how much they understood."

"Why did you let them hear that?" Paul says to both of them and neither one of them in particular.

"Because it all happened so fast," Lavinia says. "The children followed us in there and we could hear the two of you talking as clearly as if you were standing there in the room with us and we froze. I could no more have moved right then than I could have flown to the moon."

"The children already knew what had happened," Mae says. "They knew long before that coward Ben Eavers walked into our yard."

Paul's eyes snap up at Mae.

"He is a coward. I don't like saying it, but that's the truth of it. They're all cowards and Ben Eavers is no less so for coming here to warn you. And that was no warning, that was just making sure you'd gotten the message they'd all sent through their children."

"You didn't see his face," Paul says.

"I didn't have to. I heard his voice and I heard the truth you got out of him out there. He was here to ease his own conscience."

"Ben's one of my oldest friends."

"He was your friend," Mae says. "He's not anymore."

"I know that!" Paul bangs his hand hard on the table. "Let me get used to the idea."

Mae exhales and finally sits at the table with Paul and Lavinia. The only sound is insect song coming through the open windows.

"What on earth do we do now?" Lavinia asks.

Paul has never reckoned on this. He's never figured on everyone looking to him any more than Ruby and Ellis would turn to Homer for help in solving a problem. "I don't know if there's anything we can do but wait," he says.

"Wait for what?"

"Wait them out. If folks were trying to make a point, they've made it."

"They're not making any point, they're punishing us," Mae says. "The storm didn't take this house, none of us died, and they're all bent on punishing us for it."

"I don't understand it," Lavinia says. "I don't understand why we lost nothing at all. This is a well-built house, but no better than any other good house in town was. It was just dumb luck, that's all. How anyone in his right mind can blame us for that, I don't know."

Paul has stopped speaking and neither Mae nor his mother seem to have noticed. He could tell them that he doesn't think waiting is any more a solution than they do. He could go to the foot of the stairs in the living room, look up to the dark landing where the children are surely listening and call, "Go back to bed." He could drive out to the burn site and see for himself that the remains of his lumber, charred and cold, look no different really than what was left after they burned the wreckage last spring. He could tell them about the shipment he just took delivery on from the mill in Carbondale and the payment that's due to the bank on it in less than thirty days. He could say that he's waiting to feel numb, as if he's hit his finger with a hammer and the pain is just now beginning to recede. He could even try to explain that Ben Eavers is responsible for the strange smile on his face. Not the Ben who came to him tonight in secret after dark, but Ben as Paul remembers him at sixteen or seventeen, right there ahead of him on the running track, his arm stretched out and his fingers splayed for the relay baton, grinning back at Paul and waiting to run.

30

There had been many nights when Mae was a child that she had woken to find her mother sitting on the edge of her bed, looking out Mae's window at a full moon. The curtains open, her mother sitting silent, wrapped in her shawl, their two faces bathed in the astonishing light. Her mother did not chart the moon's waxings and wanings, never drew crescents or circles on the kitchen calendar as she might have done, but let it take her by surprise instead. And whenever it appeared, ripe and white, she would watch for hours with the curtains thrown apart wide.

There had been other nights when her mother had carried Mae outside wrapped in a blanket to look at the girl in the moon. It wasn't enough to see it through the window, her mother had said. You had to get on the other side of the glass and feel the night air on your skin. Mae remembers her head on her mother's shoulder, her hand gliding over her mother's unpinned braid, the cold night air on her bare feet under the blanket, and her mother saying, "Look!" as if the moon had never before been full, as if it had never before sailed above their house.

"Can you see her?" her mother would ask then.

"Yes," Mae would answer.

"Can you?" her mother would ask again, as if it were the first time. "Tell me what you see."

"A sideways girl."

"And?"

"A big flower and her hair blowing like it's windy."

They could never, either of them, see the man in the moon, only this girl of her mother's. Mae has tried many times since to show it to Paul, standing outside and pointing to show him which part was the girl's dress and which part was her hair flowing out behind her. She's even drawn it on paper, trying to make him see, because this is her best way of explaining her mother, but he's never done more than smile and shake his head. He can't see it and he never will.

Mae remembers her mother's lips moving silently those nights her face was tilted up to the sky. As a child, she had never questioned what her mother might have been saying or to whom, and later she never thought to ask. She had been transfixed by her mother's face, if only because while her mother was occupied with the moon it had been possible for Mae to watch her more closely than usual. She had thought her mother even more beautiful on those nights, like a storybook princess under a curse, forced to wander in another shape until the full moon when she would turn again, briefly, into her authentic self.

Now there are clouds racing across the face of the October moon and Little Homer is on Mae's lap, wrapped in the plaid blanket he had been dragging behind him when he found her out on the porch. He twitches in his sleep. Mae tucks the blanket in again under his feet and presses her mouth against his hair that smells of a faded tang of sweat. Sitting outside like this it's impossible to stop herself from thinking of the time before the storm and all the other fall evenings they've spent out here on the porch, the nights when it was too chilly to be comfortable, nights that finally forced you to admit that Indian summer had gone and there were only cold days ahead. Back then, of course, Mae wouldn't have had to bring this straight-backed chair out from the kitchen, and she and Homer would have had the porch swing to sway on. Before the storm, Ruby and Ellis might have followed Homer when they heard him leave his bed to find her, but then again before the storm none of the children would have had much need, and Paul would have been out here with her instead of reading the evening paper inside. He's switched on the lamp near the living room windows to let her know he's there and not in the kitchen. Mae supposes he saw the chair missing from the kitchen and figured out where she got to. He won't come out here, she thinks, not now. She would welcome it tonight and greet him with a smile, but he can have no way of knowing that. He's learned by now what an absent chair usually means.

It's getting late now, and colder and lonesome with only Paul's lamplight spilling out over the porch boards for company. The light stretches away from the windows as if it is bent on getting away, much the way Mae sees her shadow toiling outside of an afternoon, stretching itself out long and thin on the pavement in different directions by turns as if by perseverance alone it will one day surprise them both by snapping and rolling away. Mae thinks her mother must have felt fettered this way, chained to life by her burdens, like a hot-air balloon staked to the ground and forever prevented from rising.

When her mother escaped her burdens by dying suddenly at the age of forty-three, the doctor had blamed her heart. It had likely always been weak, he'd said, and had finally given out. It would likely have killed a laboring man sooner. Mae had nodded, but she couldn't agree. She'd never told her father, who had been too occupied with grief to have heard her anyway, but she'd believed her mother had been exhausted by her life and that her body had simply given up struggling. It had been easy enough to go along publicly with the idea of a weak heart, if only because her mother's heart probably had been growing weaker through the years along with the rest of her, defeated as she was by each succeeding day. In any case, it was her father's heart that had turned out to be weak, and he had entered his own grave five months after. "A broken heart," Mae heard a woman say at the funeral, shaking her head at the waste of it all.

It seems likely to Mae that her mother had never comprehended her own life, just as it was certain her bewildered father had not. They had no doubt been able to remember a time before their lives had become so diminished, or perhaps they had only been able to look back and see a time when they hadn't yet understood what was happening. After she died, Mae's mother hadn't looked peaceful, at least not in the way Mae had been hoping she would. She had looked as if she were finished with something more than that she had finally understood it, as if she were simply done. "I did used to think it would all amount to more than this," she had once said.

When Ruby was born, Mae's mother had refused at first to hold her, so Mae had sat right next to her mother on the davenport and held Ruby so that they both could look at her. Paul and Mae's father had sat on chairs opposite them, and they had all just looked at the baby without speaking. Her mother's hands had twitched now and then, beginning to reach for the baby, but she had stopped them each time and squeezed her handkerchief instead. Mae had finally said, "She won't break," in a soft voice, and her mother had gone as far as to lay her hand on Ruby's feet through the blanket she was wrapped in. Mae wondered at the terrible expression of dread mixed with longing on her mother's face, as if she were worried she'd hurt the baby somehow, or that she was simply overwhelmed by the possibility of joy; of what might happen if she just once touched the baby's skin.

A night like this one would have given her mother some ease. How wearying it must have been, knowing that each reprieve would be a short one, so short it must have made her mother doubt they would recur at all. Mae is weary herself, tired of grabbing hold of every last thing she feels and shoving it behind her back as if her feelings were unruly children threatening to bolt each time she opens a door. She's beginning to feel it's dangerous, holding on like this. Something will surely break. She'd let her thoughts wander to her worries one night in bed, let the indignant, accusing faces she sees all over town swim up before her, and suddenly she was biting Paul's lip so hard he hollered. She'd felt his lower lip between her teeth, she'd simply shut her own teeth together on it, not thinking what it actually was. They'd looked at each other, aghast, Paul with his hand on his mouth to feel that his lip was still all there and Mae with her hand on hers from the shock of it. She'd apologized and he'd reassured her, both so genuinely that they'd then proceeded, agreeing somehow to pretend it had only been passion though Mae thought privately that they were both surprised she hadn't drawn blood.

Mae's burdens are her own. Curtains and windows are nothing more to her than curtains and windows, except in the way they recall her mother and her mother's way of always having to close them. It's mirrors she can't abide suddenly, and she's taken to washing her face and brushing her hair without ever meeting her own eyes. She knows what she should be feeling, she sees the way they all hope she'll remember to feel each day, as if remembering were as simple a thing as putting on a blue sweater instead of a brown one.

Little Homer shifts in her lap and Mae feels his breath on her neck.

"I saw her, Mama," he says, and Mae answers, "I know."

It's not surprising to her that Little Homer was the one to see her mother's girl on the face of the moon, not surprising at all. She exhales while he settles again, falling back asleep. She'll stay here holding him as long as she can because tomorrow morning when she wakes in her bed, this will all have gone. Tomorrow, she'll be unable again to see a beautiful thing without wanting to look away. Tomorrow, someone will accidentally slam a door or drop something and they will all look at her first, before allowing themselves reactions of their own. Tomorrow, the children will want something from her and Mae's eyes will betray her, Lavinia and Paul will give her their looks of suffocating pity and tell them, "Leave your Mama be," while Mae spends her day waiting for the clock to show that she has come through another day and can disappear into sleep.

Mae's father had never warned her away from her mother. He'd relied on Mae to go to her mother when he couldn't stand to go himself. "She needs you," meant that likely as not that her mother had made an attempt to come downstairs and then had frozen, mid-way on the staircase with her eyes down and her head cocked at a peculiar angle, tapping the banister with a fingertip. Mae would stand beside her mother until she'd finished and then distract her, or try to, before she got stuck tugging on a curtain that was already closed, letting go and then tugging again. Sometimes her father would manage on his own to wait her mother out and then would sit her down next to him on the davenport and hold both her hands so that there might be a chance of conversation. But then increasingly, toward the end of her mother's life, his face would simply fall and he'd hurry from the room because the heartbreaking choice between seeing her and pretending that he didn't see was no choice at all.

They had turned inward, the three of them, in most ways over the years because it had been easier to do so. Slowly at first, then quickly, her mother's pleasures had receded until she no longer noticed the trumpet vines winding up the white porch columns and no longer cared to put her raspberries up as jam. She even left the piano music Mae's father still ordered for her from St. Louis standing unopened and unplayed on the upright. Unable to risk sitting down at the bench, afraid she'd be trapped by lining up the edges of the sheet music or counting the keys and never manage to play a single note, she had simply stood in front of the piano and looked at the music instead. All of this had made her mother's habit of going outside to look at the moon on clear nights in any season something of a miracle when you considered that she had stopped going out for much of anything else.

And now Mae's breathing, her beating heart, this house, even Little Homer's weight on her and the chair she's sitting on all feel like lengths of rope, stretched out taut and holding her to earth. "I thought it would amount to more than this, too," she says in a quiet voice. She's crying now but she makes no attempt to dry her face. It's another burden, to carry regret. Mae wonders if regret is really the word she's looking for. You can regret that your life is not what it could have been, not what you'd hoped it would be. But to regret a thing is to say that you should have chosen otherwise and did not. It must be called something else when circumstances force a change upon you. Then, perhaps, you mourn a thing or even deplore it. If so, then Mae mourns the change the storm has brought upon the town and the people in it. She deplores the knowledge that her life here has become intolerable and that she feels she must leave and go somewhere else. She feels certain she will never regret it if she does.

She mourns, too, that there's so little left of her mother and father, so little evidence that they lived their lives out in this town. One daughter, three grandchildren, and two names on a headstone in the Mitchell family plot. They had only been alive for a year after Ruby was born; Ellis and Homer had never known them at all, which unfairly made it seem as if they didn't belong to each other in the same way. Mae thinks she sees flashes of both her parents in her children's faces from time to time, something in an expression or the angle of the head, but when she looks in the photo album at the portraits of her mother and father taken when they were children, she wonders each time what on earth it was she thought she saw, because they are not alike at all.

It seems clear, then, that although each person is marked by the life they have led, by each sight and taste, the imprint they leave is not theirs to decide. Mae can carry with her the knowledge that her mother had always seen the picture of a girl smelling a flower on the face of the moon. She can stand outside with Paul and point, she can draw it on paper, she can do her best to make him understand that all this is terribly important in describing her mother, and he will still stand smiling and shaking his head, because he cannot see it and he never will.

She'd given up with Paul long ago, but then tonight Little Homer had surprised her and made her mother's imprint vivid again. The surprise of it was key. Like the tiny snake Mae had once seen pressed into the surface of a dirt road, flattened by the tire of a passing automobile. She could easily have missed it, walking along, but she'd happened to look down and the strange sight of it had made her stop. It couldn't have been there long—she could see the shape of its head and body and the pattern on its back quite clearly. It's scales had been iridescent in the light coming through the trees, and the snake was as beautiful a thing as Mae had ever seen. It had seemed an odd notion, but she'd thought at the time that the snake's skin had been iridescent precisely and only because it had been ironed out flat, and that, alive, it would have seemed a more ordinary thing. Imprinted on the road, jewel-like, it was a memory; unburdened of its flaws and more beautiful than it actually was.

The imprint of child on mother, and mother on child. What was she before I was born, Mae wonders, shifting Homer's weight on her lap. What was I before you? It's barely a question, Mae thinks, since it can have no possible answer. It's just time, after all, carrying you along and opening your eyes so that you can see the people gathered around you at your birth and watch as they're carried along with you, watch as they fade away in their turn. And at the end there are still people around you, the ones you have gathered to yourself who will be carried along in turn as you subside.

Mae looks at the boards of the porch floor, now dark, and realizes she doesn't know when Paul turned out the light. He will have left a light on in the upstairs hall so that she can see her way to bed. His switching off the lamp in the living room was nothing more than a signal that he had gone upstairs and that she could come in now without fear of having to talk to anyone. A signal that if he is not yet asleep when she comes in, he will not comment on the pretense when she gets into their bed quietly so as not to wake him. That he will not touch her first.

Mae shrugs the blanket off from around her shoulders. She'll carry Little Homer back to his bed now. She'll look down as she walks through the house, avoiding mirrors and glass as she does, avoiding anything that shows her to herself. She'll leave the chair out on the porch, and the blanket, because she might still be unable to sleep. She might wake and want to steal back downstairs. She might wake again and spend the night feeling like her heart is full of pins.

31

Lavinia looks at Pastor Aufrecht sitting open-mouthed across from her, his fork forgotten in his hand, saying, "Surely not." Her stomach sinks then with the realization that she must now convince him of something she had hoped he already knew to be true. She turns the cake off the server and onto her plate and looks back at him.

"Paul heard it himself from an old friend, standing right here in our backyard," she says.

"Is it possible he misunderstood?"

She'd been waiting for this question. She supposes it's a fair one, and one a minister would be honor bound to ask. Still, she feels wretched at having to answer it. "I heard it myself, from inside the house. So did Mae. There's no mistake."

"This is a very serious accusation."

"I know it," Lavinia says.

Aufrecht looks at her, blinking in his amazement. "People burned your lumber rather than use it? Whatever would possess them?"

"I believe they mean to ruin us."

"I can't believe that," Aufrecht says, shaking his head. He looks hard at Lavinia to see how deeply she believes it herself. "No," he says to convince himself, even as anguish settles in his face.

"I wouldn't have believed it myself if I hadn't heard it with my own two ears. The children are even being taunted about it at school."

"But why? Why do such a thing?"

Lavinia looks down at her plate, uncertain of what to say next, and when she says, "Mae thinks it's a punishment," and Aufrecht only continues to stare at her in bafflement, she says, "A way of making us lose something, same as they did."

They sit silent then, and Lavinia begins to eat small bits of her cake while Aufrecht only stares at his plate. She had been seeking advice when she asked him to pay this visit, hoping for comfort and reassurance, even to be told flat out that she was wrong. But Aufrecht's ignorance is making her relive those moments of listening through the window when Ben Eavers came to say his piece and all the moments since that night when she's had to hurry thoughts of Ben and Paul out of her mind. Ben and Paul coming and going along the road together, grown tall as men overnight but still really nothing more than spindly boys. Ben so often at her table, sitting between Paul and John, eating her food till the night he forgot himself and made them all laugh when he said, "Thank you, Mama," after she cleared his empty plate from the table.

That the storm had been a reversal of fortune for the town had been evident, but Lavinia would never have believed it capable of turning old friends into cowards who faded back into doorways and shadows rather than behave honorably. Honor is the thing she keeps coming back to. She had believed herself to be surrounded by decent, honorable people, and now seeing them turn with such ease, seeming even to decide to turn their backs on the idea of honor, leaves her feeling only outrage and disgust.

"I never suspected anything like this," Aufrecht finally says. "I look down at people's faces every Sunday, I look them right in the eye and shake all of their hands when they go out the door. Believe me, I've seen some terrible things in people's faces since the storm, but never this."

"I didn't see it until it was pointed out to me." Words run in a chain through Lavinia's head—revenge, vengeance, retribution, reprisal—and she wonders if she failed to recognize the looks she was seeing in people's eyes because she had never seen those looks before or whether she had simply been unwilling to recognize them.

"'He feedeth on ashes: a deceived heart hath turned him aside,'" she quotes with a wry smile and makes Aufrecht shake his head again.

"But not everyone. You can't believe that everyone feels this way. What do your friends say?"

Lavinia looks at him in frank disbelief. "When it's your friends coming to you after dark with news like this, a person doesn't go looking for their friends."

"You're not friendless," Aufrecht says.

"It certainly has begun to feel that way."

Aufrecht pauses. "I assure you that you're not. Things will turn around. Folks are just too frightened or worried to take a stand."

Lavinia takes up her cup and blows across the coffee, though she knows it's gone cold. "It amounts to the same thing."

32

Paul sits at the table watching the children stare out into the room, watching Lavinia put the serving dishes in the center of the table. A plate of cold sliced ham, scalloped potatoes bubbling in their dish, green beans shined up with butter and heaped in the old oval bowl. Mealtimes are mostly silent now, apart from saying grace. There's not much they need to say to each other at this time of day, and it's often easier to keep whatever news they might have to themselves, seeing as none of it's good.

"I want to donate some lumber," he says, breaking the silence.

Lavinia folds her apron and lays it on the counter. When she goes to pull the curtains shut, Paul catches her eye. "It's darker outside than in," Lavinia says. "I don't want to be on display while I'm eating my dinner."

Paul has spoken his mind by way of a statement, although he phrased it as a wish and not as intent. He knows it was this that provoked his mother into closing the curtains. She'd heard the words "I want" as the loudest part of the sentence, and her closing the curtains was her way of beginning the discussion, of closing them in on themselves. Paul hopes now that the worst of it is over, that having unburdened himself of those surprising words, the dinner can be eaten with something like relief, the children can be excused from the table and not merely sent from it when their plates are clean, and that the three of them can sit together under the ceiling light at this table his father built and come to an agreement.

Lavinia picks up her knife and fork but then puts them down again on her plate and lays her hands in her lap. "We were sitting at this very table the night you boys asked your father for a loan to start up the lumberyard," she says. "Do you remember?"

Paul feels a slight consternation at her turning the conversation like this, even if he is unsurprised. "Of course," he says, knowing that in order to discuss the thing at all his mother might have to have her own place to begin.

"You surprised us both with that one." Lavinia smiles, "Oh, don't mistake me; neither your father nor I thought you boys were interested in the farm. We knew it was just a matter of time before you went off on your own, but we'd guessed that you'd each strike out in a different direction. We believed you were too different to end up together, here. You see, we were determined that each of you should lead your own life, and we'd already resigned ourselves to the loss of the farm, so it came as quite a revelation, quite a relief when we learned that we'd guessed wrong and that the two of you had planned to stay together and only go as far as Marah."

"But you weren't wrong. Not entirely."

Lavinia watches Paul and the sad, fond smile that has overtaken his face.

"Johnny never wanted to live in Marah," Paul says. "It was his idea to start up a lumberyard, but it was my idea to build it here. He'd been dreaming of California for years by then, ever since we were kids, and just never let on. I talked him out of it, or at least I thought I had. He'd wanted me to go out there with him all along. And even after I bought him out and they'd moved, he wanted me to sell up and move, too. I expect he still wants all of us out there."

"And so you boys fell out with each other."

"Johnny lost time by starting up here."

"You were hardly to blame. I suppose you both were still

young, but you were grown men and he made a decision to stay."

Paul shakes his head. "I should have let him go when he wanted to. You were ready to let us both go, but I was afraid to be alone and fear made me play dirty."

"You stop that right now. I won't listen to you talk that way about yourself. You were never alone and you've never done an unfair thing in your life."

"But I was alone in a way, or knew I would be. Dad couldn't live forever, and if Johnny was clear out in California, I'd be left to be the head of the family here. I told him if he couldn't stay for me, then he should think of you and Dora's family left behind here."

"Oh, Paul—"

He gives Lavinia a wry smile and then looks away quickly at his plate. "He never intended to stay. He was only postponing for a while."

"Whatever do you mean?"

"I wanted to call the place Graves Brothers Lumber. Did you know that? But Johnny said no. He told me to leave out the 'Brothers.' Graves Lumber was enough, he said. It would look better on the sign, and besides, everyone in town already knew we were brothers." Paul smiles, blinking hard, and pushes at his food with the back of his fork. He looks up at Lavinia again and says, "He didn't want me to have to change the sign when he left."

All these years, Paul thinks, that he and Johnny had thought themselves blessed for having such parents as they had who would never let on they were disappointed, all the years he'd spent hoping they hadn't disappointed them too much. There was guilt, too, that turned out now to have been unnecessary. His parents had certainly hoped that one of them would want to work the farm, but had managed nonetheless to understand before either of their sons the indefensibility of choosing the *where* and *what* of another person's life. Johnny had understood it soon after them and long before Paul, who had taken years and was really only now just beginning to comprehend. Johnny, who had seen that Paul was too uncertain of himself to take a chance on leaving Marah. Who had known that Paul didn't trust himself to enter adulthood alone because everything he'd done in his life up to that point had been done in emulation of his brother. Johnny, who had waited, who had deferred on a promise to himself until he'd seen that Paul was shored up with a business, a house, and a wife.

Paul smiles. He must have had a peculiar expression on his face, he thinks, to make Mae look at him like that. He can't remember having seen that particular look on her face before that's making her seem to be looking right through him now, or past him at something else entirely.

"What's this about donating lumber?" Lavinia asks.

"If it's an idea of Paul's, it has something to do with responsibility," Mae says out of nowhere and startles them both. "Or more likely, it's entirely to do with responsibility."

Well, yes, Paul thinks. He'd realized the very moment the thought had entered his head that it had to do with responsibility and whether the responsibility was to others, to an idea, or only to himself had been of little consequence. Still, he'd puzzled it out all the same since then and had decided that he was thinking only of himself. He had felt both satisfaction and relief at this, understanding that, in this case, thinking of himself did not mean he was being selfish. The idea of donating wood had nothing whatever to do with how others viewed him or his standing in the town, and although those things had once held importance for him, the fact that he's now been stripped, slowly and deliberately of public regard since the storm has left him distrustful of anything resembling vanity. He regrets that understanding has come to him so late, since that will have cost Mae and his mother something as well.

Paul takes his arms off the table and leans back on his chair. His legs slide out under the table, and as his thumbs hook themselves into the belt loops on the front of his pants he realizes he must be the image of his father. Give him a duck call to chew and he could make his mother cry. "You done, Homer?" he asks, and Little Homer nods. "Put your plates in the sink and go on upstairs, all of you." Paul knows the children will likely only pretend to be playing once they're upstairs, that they'll go into one bedroom or other and make a little noise and then creep back to the landing to sit with their shoulders against the railings and listen.

"The Methodists haven't decided whether they're going to rebuild yet," Paul says. "Last I heard, they were thinking of going over to another church instead. Maybe our church or maybe the Baptists. There's hardly enough of any one congregation left to warrant much building."

"Then why give them lumber?"

"So they can build."

"It might be too late," Mae says. "People might think— well, they'll think a lot of things."

"I know it, but folks will think what they want no matter what I do. It seems that I've done absolutely everything wrong. I hauled what wreckage I could out to the burns alongside the rest of them. I hardly slept those first days. I just cut wood and cut wood for coffins. I thought that was what I was supposed to do. Cut wood because people needed it. Look them in the eye and do business with them and help them to keep their dignity. I was only trying to be mindful of their pride, and now they've got it figured as greed."

"It could be the last straw," Mae says. "It could break us."

"I believe we're pretty near broken already," Lavinia says.

Paul nods and looks away, although there had been nothing of reproach in his mother's voice.

"They might refuse the offer," Lavinia says. "Though that's no reason not to make it."

Paul looks back at her and sees as tender an expression as he could hope to see in her damp eyes. "I realized one day I couldn't look at myself in the bathroom mirror," he says.

"You haven't done one single thing to be ashamed of. You hear me? I've been right here the whole time, and not once have I been ashamed."

"Well, I have. I'm pretty sure it was shame I was feeling when I wrote my last letter to Johnny." Paul leans forward again with his arms on the table, clasping his hands in his old attitude of uncertainty. "It was his work as much as mine that built the lumberyard, and I couldn't even manage to keep it going."

"I'll never know what you could have done differently," Lavinia says. "Not as long as I live."

In the silence that follows, Paul's mouth tightens and his eyes begin to burn. He keeps his hands folded close to him on the table so that his mother can't reach out and take hold of one. There are no voices, no sounds at all coming from upstairs. The children have begun to listen to their conversations so openly that Paul wonders whether they would even bother to hurry from the landing now if they heard him coming or if they would simply remain there, a jumble of elbows and knees, a row of sober faces. Mae is staring at the table, eyes unfocused, agitated in spite of her stillness, as if she might bolt from the table at any moment. Paul sees that she's holding something back, he sees that she's barely able to contain it. What would he have said the day they were married if someone had told him he'd one day look at his wife and be unable to say whether it was elation or panic she was stifling on her face. He winces and looks back at his hands.

His mother has no trouble reading his face and says aloud for him the very thing he has been unable to bring himself to tell her. "You've been paying them out of savings," she says, and he nods. "How long?"

"A month."

Of course she knew, he thinks. She's either seen the passbook or been down to the bank herself and found out there. He feels a hot prickle on his neck at the thought of her standing there at the teller's grill. *No, ma'am. There's no mistake.* One month's pay for Clarence, Lon, and Irene. Payment to the bank in full for the last shipment of lumber from Carbondale.

"They asked me if they should be looking for other jobs," Paul says.

Lavinia raises a hand. "You don't owe me any explanation."

"It's your savings, too, Mother. What you put in from the sale of the farm. You had a right to know before now."

"Well. I don't know that I would have done any different."

"I suppose I owe it to them to tell them to start looking now." He laughs in a short sputter. "They'll start looking as soon as I start donating lumber."

"I'm not so sure."

"Well, they should. I don't know why they've hung on this long as it is."

"Of course you do."

There it is again, Paul thinks. Loyalty. He'll think it, but he can't say it out loud anymore. There's nothing to do at the lumberyard most days; they all just tidy things up all the time. Oil the saw blades, move the lumber from here to there so they can clean places they've never had time to get to before. Sweep the baseboards, sweep the floor, straighten the papers on the desk, check the file cabinet again and again. Time was Paul would have asked their opinion on how to proceed, but now they all just watch him the same way the children do. Keeping busy, keeping quiet, and watching him to see if he'll break. He'd finally taken down the bell from over the door when he realized they were spending too much time looking at it, waiting for it to ring.

"I forgot about them all after the storm," he says. Lavinia gives him a vexed frown, as if he's talking nonsense. "I got up off the ground and didn't give them another thought until the next morning. Mae remembers."

"They didn't need you," Mae says, shaking her head. "You went where you were needed."

"No, I came here where I wasn't needed either."

"You didn't know that until you'd seen us."

"Stop it, Paul! Stop it right now!" Lavinia pounds the table with her palm and makes the cutlery jump. "I said you'd never given me cause to be ashamed, but I didn't say you'd never made me angry. If you're determined to blame yourself for absolutely everything that has ever happened in this town, I guess I can't stop you, but I won't stand by and say nothing while you wallow in it. You haven't let anyone down, but you're on your way to letting yourself down. Give away your lumber if they'll let you. Give it all away. Tell everyone at the yard to find new jobs or empty out all our savings so you don't have to. You've had to make some awful decisions lately, but you've chosen right every time."

Lavinia exhales and looks at her hands. When she speaks again, her voice is soft. "You'll choose right this time. You'll choose right for us all."

33

S itting in the borrowed church, Lavinia feels as if she is on display, as if she's been picked out by a blazing shaft of light there at the end of the pew, though the air in the church is dim. Half the windows in the church are boarded over, waiting for new stained glass from St. Louis, and the other half give only dull light from a clouded sky, but still she feels as if she is in the center ring, a curiosity for any and all to view. She should have contrived to sit where Mae is sitting, she thinks, at the other end of the pew, away from the aisle and all the eyes she feels turning to look at her.

Pastor Aufrecht is reading from Isaiah. That he could be so artless and that she herself might have sown the seed leaves Lavinia breathless.

"'He heweth him down cedars, and taketh the cypress and the oak,'" he reads. Lavinia's eyes close, and she wonders if Paul will understand that this is no accident, whether he will also see the straight line that runs from her, sitting with an open Bible at the kitchen table, to Aufrecht's visit, to this. "'He burneth part thereof in the fire . . . yea, he warmeth himself, and saith, Aha, I am warm, I have seen the fire.'"

Paul is next to her, with the children in a row between him and Mae. Lavinia looks sideways at the children, who are very still, then up at the row of windows interrupting the white wall. She sees young Pastor Ollery sitting off to the side in the front, listening to another man preach in his church. She watches him closely; his head is bowed, he seems to be listening attentively, solemnly, but Lavinia thinks she sees something of sadness or resignation in his downward glance. She could well be imagining it, she knows, hoping to find the dismay she is feeling on another face. Whatever she had intended when she opened her door to Aufrecht and set cake and coffee in front of him is unraveling now and turning into something else.

"'And the residue thereof he maketh a god, even his graven image: he falleth down unto it, and worshippeth it, and prayeth unto it, and saith, Deliver me; for thou art my god.'"

If Lavinia looked at Paul for just a moment, she would be able to tell what he was thinking, whether he realized how horribly Pastor Aufrecht was blundering even as he sought to chastise and instruct, adding still more fuel to the pyre they'd all been lashed to. It was a foolish use of Isaiah on top of everything else. She would never have said before that this is what she meant, but then doubts herself as Aufrecht continues to read, "'He feedeth on ashes: a deceived heart hath turned him aside, that he cannot deliver his soul, nor say, Is there not a lie in my right hand?'"

She stops listening then and, without even looking up at the pulpit, simply sits motionless, waiting for it all to end. Was it possible she had thought this in her heart, she wonders now—that the men who burned Paul's lumber had fashioned themselves a false god of righteousness? Lavinia is roused from her thoughts when Aufrecht's voice begins to rise. "'Follow peace with all men,'" he calls out. "'Lest any root of bitterness springing up trouble you, and thereby many be defiled.'"

Lavinia forces herself to look at Paul as they stand, relieved that he is only frowning as if he is puzzled. She feels a twist in her stomach and looks away, reminded of the sound of breaking glass when she'd tried to get at her mother's candy dish as a child and sent it crashing to the floor, and then of her mother's voice when she'd found the pieces later and blamed herself for setting it too near the edge of the shelf.

She looks around cautiously at the people going past them as they leave the church, but there's no mistaking the looks she sees. Some people meet her eyes only long enough for her to see their outrage at having been made an example of, a few give her contrite smiles, but then look away. Lavinia pushes her way into the aisle, sickened by the passing parade. She reaches Pastor Aufrecht and his outstretched hand, wanting nothing so much as to slap his smiling face.

"Pastor," she says, looking at him hard and refusing his hand. She catches Pastor Ollery's eye before she turns on her heel. Paul hurries after her and catches her by the arm.

"Mother, what are you doing?" he whispers.

"Me?" she says, walking faster, listening to her heels strike a ringing sound on the sidewalk. "I'm thinking of becoming a Baptist."

34

Paul pushes the gooseneck lamp up some, away from the clock, and squints at a detail in the wood.

"Pass me those toothpicks, will you?" he says to Lon, and Lon looks up from his mirror frame long enough to push the toothpick holder across the table.

"I wish I knew what possessed my father to paint this clock," Paul says. "Every time he painted the kitchen, the clock got a lick, too."

Paul pushes a line of softened paint along a groove on the clock's base with a toothpick. If Little Homer were there to see, he'd tell him it looked to him like a giant's hand, skimming dirty snow with a shovel.

"It'll be real handsome when you're done," Lon says and Paul nods. "I'm almost finished here. I could give you a hand and work on the other side."

"Might have to if I'm going to get this carving clean before I'm old."

Paul looks up at Lon rubbing his mirror frame with sandpaper and then stroking it with his palm, looking at it with his head drawn back, turning his face this way and that as if it's a drawing he's executing in charcoal.

"That frame's looking real good," Paul says.

"I guess it did turn out all right. We only saved it to save something. There wasn't much left, just some pots and pans and this. I wanted to chuck it on the burn pile when I found it lying in the wet, but Essie wouldn't let me."

"Things keep up like this much longer, maybe we could open an antique store," Paul says with a wry smile. "Course we'd have to open it somewhere else and use your name on the sign if we wanted any customers. Maybe even keep me hidden in the back so I wouldn't scare folks off."

"Boss, I . . . " Lon falters and Paul looks up at him.

"What is it?"

"Maybe we oughta get Clarence in here."

"All right," Paul says slowly and folds his hands to wait while Lon goes out to call Clarence from the back. It's finally happened, Paul thinks. It's all over, and they're having to end it for me. He watches Clarence follow Lon back into the room. They give Paul quick glances, sheepish as a pair of boys caught chucking rocks.

"Sit down," Paul says. "No, hang on a minute." He goes quickly to the door and hollers, "Irene!" and sits down again. "You can all quit together," he says, pressing his hands together under the table to stop their shaking.

"Boss . . . "

"No," Paul says. "Wait for Irene. She should be here for this."

"She doesn't know anything about it."

Irene is there, suddenly, frowning at them from the doorway. "Doesn't know about what?"

"Quitting," Paul says.

"No one's quitting," Lon says. "We don't want Irene to quit and we don't want you to let her go, either."

Paul looks at Lon, then Clarence, and shakes his head, baffled. Lon sits down and says, "Clarence and me have been talking, and we want you to stop paying us."

"What?" Paul looks between Lon and Clarence at their worried, earnest faces. "What do you mean?"

"We both had the same idea when we figured how you'd been making payroll," Lon says.

Clarence speaks finally, in a quiet voice. "When that last shipment came in and there weren't any orders, we figured you had to be paying us out of your own savings."

Paul clears his throat and takes out his handkerchief to blow his nose. Everything moves slowly for him as he takes in their faces, shocked that things have come to such a pass that he's surprised by kindness.

"I can't stop paying you," he says finally.

"You'll have to stop soon, one way or another," Lon says. "We figured we could buy you some time, so to speak, to try to turn things around."

"Mother and I have our savings," Irene says. She's standing there in the doorway with her arms folded across her chest and the same look she gives him when she's tired of telling him to go home for the night.

"This is more than I deserve," Paul says, shaking his head. "I've let you all down, over and over again. I've let this place fall apart."

"It's not you that fell apart, boss. Everything is here, waiting to be sold and we're here, ready to sell it. We just need more time."

They're looking at him expectantly now as if he's got a solution and they're only waiting to hear it, as if the telephone will ring any moment and the bell will start jingling as soon as he hangs it back up above the door. But those hopeful looks fall away quickly, and he sees the fear they're all trying to hide from him behind their staunchness.

Paul knows what they'll tell him if he lets them keep talking. That they've been together, all of them, since the beginning, since he and Johnny took their father's loan. That this is the first and only job Irene has ever had, and none of them can hope for better. That there's been something more than a paycheck making them walk through the front door every day.

"I did have an idea," Paul says. "Something that might start to turn things around."

They allow themselves hesitant smiles, and Irene lets her arms drop. Clarence and Lon rise from their seats to shake Paul's hand and Lon says, "That settles it, then."

35

It had seemed so simple when she'd heard Paul say the words, but now that Mae has repeated them, now that she has reconfigured the words *sell, move, John,* and *California* as a question she realizes she has used her one and only opportunity to say them. She had known somehow before that there would be just one chance and had saved up the words, hoarding them, afraid all the while they would erupt out of her in the wrong place and at the wrong time. Now she sees that there was no right time because Paul is looking at her with an expression so bewildered she wonders if she said something else entirely and announced a truly impossible desire. His expression shifts and still he hasn't said a word. He looks at her as if he's injured, as if she's somehow betrayed him and then he looks down and walks away.

Mae goes back to her work as dazed as a reprimanded child, burying her shame in industry. She goes to the pantry and scrubs at the wooden countertop in the same pattern she wiped it earlier that morning. She lifts the canisters to get at the corners, wets the rag again with water so hot it hurts her hands when she wrings it out, and watches the dry streaks unfurling like the wake of a boat where she's just wiped the cool boards. Mae looks at the shelves above the counter, the floor, and the walls. She could clean it all. She could keep busy in here for an hour or more and no one could fault her. No one would dare disturb her, either, even knowing as well as she does herself that there isn't a speck of dirt or a crumb anywhere to be found.

She can't think how else she could have done it. She might have deserved that look if Lavinia or, worse, the children had been standing there with them. But she had been careful, she had been discrete. The children had left for school and Lavinia had been upstairs somewhere making one bed or another and Mae had simply asked in a lowered voice, "Can't we please sell up and leave here? Can't we move out to John in California?" She had not thought, she realizes now, to prepare herself for his response. She had not considered any response beyond grateful surprise. Mae had believed it was plain to everyone that they were beat, that there was no longer any use in shamming, no way to recover, and that this alone could save them all. She knows Paul has wondered what she's been thinking, all the long quiet evenings leading to this moment when she tried to brush off her desperation and pose a simple question. She had thought that the truth of it was clear: that, in its way, the storm had devoured them and the life they had led just as surely as if they'd been snatched up bodily into the cloud. They were lost, each of them, changed beyond recognition and, worst of all, they were lost in the very place they always had been.

Before the storm, it had seemed to Mae that Paul could do anything. Before the storm, he'd been a man who never met a stranger, never seemed to doubt himself. He could run faster than anyone; there had been joy in his movements, his world was full of possibilities, and he'd stood taller than he actually was. Like a house cat, Mae had once thought privately, who discounted the rumor of tigers. Now, with his defeated shoulders and wary eyes, he's as unrecognizable to Mae as he must certainly be to himself. He's aged a decade since the storm, and there's more pain in his face than any man of thirty-four should have to carry. He looks around, bewildered that he has been unable to halt the ruination of their lives, unable to see what Mae sees quite clearly: that the townsfolk have shunned them

forever and mean to exact a price as surely as if they were gathered in a ring outside their house for the express purpose of
burning it down; that she has taken hold of the lifeline he so
casually mentioned and dismissed; and that she has it firmly in
her hand and is holding it out to the rest of them.

Mae thinks it's odd in a bitter, funny way that she should be
the one to see this. She understands now that, although she
only meant to say they should begin again in a new place, Paul
heard her ask him to flee a failure. Always one to go along,
she's waited too long to ask for something monumental, and
now she's botched the manner of asking. Perhaps she can cor-
rect this much, she thinks, and she's reassured suddenly that
she can put it to him another way and say that it's his successes
she means for them to take with them to California. That if
Paul and John Graves once built a business together from
nothing, and if John has truly been hoping all along that they'd
follow him, there can be no shame in leaving.

She calls his name, "Paul?" drops her rag in the bucket and
dries her hands on her apron. She finds him upstairs, standing
in front of the linen closet in the hall with Lavinia. Mae can see
in their faces that Paul has told Lavinia already, and that
Lavinia has made up her mind. They're both disappointed,
sorrowful somehow, in the way they're looking at her, like parents warning a guilty child against compounding her disgrace
with denial. Mae's momentary assuredness unravels, as if she
has wet herself publicly.

"I have no family left anywhere to take us in," Mae says.

"We are your family," Lavinia says.

"I know that. Don't you think I know that?"

"I'm not sure you do. Not if you're behaving like this, making decisions for all of us and not taking anyone else's feelings
into consideration."

"What do you mean? That I'm thinking only of myself?"

"I can hardly live here alone if the rest of you pack up and run away to California! You didn't ask me. I live here and I was born here. So were all of you, at that rate. You never asked me."

"I asked Paul," Mae says. It is a simple statement, only three words, and contains everything Mae must now leave unsaid. That Paul is the head of the family, that asking him first was only a beginning. She had thought they would ask Lavinia together. Mae had known her own mind at once when she'd heard Paul say that John had wanted them out there all along. Moving was a way of making their lives match up again with the picture of their lives, with the memory of it. Moving would mean reuniting their family with John's, and giving the children a fresh chance to be whoever they wanted to be, relieved of the burden of the storm. Of course she'd always intended to ask Lavinia, but she could hardly have asked her first. That must be obvious. How much worse would Paul have taken the news if he'd learned that his mother had approved of the move and they'd gone to him together, the females of the household, armed with a foregone conclusion?

Mae sees there's nothing left to be said, not now at any rate. The only thing left is for one of them to turn to leave the hall and go about the day's regular tasks. Mae realizes that they're both waiting for her to be the one to leave, not because they need to confer once her back is turned—they have nothing left to say to each other, either—but because leaving first will somehow serve as an admission of fault. Mae turns and, in the next moment, Lavinia closes the linen closet door as if to say, This closet contains this family's sheets, blankets, and quilts and it always will, as surely as closing this door is part of my work and always will be. Mae goes back down the stairs, aware that they are watching her go. It's not as if they've closed ranks on her, not as if their standing together like that was meant to remind her that they, mother and son, were related by blood. It's more that they intended to shame her, to remind her that by marrying Paul, she had committed herself, like Ruth to Naomi, entirely to them. But she doesn't feel shamed, and she no longer feels like a child. Something shifted in that last moment of unraveling when she turned away from them. She's sure of that, even if she has yet to discover what it was exactly that changed.

The three of them avoid each other for the rest of the day, Paul by leaving for the lumberyard, Lavinia and Mae by performing their work. There is little need for the two of them to talk; they operate around the house as if they are two halves of the same person, not so much doing the tasks they've assumed as their own as doing whatever work needs to be done and then looking about for the next undone thing. The marketing is done, today's supper was decided yesterday evening, and what remains is the execution of the mundane and the obvious. When they do speak to each other, it is with the heightened courtesy of acquaintances on a social call. Lavinia passes Mae in the hall upstairs, pulls the corners of her mouth into a sort of smile and says, "Is your bread out of the oven? It certainly smells good," but then Lavinia's eyes dart away from Mae's, too soon. Mae wonders why Lavinia and Paul should be so disappointed in this, why her uttering a wish should so immediately upset things when the unreliability of her moods has not. When Lavinia tells her, "The children will be home soon," she is not saying, "Look at the time!" she is reminding Mae of how to behave. Everything in Lavinia's manner now is intended to say that they can and will continue as before, but a basic trust between them has been broken, and that their former ease will be replaced for a time by civility. Mae does her part and is civil in return. She knows she is expected to understand.

They eat their dinner at the customary time, prompting the children to clean their plates in the usual way, the usual number of times. A certain amount of food is left uneaten to be packed for Paul's lunch the next day, and Lavinia and Mae scrape and wash the dishes in silence. When the table is wiped and the floor swept, Mae hangs their aprons together on the hook on the back of the kitchen door and they settle in the living room with Paul and the children, each with their solitary occupations. Mae takes up the sock she is knitting from the basket beside her chair. Her thoughts do not wander as they usually do; she jabs the needles into the sock as if her only purpose in knitting is to try to distract herself from a period of agitated waiting, as if she will soon be called in to the doctor's examination room. She looks up occasionally at Lavinia and then at Paul. She knows what each of them must be thinking, the speeches they are rehearsing even now in their heads that they will deliver to her once the children are in bed. She could be difficult, she thinks, she could interrupt and say their respective speeches for them. She could serve their very thoughts, every reason and justification, up to them and watch the astonishment overtake their faces. She could, but she won't, she thinks; she'll hold her tongue. There would only be more dismay at her impudence.

Mae puts the children to bed herself, early, so as to not prolong their waiting, and returns to her chair. She takes up her knitting again without looking Paul or Lavinia in the eye, knowing that they will wait, silent, until they are certain all three children are asleep before they each say their piece on the subject of moving. Sitting together like this should be a comfortable thing, Mae thinks. But the ticking of the mantel clock seems too loud, and she's bracing for the moment when the mechanism will catch and the clock will sound the quarter hour. Paul's turning the pages of his newspaper should be so familiar a sound that she forgets to hear it, the way she forgets to hear her own breathing or the rustling of leaves in trees. She should forget to hear the clicking of Lavinia's and her knitting needles because she hears it nearly every evening, but the click-clicking has turned sharp, like an angry finger tapping on wood.

Once the quarter hour and then nine o'clock have struck, Mae goes upstairs, first to Ruby's room and then to the boys', to listen to their breathing. Ruby sleeps curled up on her side, with one foot outside the covers, as she does every night. Ellis is on his side with his back to the room, exactly like Ruby, and Little Homer is on his back, breathing loudly through his open mouth.

Mae stands in the doorway of the boys' room, looking at them in their beds. She feels an overwhelming sadness when she sees that Ellis is not merely lying on his side; he is curled up tight, turned in on himself, and wary of uncoiling, like the pill bugs he jabs on the sidewalk. That Little Homer lies motionless and slack-mouthed, struck senseless by sleep as only a young child can be, is no comfort. He'll be twisting himself into a coil on the bed like the others soon enough. She resists the urge to enter the room and touch each boy as she usually does, barely resting her fingertips on their covers. She resists the urge again when she passes Ruby's door.

Paul is the first to speak when she's back downstairs and seated in her chair with her knitting. His paper refolded and laid beside him on the davenport, he says, "This can't last forever. It simply cannot go on like this forever, maybe even not much longer. People will see that. They have to, eventually. What if we moved and didn't do as well in a new place as we could do here by staying? We'd be well and truly stuck, then. We couldn't come back."

Mae keeps at her knitting, calmer now, grateful that she has her work to look at and does not to have to meet Paul's eyes while he speaks. What will she say herself, she wonders, if she says anything in all of this? What would Bess have said if she'd told her she intended to move away forever? Bess, oh, Bess. She'd have said, "You can't move away, you know," but she would have said it with a sad smile and she would have helped Mae with packing and she would have been there when they finally drove off for California, her hand waving high as long as she could still see the car, as long as Mae could see her.

Mae can feel them both watching her, Paul with his hands folded and Lavinia with her hands resting in her lap, still holding onto her own knitting.

"I don't like the thought of leaving this place, however unpleasant it has gotten to be here at the moment," Lavinia says. "My family are all from these parts. The children are the fourth generation to be born here. You'd be telling them to start over from scratch, too, you know. I don't think any one of them would say yes if you asked if they wanted to leave this place. Their whole lives are here, and they can't imagine anything else. As for me, you might think my selling the farm would make it easy for me to leave, but I can tell you it doesn't. Even if another family is out there now, working my grandfather's land, even if the house my father built got blown to kingdom come, I wouldn't want to leave it. I'd no sooner leave that land behind than I'd leave the family plots behind. There wouldn't be a soul left to tend those graves. Your family plot, too. We three sitting here in this room and those three children asleep upstairs are the very last of the Walkers, the Mitchells, and the Graves in these parts. The very last."

The justifications continue like a radio play Mae has heard before. She wonders how all of this would sound to another person, someone entirely unrelated and unknown to them, hearing each argument for the first time. What am I now, Mae wonders, what is the sum of me? What am I, she wants to ask, if I cannot continue here and you will not leave with me? What can I possibly fill this emptiness with, if I cannot fill it with myself?

Mae feels as if she is receding from the room, as if she is being drawn backward into a tunnel, watching the circle of light that holds the picture of Paul and Lavinia sitting there together on the davenport fade in brightness and grow smaller.

She wonders if they can see her receding, if they can still make out the placid expression she wears on her face or the color of the ball of yarn in her lap. She can still just make out their voices saying things like *couldn't hold my head up*, and *ride it out*, but all she sees in that circle of fading light are a prideful man and a frightened old woman.

She had thought while she waited for this moment, waited all day for this moment, that she would feel more desperate when it came. It surprises her, this feeling of understanding that's coming over her and the way it's spreading out from her core like warmth. She wants to hold very still while it's happening, even to slow her breathing to prolong the moment of realization. If she were to inhale deeply or even simply point her needle through the next loop of yarn it would be gone. She's aware now of a sensation of intense relief, as if she's lain down, cold and exhausted in her bed and has realized she is beginning to get warm, that it is time to submit to sleep.

Mae hears Paul's voice asking her, "Do you see?" and she feels herself nodding a little without looking up or altering the expression on her face. *Yes*, she could say, *it's all quite clear. It wasn't clear before, but it is now. You won't leave. You won't save yourselves and you won't let me save you. But I can make you leave. I've got one last coin to spend.*

Mae is tired suddenly, overcome by weariness, and there's nothing more she'd like than to lie down right here on the floor. The fire in the fireplace would burn unattended for a long while and the others could simply leave her there when they were tired enough to go to bed. She could lie with her face against the cool wooden boards and watch the fire, watch it diminish and fade like the light in the lanterns that people set out all over town those first nights after the storm. The lanterns that cast their feeble light a few feet in each direction, struggling to illuminate houses and people that were no longer there. People disappear sometimes, Mae thinks. A wind snatches a baby from its mother's arms, a mother becomes exhausted and stops trying to live, a father's heart simply breaks. You can watch it happening if you're brave enough to look, if you don't avert your eyes in that brief moment before the lantern's precious, fragile light ceases flickering and goes out.

36

Paul leans back with his hands still on the steering wheel and looks out across the January fields.

"I don't like it, Mother," he says. "Why can't I just pull off the road up ahead there and come with you?"

"Because I don't want you to, that's why."

"Well, I think I need to. I don't like the idea of leaving you out here, even if it is for just an hour."

"Two." Lavinia gets out of the Ford and shakes her head at Paul. "One and you'd no sooner get home than you'd have to turn right around and come back for me. Two hours. I am dressed in every last woolen thing I could find, and I will be fine."

Paul opens his mouth to speak, but then closes it again in frustration and simply gestures at the white expanse in front of them.

"I was born on this land, and so were you, for that matter," Lavinia says. "I'm surprised at you. I thought you knew I was just a tough old farm girl."

Lavinia slams the car door shut, takes a step back, and nods at Paul who holds up two fingers and mouths the word two at her until she flaps a hand at him as is she's shooing off a fly.

"Land sakes. You'd think I was a child." She stands watching until he's driven off in the direction they came and sounded his horn.

But when she turns to continue up the road, she finds she must fight to keep her mittened hands in her coat pockets, to

keep them from flying to her face to cover her mouth and sti-
fle the choking sobs that have overtaken her. She keeps walking with her back straight, managing not to shudder so that
when Paul looks back at her in the Ford's mirror, as he certainly will, he will see no reason to turn around and come after
her. She can cry all she wants to out here, as loud as she wants.
There's no one to see or hear her. This thought provokes a wet
sputter that becomes a laugh and Lavinia wipes her eyes and
nose with the hankie she has ready in her coat pocket.

"In all my years—" she says aloud. Who would have
believed she'd one day ask to be let off on this county road in
the middle of January to wander alone for two hours before
being fetched home? Who would have believed that this particular landscape could be so altered? She'd known that many
of the farmhouses and outbuildings would be gone, but the
stand of willows along the river is gone, too, and without them
there in the distance she is utterly lost. She could be anywhere.

There's nothing to do but walk to keep warm. She checks
her wristwatch and decides that she will simply walk west and,
after one hour, turn and walk back east again until she meets
Paul on the road. There's no wind to speak of, but there's no
sun, either, and she's beginning to feel the cold. The sky is solid
grey. Lavinia thinks it will likely snow. She's regarded these
very fields often enough in winter, but always from inside.
When there was outside work for her to do on the farm in winter, she'd always hurried along and done it and saved staring
into the distance for the window over the kitchen sink. The
white, sleeping fields reaching out endlessly from the house,
the sleeves of her old, blue cardigan pushed up for work, the
click of the vegetable peeler on the slick, white ball of potato
in her hand, the coffee pot and her cup still left to wash. A
glimpse of Homer from the window.

This landscape that had always seemed benign, even in the
harshest winters, stretches out away from her now, austere and

heedless. Lavinia had always believed that the land remembered. It had been her way of explaining the seasons to herself when she was a child: the delighted shock she felt each spring at finding crocus leaves piercing the last crust of snow, and the corn's yearly progress from a green haze of seedlings to a forest so towering and expansive a child could be lost in it. Then the stalks would stand in their rows, brittle and dignified as old men who have refused a chair, waiting for the harvest. There had always been summers that were too dry, springs that were too wet, spindly and even stunted crops, but each year, good or bad, her father had brought the crops in and turned the soil and the earth had remembered that it was time to sleep. Lavinia had watched all this as a child from the house her father had built and then as a bride when Homer came to live in that house and work beside her father in the fields. It had been sufficient, and she had wanted nothing else.

She thought she'd braced herself for this, for seeing that the storm had indeed erased almost every sign that she'd lived most of her life here on this land. Lavinia's father had lived out his entire life here and had often repeated the story of Lavinia's grandfather arriving in Illinois from the east, he and his bride both all of eighteen, traveling further and further south until they found themselves in Little Egypt, where they'd agreed it was time to stop wandering. Lavinia's grandfather had liked the look of the land, and he thought that names like Little Egypt and The Big Muddy had a certain weight, a ring of significance that was equal to what he had now left forever behind him back East. Lavinia had always been sure she looked at the land as her grandfather had, that she felt what he had felt when he first laid eyes upon it. *Didn't I live here?* she wants to shout now. *Didn't I have this soil under my fingernails and on my knees? Didn't I force this land to give us food?* The landscape now seems purely hostile; she cannot conjure her former pride. The winter fields had always moved her before—more, in their way, than they did in summer—because of the unspoken promise between the farmer and the land, because of the abundance that would surely follow the thaw. This notion curls her lip now, even as she sullenly acknowledges it was the wind that changed the land and not the land that changed itself to spite her.

There's someone walking toward her, a man, still far off and waving. Lavinia recognizes him first and waves back to signal that she has seen him and they continue towards each other. He calls out to her when they're close enough for their voices to carry.

"Are you broke down?" he yells, "Where's your car?"

"No, I'm all right!" she calls back. "It's me, Arthur. It's just me."

Arthur Coffman slows for a moment, then hurries toward Lavinia.

"I never . . . " He looks at her with watery eyes as if she's an apparition, a revelation for which he is profoundly grateful. He squeezes her mittened hands through his gloves.

Lavinia is crying, shaking her head. "I could have come sooner. I should have come sooner," she says.

It's starting to snow. Arthur puts her arm through his and when they've reached his house, he hangs her coat to dry on the back of a chair pulled up to the kitchen stove.

When they're seated at the round kitchen table, Lavina skates her hands across it's surface.

"A person could be forgiven for thinking it was the same table," she says.

"Homer helped me build it."

"I remember. I don't think either of you had a choice, once Sadie saw ours."

"You know, I was riled for the longest time when you sold out," Arthur says.

Lavinia clucks at him.

He holds up a hand and says, "It's only the truth. And I've had reason since to be glad you did."

"So have I," Lavinia says.

"I've seen a number of things in my time," says Arthur, "But never anything like the sight of my own metal water trough, coming end over end toward the house, fast as a car on the highway. That cloud was coming for us right behind the trough, but I tell you in that very moment I was more worried about what the trough would do to the house."

They're silent then, with their hands resting lightly on their coffee cups and the plate of oatmeal cookies standing untouched on the crocheted doily at the center of the table. Lavinia looks at Arthur, at his good face that is still as familiar as if he were family. It was Arthur who reached her first when the hired hand found Homer dead in the field, Arthur who'd helped to carry Homer into the house, and Arthur who'd found her trying to right the corn stalks that had bent where Homer had fallen and gently led her away. Arthur had brought in the harvest for her that year, along with Paul and a few hired men. It would have rotted in the ground if it hadn't been for them, she'd told them, and then the sight of Arthur rushing back to his own crops and Paul rushing back to the lumberyard and only the hired men left in her kitchen eating pie was all it took to force her to sell.

"Am I allowed to ask what you were doing out there on the county road alone in winter?"

"I'm not certain, myself," Lavinia says.

"I suppose you had to see it for yourself," Arthur says.

"I've seen what happened all over town, but this is something else."

"Out here's where you lost something, too."

"Yes," Lavinia says.

"I won't lie to you. We've heard talk out here, not much, but some." Arthur shakes his head and turns his cup in a slow circle on its saucer. "It doesn't amount to much, probably because out here people can see with their own eyes that there's nothing left of your old place. But I guess not everybody sees it that way in town."

"Even if they did, they'd still say it wasn't the same. It wasn't my farm anymore. I'd sold it, I had the money, and it wasn't mine to lose."

Arthur looks at Lavinia with a sad smile. She says, "I know," and looks down at her hands folded on the table.

"I've seen that expression on your face before," Arthur says, and Lavinia looks back up at him, curious. "Just the one time. I couldn't figure it then, but I realized later it was the moment you decided to sell up. Funny thing about letting go. That storm peeled a little part of this house clean off—just wasn't there anymore—but once it was gone, we decided to keep it that way. Oh, we closed up the hole and prettied it up so it looked like it'd always been like that, but all we rebuilt was the barn. Sadie always said the house was too big for us, anyway."

Lavinia has the sudden feeling that Homer is there in the chair next to hers, smiling at a hand of cards he's reordering, hooking the toe of his boot around her ankle under the table. She feels time folding in on itself then and collapsing on top of her and it's impossible to think that it's not all still happening: that her father is out there somewhere, leaning on a hoe; that Homer is right here beside her; that her mother is standing in her kitchen garden, filling a bowl with green beans and pea pods.

"You wouldn't have to leave, you know," Arthur says. "Not really. Your land is for sale."

Lavinia's breathing goes shallow and, as much as she wants to look away from Arthur, she can't.

"They're selling out and heading for Chicago," Arthur says.

Lavinia shakes her head and exhales. "Paul is no farmer and my time on this land is past."

"I'd feel better knowing you were near friends."

Lavinia laughs. "So would I."

"Paul will be coming for you soon," Arthur says, rising from the table. He helps Lavinia on with her coat, then puts on his own.

"Oh, I can go by myself," Lavinia says. "Wouldn't you rather stay here in the warm?"

Arthur smiles at her. "No, I wouldn't."

They walk slowly, in the direction of town, watching for the Ford on the horizon. Snow is still falling, thick and soft, and, except for the sound of their footfalls on the road, everything around them is utterly still. They stop when a car comes into view, though it's still far off, and Arthur says, "That'll be your boy."

Fear comes over Lavinia as Paul approaches, too quickly. It's the same fear she felt when he came to collect her that last time from the farm, when he moved her in to town, or perhaps only the memory of it. There are endings all around us, every day, she thinks. It's a mercy we don't see them for what they are. How else could you stand to put a child down if you knew he'd just asked to be picked up for the last time? How else could you absently accept a whiskery kiss if you knew it was the last time a husband would thank you for breakfast? She wonders now how she will lift her feet from the asphalt and step into the car.

Suddenly, Paul is there, waiting on the other side of the road for her. Arthur opens the passenger door and reaches in to shake Paul's hand.

"I guess she kept warm, after all," Paul says.

Arthur hands Lavinia into the seat, and time folds in on her again, slamming together like a telescope.

"Sadie will be fit to be tied when she gets home and finds out you were there," Arthur says.

Lavinia takes hold of his hand again and, when she looks up at him, she finds that she can't speak.

Arthur nods at her and steps back. He closes the door, saying, "You take good care of this old girl, son," and walks swiftly back in the direction of home without waiting to wave or watch them drive off.

After they've driven a mile or two, Lavinia says, "You're a good son, Paul, but what were you thinking, leaving me out there like that?"

Paul shakes his head in mock exasperation and Lavinia laughs until she must wipe her eyes. She waits until they are parked in the driveway at home before she says, "I was wrong before, Paul."

"What about?"

"About leaving Marah."

Paul's hands stiffen on the wheel. He does nothing to hide his dismay, and turns to Lavinia and says, "I honestly don't know whether I'm coming or going with either one of you."

"Don't you understand why I had to go out there today?"

"To see the Coffmans."

"Don't you sass me, young man. You'll never get so old you can sass your mother. I had to find out if I could leave this place behind, leave it truly behind, and never see it again. I can imagine you're surprised. Lord knows, I've been busy enough listing all the reasons to stay. But I want you to think about this and think about it hard."

"Mother, when I drove up and saw you and Arthur standing there, you didn't look to me like someone who wanted to leave. More like someone who'd just as soon bolt as get in the car."

"I was saying good-bye."

"You never said a word."

"I've known Arthur Coffman all my life. Surely, you've lived long enough to know that two old friends can say a thing without opening their mouths."

"What happens if I still don't think we should move?" Paul says.

Lavinia looks at her hands in her lap. "Then we won't move."

"What am I supposed to tell Mae?"

"Don't tell her anything. Not yet, anyway. If you decide we're staying, there won't be any need, and if you decide to leave, well, I should think that would be an easy thing to tell her. We already know what she wants."

Paul opens his door to get out of the car, but Lavinia stops him with a hand on his arm. "She doesn't want it, she needs it. I'm not the only one who can say a thing without opening my mouth."

Paul nods and Lavinia finds she can't say the next words; that when they drove away from the spot she'd been standing on the road with Arthur, she'd felt relief and even elation when she realized she'd made up her mind. She'd expected then to think first of John and of living near both her boys for the first time in years, and instead she'd thought of Mae. That this should be so moves her profoundly and fills her with remorse. Paul opens her car door for her and offers his hand, but she waves him off, saying, "I'll be in directly." She's wiping her eyes again and he knows better than to argue, but says, "That's twice today you've told me to leave you behind out in the cold," before he goes into the house.

She'll go in soon when she's managed to get control of herself again, when she can face Little Homer who will see her face and want to know why she's been crying. She'll go inside when she can think how to tell him that she wants him to come back to this place one day when he's a grown man, that she wants him to come back to see his first home, no matter where he's living. She'll tell him that when he stands in front of this house as a man he'll be overcome with the certain feeling that they're all still inside, his whole family, waiting for him. It will seem like more than he can bear, the feeling that every moment of his life is still taking place, and that he is nonetheless pow-

erless to see it, forced to stand outside with no way in. Lavinia
knows that she can tell him these things without frightening
him, that he'll understand in his way when she tells him that
memory is something more than recollection; that the idea of a
moment can sometimes seem as real as the moment once was
itself. *Come back here when you're a man*, she'll say. Press your
hands against the trunk of the post oak by the street but don't
think about how much you and it have both grown since you
saw it last. Put your fingers into the fissures in the bark and
remember that your own father planted it there. But know that
memory can beguile; it can draw you to it the way you are
drawn to the skin of new ice on a pond, tempted against your
better judgment to walk across it to see if it will hold. Remind
yourself then that memory can lose its power to harm if you let
it alone a while. If you leave it to ripen, like ice.

37

Paul stands alone in the office, gripping a shelf and weeping. "Thank you," the Methodist minister had said, over and over again. "Thank you, indeed, but we couldn't see our way clear to accepting any lumber. Couldn't be seen to benefit where others have not." It's a curious feeling, knowing he has exhausted all of his options, knowing that he has literally tried everything he can try. For the first time, Paul thinks that it would have been better if they had lost the house or the lumberyard in the storm. He has never allowed himself the thought before, banishing it when it came creeping around the edges of his thoughts as mere foolishness and dangerous wallowing. But now he is gripping the shelf with such ferocity that it begins to come loose from the wall and he wrenches it harder until he has pulled it off entirely and he is standing there with the shelf in his hands and the books and boxes that crashed down off it around his feet and the sound of his own wail dying in the air.

He hears a door close and realizes that he is not alone. He goes out quietly into the yard and finds Lon there, shuffling among the piles of lumber trying to invent an occupation for himself as if he'd gone out there with a purpose other than avoiding the embarrassment of meeting Paul's eyes.

Paul stands there in the doorway where Lon can see him, too weary to find something to say that will dispel the tension for them both. He should tell him to go, tell him to just get the hell out and find himself another job. He should force him to go as he forced Irene and Clarence when he finally pushed them bodily out the door and told them to try their luck at the banks and the rail yards and any town merchant they could find.

"I'm going home," he says and he turns to go as soon as Lon has nodded his already lowered head.

Out on the sidewalks, Paul is invisible. People pay him no notice at all, anymore, like children who have prodded an insect to death and then abandon it, bored, because it no longer offers any resistance. He can recall the exact moment it first occurred to him that he was meant to be upset by the stares and the manner of staring he encountered around town. His mother had been indignant when he'd tried to put it down to an absence of manners or some odd sort of provincialism. She'd railed loudly and exhaustively against that notion, letting him know that all the people rubbernecking at them around town were no more or less sophisticated than they were themselves. "Oh, no," she'd said, "We've all been reared on the same moral code and if people watch and whisper as we pass, it's because they've chosen to do so." He'd taken to averting his eyes after that, to avoid witnessing his neighbors' abasement, to avoid admitting how those looks could scald.

He's been rendered nothing more than a ghost now; a vapor, the suspicion of a man who once inhabited this place. Paul laughs a short, bitter laugh. All that will be true soon enough, once he's sent the letter he has in his pocket. It will need to be written out fresh—it's been riding around in his coat pocket so long the paper is wearing away at the creases from his worrying it—but that's a small enough thing. He knows it by heart. *Dear Johnny . . . Mae's nerves since the storm . . . Can't find peace here anymore . . . invest in your lumberyard . . . partners again . . . rent a little house near you . . . Don't like to leave . . . things are real bad . . . Please write.*

He'd taken time, at his mother's suggestion, letting go by

degrees. "Once you let go a little bit," she'd said, "you'll find the next bit gets easier, and you'll wonder what it was you were afraid of in the first place." Yes, Paul had thought privately. And when you remove a finger from the edge of the cliff, you find the next one comes off faster and it's that much easier to fall. He wrote the letter to see how it felt, to see what it looked like on a sheet of paper and, when it was done and lying there on his desk at the lumberyard, he'd still thought it so empty and cowardly a thing that he'd wanted to crush it into a tight ball and hurl it into the stove, but had folded it and jammed it in his pocket, instead.

Having decided to mail the letter, Paul finds he is looking differently at the town, looking at it with the heedful eyes of a man taking his leave. More than anything, Paul thinks, the town has now come to resemble a boomtown. It does not, in any case, resemble itself. If, a year ago, this place had been a frontier town and gold had suddenly and improbably been discovered on someone's land and the requisite number of prospectors had stampeded in to unearth their share, the alteration could not have been more remarkable. Paul wonders if people can see things as he does or if they are just keeping busy scurrying around town trying not to see the way the rows of new structures are punctuated reliably by holes in the ground where nothing has been rebuilt. It's easier, certainly, to ignore them, signaling death as they do, a family's abandonment of the town, or both. Paul wonders, though, if people even see how leery they've remained; the way, when a friend or acquaintance greets a person or says a funny thing, the smiles slide quickly off both faces, as if an ordinary smile had become too suspect to sustain.

Despite walking slowly, despite taking the long route home, Paul arrives. He stops at the bottom of his own front walk. To continue up the walk will be to admit that he's beat, that there's finally nothing anymore to be gained by turning

on his heel and going back downtown to try again. That the
bit of land this house and family all ride on is still his, but only
for the present moment and only in the sense that it will be his
job to hammer the "For Sale" sign into the ground by the
curb. To continue up the walk will be to admit that they had
been scoured from this place as surely as if they'd been hit by
a thousand such storms. He imagines that when he tells his
family the news about the move they will wonder at his
expression. They'll just have to wonder, he thinks. None of
them, not a single one of them will understand that, even if he
no longer denies that the children will thrive only after a new
start in a new place, even if he can toil at other work and put
another roof over their heads in another place, he can never
rebuild his idea of himself.

Lavinia opens the front door and calls to him in a low voice,
"You're making a spectacle of yourself, standing there." Once
he's inside, she hangs up his hat and coat and says, "Was he at
least polite about it?"

"Oh my, yes, he was polite. It was almost unbearable. He
shook my hand and then shook it again so hard it hurt and he
smiled at me so earnestly I believe he'd even convinced himself
it was my idea for him to turn down my offer of lumber."

"I'm sorry. I know how you were hoping he would accept."

Paul looks at Lavinia, expecting to see hesitation in her
face, expecting to see her wondering what interval she should
let pass before she asked him what he intended to do next. But
he sees nothing of the sort, only a mother who is anxious for
her son. He tries a smile and squeezes her hand and the tenderness of her gaze is almost enough to make him blurt out
that he's already written the letter to John and is now ready to
copy it out fresh and send it. Something stops him, though,
and he decides that he'll tell them all—Mae, his mother, and
the children—when he can show them John's reply. He knows
what John will say and even how he will likely say it, but the

exchange of letters is somehow a necessary formality; the first event of their renewed partnership.

"Why don't I heat you up a cup of coffee," Lavinia says.

"I don't want any coffee, Mother, thank you. Where's Mae?"

"In the basement, cleaning."

Before Paul can ask, Lavinia answers his question, "I don't know why, but she's a good deal less agitated when she's occupied, so I don't like to ask."

Upstairs in his and Mae's bedroom, Paul closes the door behind him. The bed is immaculate, each pillow plumped to identical thickness and the chenille bedspread creased under them. The wooden bedstead, the tables, and the floor are gleaming and the curtains hang starched and smooth, parted evenly in front of the polished window. Paul looks around him for a moment, feeling that he hardly belongs in this room, that no one could belong—let alone sleep—in a room so pristine. He decides that he has been preoccupied, that the room certainly always looks like this, and he sits down at the small writing desk beside the bureau to recopy his letter. Once he's finished and signed the letter, he reads and rereads it, staring at the words *sell . . . failed . . . move . . .* finally sealing it inside an envelope and addressing it to John. He leaves through the back door when he is finished, tossing the first copy of the letter into the cold stove in the kitchen on his way out. He shouts, "I'll be home before supper," to anyone who can hear him and walks quickly toward the post office.

He's consumed by thoughts of Mae for the rest of the afternoon: of her way of running a palm over the surface of a newly made bed, of her bending to take one of the children's faces in her hands. He wonders if there are flowers all year long in California. It's surely warm enough. He never thought to ask before. It would please Mae, if he could tell her that there were.

When he comes home again into the kitchen through the back door, Mae is there. He smiles, but the confounding expression on her face stops him cold. He closes the door behind him and turns back to face her.

"Could you tell me how to back the Ford out of the garage?" she says without greeting him.

"What?"

"I wondered if you could tell me how to back the Ford out into the driveway."

Paul looks at Mae standing there. She's bunched a dish-towel in her hands, looking as though the wrong answer from him will cause her to splinter into shards.

"Do you want me to teach you how to drive?" he asks.

Her eyes fall and she shakes her head, turning away from him.

"No, I don't," she says. "I've gotten an early start on spring cleaning and I thought I'd clean out the garage tomorrow is all. I didn't want to have to bother you about moving the Ford."

Paul takes a step closer and, when Mae doesn't move away, he stands behind her and holds her arms. He lays his cheek against her hair and says, "You can just ask me to move it for you."

"I suppose you could do that."

"I could show you how to put it in neutral, but I don't know if you could push it by yourself. Why don't we just say that I'll move it out on my way downtown tomorrow morning."

"If you think that's best."

When she turns, she's only able to look up at him with difficulty before her eyes dart away. Paul feels as if he is burning. If he could, he'd ask her how they got this way, how it is that they're standing toe-to-toe and he can't ask her to tell him what she's thinking, can't ask why they're talking about spring cleaning, can't kiss her, can't seem to ask her a thing. The girl he kissed in the apple orchard is now so remote a memory he might just as easily imagine that he and Mae fell in love sitting in the mud together as children, he in short pants and she in bloomers, making pies.

What would he say to her with his eyes if she would truly look at him? What would he tell her if she would listen? That if he's become a ghost to the town, she's become a ghost to him and maybe to herself. That he feels something like surprise each time he looks and sees that she's still there. He could tell her that he watches her at night and that, even though she lies with her back to him, he knows when she's not sleeping. He knows that she leaves their bed each night to lie on the floor in one of the children's rooms, to go downstairs, even to go outside. He knows all this because he tries not to sleep, because of the dream of the coffins that will come if he does. He smells the new-sawn wood and hears others at work around him, hammering at coffins. He hurries because there are so many coffins to build and because, suddenly, the others are no longer there, and he's left to build them alone. He can't see anything anymore but coffins in teetering stacks all around him, and when he finishes joining the pieces of the very last lid and lifts it to set it on the last coffin, he turns and sees a shrouded body on the ground, but there is no more wood now and no way for him to get any. He wakes in a sweat each time he has the dream, alone and wondering if Mae will come back to bed before dawn.

38

Homer is rushing home. Ellis and Ruby are ahead of him, like always. They don't pay him much notice these days, not if no one is looking. They walk to and from school faster than they know he can, forcing him to skip to keep up with them. He stopped complaining long ago. No use pleading with them, no use telling on them at home. Today he's almost managed to keep up, but hearing him close behind has made them walk, if anything, even faster. It's always the same. Try to keep up. Eat your bread and butter at the kitchen table, try not to get nabbed for a chore before dinner. Stay out of Mama's way. Stay out of Gran's way, too, because she'll just tell you *don't bother your Mama*, or give you a chore to make sure you stay out of their hair.

Homer stops at the little spit of sidewalk above where the driveway descends into the street. Ellis and Ruby are already in the house, the front door slammed against him. Didn't they even see it, he wonders, looking at the black Ford standing there in the drive. Homer looks around him, up and down the street, but the sidewalks are empty. He stares at the car. Daddy never leaves it outside, has not left it outside one single day since the storm, but there it stands, spotless and shining, parked facing the garage door as if it's waiting to be let in.

Homer knows that his Gran is inside the house, giving Ellis and Ruby something to eat. They'd have come out again if Gran hadn't been there waiting for them. Why is it, then, that no one else has noticed the car? Daddy walks to work, and Gran and Mama walk, too, to do their errands in town. If the car stands out, it's only because Daddy is washing it and Homer and Ellis are watching him tip buckets of clean water over the black, soapy metal, waiting to help him rub it dry.

He walks between the house and the garage and stands on tiptoe, trying to see in through the small four-paned window on the side. He can't see well enough, so he goes around back to get a crate he can stand on, but even when he's higher up, cupping his hands against the glass in a hood over his eyes, he still can't see so well. He could go get someone to raise the door for him, but Gran can't manage the heavy door any more than he or Ellis or Ruby can.

Homer steps down off the crate and stands back to look at the garage's side door. Daddy has taken to locking it, although he never used to. He leaves his lunch pail and books beside the crate in the grass and goes to try the knob. He closes both hands over it and it turns. He pushes lightly against the little-used door until it's open a crack and he stands there, his stomach muscles shaking. He closes the door again and stares at the knob and then finally turns to run to the back door and into the house.

He forgets to catch the storm door and it cracks shut behind him. Gran winces at the noise and snaps, "Hands!" at him so he'll go to the sink and wash before he sits down at the table. His bread and butter is there on the plate at his place and he chews and swallows his first bite before he asks, "Why is the car parked outside, Gran?"

"Hmm?" She drops a peeled potato, slick and white, into a pot of water by the sink. "Your mama is cleaning in the garage today. I guess she wanted the car moved out so she could get at everything."

Homer frowns and asks, "Where's Mama now?"

"I expect she's still out there. Didn't you see her when you came home?"

"No," Homer says.

"Well, if you saw the car . . . Didn't you two see her?" She points at Ruby and Ellis with the vegetable peeler and then looks at the kitchen door when they shake their heads no. She drops the peeler into the sink and her voice trails off, saying, "Where in the world . . . " Her wet hands bunch up in her apron and she raises a slow hand to her mouth. Homer hears her breathe the word, "Lord," and she raises a finger to them and looks at them hard. "Stay here," she says and goes out the back door.

They don't move while she's gone, not to lift the bread to their mouths, not to swing their legs under the table. They wait and watch the door, and when she flings it open again and cries, "Go get your daddy!" and none of them moves, she shrieks, "One of you run get your father!"

Homer hurtles out the door and around the house to the sidewalk. He tucks his head down and pumps his arms as he has seen his daddy do and runs harder. He runs through a stitch in his side, runs straight down White Street instead of zigzagging as they usually do, to and from school, then left on Union, all the way to the Liberty movie theater and the lumberyard.

His daddy is there in the office, alone, with his back to the door, bent over his desk, his head in his hands. Homer stands, panting, in the doorway and smiles a little. But then the smile falls away when he sees his daddy's eyes searching his face. Suddenly, the chair his daddy had been sitting in is tipped over backward onto the floor and his daddy is there, kneeling in front of him, hurting his shoulders, holding them tight. His legs and his sides still hurt from running. He has seen something like this look on his daddy's face before, when he holds his mama's shoulders, pleading with her with his eyes. And then they are running again, his daddy pulling on his hand, and the people on the sidewalk are moving out of the way and staring. His daddy lifts him up and carries him, still running, jolting down the sidewalk, then stops to swing him onto his back and starts running again, his breath juddering with his footfalls.

Homer holds onto his daddy's shoulders and watches for their house come into view. When they've reached it, his daddy sets him down in the same place Homer stood staring at the car when he'd first come home from school. Now his daddy is panting and staring at the car. Homer points toward the side door. His daddy puts his hands on Homer's shoulders, not squeezing now, but pressing down, rooting Homer to the sidewalk. Homer watches him walk away, past the car toward the big garage door. He sees him take hold of the handle and wrench it up, grunting with the effort. The door rises and Homer sees his mama there inside, with her back to him, hanging from a beam.

Homer walks toward her, wanting to see her face, wondering what expression she'll be wearing. They didn't let him see the dead bodies after the storm. They'd kept him home with Gran during the searches and then when the burials came, all the dead people were hidden in their boxes and there was nothing to see. Even when there'd been bodies in a line on the front porch, he hadn't managed to see more than a couple of pairs of feet through the muddied window glass.

His daddy rushes past him and hugs his mama around her legs, lifting her up. He's looking up at her, looking up at the rope, shouting, "Oh, no, Mae! No, Mae, no!" When he lets her down again and grabs a ladder to stand on, Homer thinks of the crate and his school books lying in the grass outside. He watches his daddy on the ladder next to her, holding her under the arm like they're dancing, sawing at the rope above her head with his pocket knife. He nearly falls off the ladder once he's gone through the rope. He throws his knife away from him, hard at the far wall, where it bounces back and spins on the cement floor. He has to let her fall, but he holds onto her arm and comes down off the ladder, and then he hurls the ladder away from him like he did the knife.

Homer still can't see her face. His daddy is on his knees, hugging her, holding her head against his neck. He rocks her back and forth, smoothing her hair with his palm. Homer remembers all of the other fathers and their wet faces after the storm. He feels his gran come in behind him, hears her cry out, and feels her fingertips on his shoulder when she tries to catch him, but he's quicker than she is, and he bolts for his mama. His daddy catches him, and they hold her between them on the floor, rocking her between them.

He hears his gran start to lower the garage door, and then his daddy's terrible voice bawling, "No! Leave it up! I want them all to see what they did."

Even holding on to her as he is, Homer's thinking of other things. His books and lunch pail still in the grass, and the crate that will need moving. He's wondering how long they can all stay here like this. How long before they must do the next thing.

He knows, somehow, that they will continue, just as the town had continued after the storm, propping itself up again as if the houses had only been paper, blown over by the wind. He knows there are boards enough to make a box for his mama, and that the cemetery is still not so full it can't open itself for one more grave. His daddy will go back to the lumberyard, and his gran will keep at the washing and cooking. They will do the things they must each day, and then they will sit quiet at home each evening. He knows somehow that he will keep growing. It won't be so different. In a way, she'd left them long ago, and only just this morning had finally said good-bye.

Homer can see the objects around him inside his closed eyes. Paint and oilcans on the shelf; the mower, the clothespin bag that used to be Gran's red apron. The toppled ladder and his daddy's open knife on the floor. The ashen light, the dark beams and rafters. He imagines himself up on that beam, beside the knot his mama made, looking down at himself and the rest of them. Gran standing just inside the door, holding Ellis and Ruby against her, not letting them see. His mama's doll body across his daddy's knees, and him, sprawled out like a starfish, riding on top of them both.

39

Lavinia leads the children back into the house and leaves Paul in the garage with Mae's body. She feels she must do something concrete for the children, so she sits them at the kitchen table and sets a glass of milk in front of each of them. She goes into the hall and looks at the telephone there on its table. She could pick up the receiver and ask the operator to place a call to California, but then the thought of hearing John's voice on the line wanting to know the what and how of it is too much, and she turns away.

"I have to go downtown," she tells them. "Only a few blocks there and back. I won't be long." She smiles at each of them out of pity and a terrifying love, touches each of their faces, and takes her hat and coat from their hook behind the pantry door.

She falters on her way out the back door, knowing that her accustomed route will take her past the open garage door, but she manages to walk past it without looking in and then manages to walk erect all the way to the telegraph office. It's a mercy, finally, to think that no one she meets will try to talk to her. In the telegraph office, she takes the form and writes the dreadful words, *Mae dead please come.* She looks at the paper for a moment before she pushes it across the counter to the astonished telegrapher who stares at the paper and then at her and then at the paper again before he begins to tap the message out over the wire to Sacramento. She unfolds a dollar bill from her coin purse and hands it to him, then puts the change in her coin purse without counting it.

Standing outside the office with her hand on the doorknob, she wonders if she is strong enough to slam the door so hard in its frame that the glass breaks. She stares at her hand on the knob, imagining how the impact of the door on the frame would feel running up her arm and into her shoulder and how her shoes would look if she were standing amid shards of glass. She closes the door carefully behind her instead and returns quickly home.

Lavinia slows when she has almost reached the garage. The children are waiting for her inside the house. She can have no way of knowing if they are all still sitting at the table where she left them, if their milk glasses are full or empty, or if they have hurled the glasses and the milk at the windows and walls and smashed them. She had thought of the children first in her haste to get home, but now it is Paul, her own child, she needs to see.

She enters the garage and, in the dim light, finds a bucket she can turn upside down to sit on next to Paul. He is there where she left him, next to Mae in her sheet, his legs splayed out and his face in his hands. The garage door is up; any one of their neighbors could walk by and look in to see them there, but miraculously, no one passes. It doesn't matter; Lavinia knows well enough that the news is already spreading throughout the town as surely as if she had sent a telegram to each and every household.

She lays her hand on the back of Paul's head and looks out to the street.

"John will be coming soon," she says.

40

Paul takes to sleeping part of the night in the backseat of the Ford. It is cramped and cold, but still the only solution to lying awake in bed all night, thinking about the garage. If he's in the car, at least he'll sleep a while and—this surprises him most of all—sleep peacefully until he goes quietly back to bed while the others in the house are still asleep. On his third night in the garage, Paul wakes with a start at the sound of the passenger door opening. Little Homer climbs in next to him without a word, and Paul makes room for him, pulling the blanket Homer is dragging all the way inside before he pulls the car door shut. He tucks the blanket in around the boy and pulls him close against his chest.

"How did you know where I was?" Paul asks him.

"I didn't," Little Homer says. "I just wanted to be out here."

Paul thinks about reprimanding the boy for leaving the house before dawn, telling him how frightened they would all be if they didn't find him in his own bed in the morning, but then doesn't speak when he realizes that the garage would be the first place he'd look if Little Homer went missing.

Paul looks down at his hand on that small yellow head that is rising and falling with his breathing. He's astounded by the way they have continued these last few days; the way they've all kept breathing and eating and drinking just enough. Most astonishing of all was the moment his mother somehow exchanged the look of horror on her face for one of resolve. Even as Paul sat there on the floor of the garage watching the terrible finality settle on the white faces of his children, his mother was the one who went back into the house for a sheet to wrap Mae in, who knew better than to insist that the children come with her but left them standing right where they had stopped when they'd seen, who knew enough of children's feelings to bring a pillow to cushion Mae's head against the gray cement before she wound the sheet around her, who spread the sheet out on the dark floor and set the pillow on top of it before she lifted Little Homer off of Mae and stood him with Ruby and Ellis, who knelt painfully on the floor to roll Mae out of Paul's arms and onto the sheet and used her own body as a shield so that the children would not see Mae's face or her purple tongue, who, having covered his dead wife, stayed kneeling and reached for Paul and held his head as he is now holding Little Homer's.

Paul knows what's waiting for him inside the house, all the things that are waiting for him this day. The first thing he will see upon entering the kitchen is the telegram from John lying on the table, which neither he nor his mother seems capable of moving, of folding, of tucking into a book somewhere, that says only *Leaving immediately arrive Carbondale Sunday*. The next thing will be the stove, which he will have to pass knowing it was there he threw out the first copy of his letter to John, which he now believes Mae found and read when she opened the iron door to light the stove in preparation for cooking their supper, which he believes she still had wadded in her hand with the dishtowel when he came into the kitchen and she asked him how to move the Ford, which she read without knowing that it was only a draft, and which convinced her that Paul had buried the idea of moving when he laid it on the ashes. In the upstairs hall will be the doors of all the bedrooms where his mother and Ruby and Ellis are still hopefully sleeping, but where the children will nonetheless have thrashed their covers onto the floor. And in his own bedroom, which is only his now, will be the empty bed and the suit and shirt his mother pressed and laid out for him to wear to the cemetery.

Paul closes his eyes and sleeps some more and after a while, when Little Homer stirs, Paul pulls the blanket away from him to wake him and then carries him into the house. His mother is there in the kitchen, standing in her housecoat, pouring milk for the children.

"There was more food on the porch this morning," she says. "Another covered dish. They must leave them in the middle of the night."

Paul looks away, wincing, at the floor. He shakes his head instead of speaking.

"I put it out at the end of the walk, just like the others, and came right back inside."

"Mother, I can't—"

"No, don't you worry about it. I'll take care of it. I imagine they'll give up trying soon enough."

Ruby and Ellis are looking up at him from their plates of bread and jam. They've come to seem so similar these last few days, as if they'd been born twins and Paul had needed to be shocked into remembering it; always together now, their faces blanching and crumpling by turns. Paul tries to smile at them, but realizes he is shaking and keeps going through the kitchen, past the table, past the stove, carrying Homer up the stairs to the toilet. When he's carried him back downstairs again, he finds he's still unwilling to put him down, and he goes to sit with Homer on the davenport where he's then faced with Mae's wing chair with her needlepoint pillow still in the seat and her basket of knitting on the floor beside it.

He wonders when he'll be able to tell his mother that he sent the letter, that his letter and John will have passed each other as they crossed the country on opposite trains. That when Johnny walks through the front door today, he will not yet have read it, the letter that Paul wrote without telling anyone and sent too late to save Mae who saw it without knowing what it was, who read it, the first letter, without telling anyone while Paul was downtown mailing the second. Johnny will be coming through that door knowing only that Mae is dead but not knowing how or the reason why. Paul will have to look at him knowing that Johnny will see in his eyes how completely Paul has failed at everything, and then he will remember the hollow feeling in his stomach when Mae looked at him with her face that was blank and terrible and asked him to tell her how to move the Ford. He will remember looking up and seeing Little Homer standing there, sweaty and gasping, in the door of his office when he should have been at home, Little Homer standing in the doorway with his face telling Paul it was already too late and Paul lifting him and running with him all the same, as if by moving quickly they could go backward and arrive in time.

He doesn't know how long he's been sitting here on the davenport. He'll have to get up soon, lay Little Homer down on the davenport to continue sleeping, and go upstairs to shave and dress himself. He'll help his mother dress the children, he thinks, and then somehow he'll drive them all in the Ford to the cemetery, or perhaps Johnny will drive them. Paul can hear the clinking of plates and glasses coming from the kitchen, but he's no longer certain how long the children have been in there eating. Johnny's not here yet. They can't leave for the cemetery before he arrives. He hears the clock on the mantel behind Mae's chair ticking sometimes with a thunking noise that seems so heavy he feels it reverberate in his chest and others with a sound so faint it seems that the clock must be farther away, in another room or house entirely.

They should have flowers. Mae should have flowers, he thinks. But are they meant to lie on the box before they've lowered it into the earth or on the mound they'll heap on top of it afterward? He doesn't know, can't remember, but likely someone else will. His mother, perhaps, will somehow have found flowers and will know where to put them. Paul looks at his hands that are trembling and feels the tremor that originates in his very core and is surprised that his core should be his heart, his actual heart, and that it should hurt so. He wonders who will carry the box and begins to count, but stops when he realizes he's not certain how many men will be present. The front door opens then, and when Paul raises his head and turns toward the sound he sees Johnny there, setting his suitcase on the floor.

In that moment, Paul ages one hundred years. No longer the little boy, running to catch the bigger one; always behind, always slower, forever watching with naked adoration the brother who might slow his pace, might turn, might smile just at him. Now Paul has truly overtaken John, run right past the first moment they were equals, outstripping and surpassing him in being the first to bury his wife. He looks at John and sees him clearly, sees in John the way he himself must have looked to others before the storm: like a man who decided early that his dreams were within his grasp, that they were neither fanciful nor more than his due, and that he could attain and keep them by means as simple as industry and devotion. He sees in John what others saw in him after the storm: a man who still had everything he'd started the day with, a man who had a wife.

Looking at his brother, Paul feels envy. He recognizes it easily for what it is, knows what name to put to it, having seen it himself in so many eyes since the storm. It leaves him breathless, this bitterness piercing him, swelling in his gut. This is what they felt when they had to look at me, he thinks. He knows he should not compare the two, that this is not what a man feels who has cultivated envy, who has beat it into a froth until it can sustain itself, but that he should now be the one to look at another man, at his own brother, with envy is especially cruel.

How strange, Paul thinks, the way the storm finally reached him as well, reached him in a way the whole town can agree upon—has agreed upon, judging from the covered dishes folks have been leaving, as if to say, *We're all the same again.* He could stay now, he knows. He could bury Mae and send Johnny off in a week or so with promises that they'd all go out and visit soon, just as soon as the lumberyard goes back to turning a profit. He could go to work tomorrow morning and hang the bell back up above the door and somebody would ring it. He could walk down Union Street midday and folks would give him a nod. Later, a newcomer to town might notice that people were extra courteous, careful even, around Paul Graves and hear in explanation, *Well, he's had his sorrows.* This is what Mae bought them all with her length of rope.

Paul spreads his hand wide on Little Homer's chest. He feels the boy's warmth and his beating heart and he knows he will not stay. Sitting there, Paul sees clearly the living room emptied of its furniture, the windows curtainless, and his fingertips skimming each bedroom doorknob in parting benediction. He sees his mother, boarding a train with Johnny. He sees himself and the children, driving to Sacramento in the Ford. This is how he will use Mae's length of rope.

His mother and the children are standing in the doorway, waiting to greet Johnny, waiting to see what Paul will do. He knows that he must be the first; that Johnny is waiting for him. He must show them that he is not broken and, for now, he can do that simply by standing up. Paul feels an overwhelming sorrow, suddenly, at having let that look of envy escape his eyes, for letting Johnny see it, if only for an instant. He looks at Johnny, looks at him hard until everything else falls away and he sees not some long-ago, lost version of himself, but his brother who crossed half a continent to shoulder a coffin. These people—Johnny, his mother, and the children—these faces are all that matters now in the world, and they must be enough. Paul lays Little Homer down next to him and rises and each step he takes toward his brother is a journey in itself that he takes slowly. He sees the pain now in that beloved other face and cries out at the tenderness flooding him. He stumbles and Johnny catches him. Paul hears his own voice, filling the room with his brother's name.

2005

A lifting breeze pushes Homer's trouser legs against his shins and stirs the canopy of leaves in the trees lining the streets. He passes a quavering hand over his hair and the flower in his lapel and then leans on the crook of his cane and watches the house. It is only mid-afternoon. There will be daylight for several hours yet and Homer wonders how long he will stand here, how long he will be able to stand in this place. Perhaps he should have come later, closer to dusk, when he could have watched the blue air settle and darken around the house and seen lights come on in its windows.

Homer remembers clearly the feel of his father's suit coat against his cheek the day they buried his mother, and the look of his child hand, curled around his father's neck. He could also say that the harsh sunlight that day had made him squint and that he remembers looking down at his mother's coffin and at the wall of earth descending into the hole beside it, but he knows he's likely pieced those pictures together from other memories of other coffins he's stood beside since.

The photograph of the house is in his billfold, taken from his bureau drawer to carry along on this trip. The photograph that arrived in Sacramento in 1926 in a letter addressed to his father, that showed the house and the garage in the shadow of the oak tree, that Homer took from his father's trembling hand and kept for almost eighty years. He's certain he's standing now in the spot the photograph was taken, catty-corner from the house.

The paint on the clapboards is still gray. A wooden swing hangs on the left side of the porch. The front door and its oval glass remain and tiger lilies grow along the west side of the house. Homer sees the garage and the windows of the house, and he remembers the light that fell into the rooms that was brighter in the bedrooms and in the kitchen than it was in the living room because of the covered porch and the trees outside. And it is no longer now but eighty years ago and Homer is not an old man, he is only five. Ellis is not lost in the Pacific, he is upstairs somewhere looking for Homer, and his mother is not dead in the garage, she is standing at the counter in the pantry in the particular gray light that comes through the window there and falls on the floor and on her shoes, and he tries to hear her voice but he can't remember it, and he hears his grandmother's voice instead calling him to wash up, calling him to dinner.

Waiting behind him in the car is his daughter Mae, his only child, who is herself beginning to grow old. A tender, curious expression overtakes Homer's face that falls somewhere between sorrow and smiling. He is staring past the house now, far past anything he can see in front of him, thinking that it is unutterably sad and somehow also lovely that, when he tires of standing, Mae will be there to drive him away. That he will be sitting in a car with a woman named Mae, leaving Marah.

ACKNOWLEDGMENTS

First and foremost, I thank my husband and daughters, who have loved and supported me in ways only they can know.

My deep thanks to my other relatives, including my father, Arthur Southwood III, who was the book's first editor; my uncle, Dennis Southwood, who proofread the manuscript; my late mother, Susanne G. Southwood, whose memories of her mother's kitchen helped stock the pantry in this book; my step-father, Thomas Barker, who provided information on building techniques and the lumber industry in the 1920s; my uncle, Robert Southwood, a retired fire-fighter who instructed me on burning all manner of types of wood; and my cousin, Mark Southwood, for his help in publicizing the book.

Many thanks to my friend and mentor, Jay Neugeboren for his abiding support, and to my agent, Richard Parks, for his kindness, insight, and tenacity. Thanks also to my publisher, Kent Carroll, for his commitment and editorial nerve, and to my friends Elisabeth Fairfield Stokes and Christy Lorgen, who generously read and commented on the book.

I am grateful to the Sallie Logan Public Library in Murphysboro, Illinois for their online archival material from the Tri-State tornado. I am also indebted to Peter S. Felknor for his excellent history, *The Tri-State Tornado: The Story of America's Greatest Tornado Disaster*, and to Wallace Akin for his riveting book, *The Forgotten Storm*.

ABOUT THE AUTHOR

Kate Southwood received an M.A. in French Medieval Art from the University of Illinois, and an M.F.A. in Fiction from the University of Massachusetts Program for Poets and Writers. Born and raised in Chicago, she now lives in Oslo, Norway, with her husband and their two daughters. *Falling to Earth* is her first novel.